CONTAMINATED 2: MERCY MODE

DON'T MISS THE BOOK THAT BEGINS THE SERIES:

Contaminated by Em Garner

CONTAMINATED 2: MERCY MODE

EM GARNER

EGMONT
USA

NEW YORK

EGMONT

We bring stories to life

First published by Egmont USA, 2014
443 Park Avenue South, Suite 806
New York, NY 10016

1 3 5 7 9 8 6 4 2
www.egmontusa.com
www.emgarner.com

Library of Congress Cataloging-in-Publication Data
Garner, Em, 1971–
Mercy mode / Em Garner.
pages cm. — (Contaminated ; 2)
Summary: The Contamination that turns people into ultra-violent zombie-like creatures is abating, but now seventeen-year-old Velvet must hide from checkpoints for the disease, to prevent the government from imprisoning her.
ISBN 978-1-60684-356-7 (hardcover) — ISBN 978-1-60684-357-4 (eBook)
[1. Science fiction. 2. Horror stories. 3. Survival—Fiction. 4. Government—Resistance to—Fiction.] I. Title.
PZ7.G18422Me 2014
[Fic]—dc23
2014007247

Printed in the United States of America.

To Unagh, who will read this,
and to Ronan, who won't. You're my best work.

CONTAMINATED 2: MERCY MODE

ONE

I'M RUNNING.

Long, loping strides, my feet slapping the soft earth in a steady pattern I don't have to think about. One foot in front of the other, over and over. My breath whistles in my throat. My fists pump with every step.

In front of me, the world expands and narrows at the same time. Every leaf and twig on each tree stand out, all in lovely shades of green, but I'm too focused on where I'm going to enjoy the woods. There's no path here, and if I don't pay attention, I'll probably wipe out. I leap over a fallen tree and come down hard on the other side, pebbles rolling under the worn tread of my sneakers. A few weeks ago I'd have landed on my face, but now I catch my balance and keep running without so much as a skip, although the stones have dug deep into my soles.

I hate running, but there's no other choice. It's ration-delivery day, and I need to get to town. I used to go in with

Dillon, but he had to leave for the early shift in the Waste Disposal Department, and driving with him, or even riding a bike, means passing through the checkpoints, which is dangerous. There's always the chance they'll pull you aside for random mandatory Contamination testing . . . and I can't risk that. So instead, I run.

I sweat with the effort. It'll leave my hair stringy and my clothes damp, and I hate this because instead of a hot shower with tons of soap, I'll have to settle later for what my dad used to call a "pits and privates," with lukewarm water and a sliver of soap so small, I'm sure it will slip through my fingers and get lost down the drain. My backpack rubs at my shoulders, but they'll be even more sore on the way home, when the pack's filled with cans and boxes . . . assuming I come home with anything from the ration station. Assuming I come home at all.

I find a rhythm, finally, just before I reach the highway. I come out of the trees on top of a hill so I can look both ways, checking for cars or army trucks, but everything's clear. Lebanon's never exactly been a shopping hot spot, and this is the road we used to take when we wanted to go the "back" way to the mall in Lancaster. There's a checkpoint a couple of miles down at the intersection of highways, just out of sight, which explains the lack of traffic. My mom used to call this stretch of road the dead zone, because her cell would always lose service here. Now it hardly matters— the only people with cell service are in the government or rich enough to pay someone in the government to allow access. Everything else has been cut off. No cell phone, no Internet, unless you're some kind of hacker. TV and radio are back, transmitted over the air like when my parents were young, but the programming's terrible. Even Opal doesn't complain anymore about it, and my kid sister has never lived in a world that didn't have kids' programming 24/7.

We read a lot of books now, instead. Fiction, of course. The Hollywood virus didn't seem to affect as many writers. Mrs. Holly from down the street says pulp fiction was really popular when she was a young woman. Not that movie with John Travolta, but real books. She says all the new books now are pulp fiction, printed on paper so cheap, they fall apart after a few readings—but the stories are all still good. Some are serials, in the way Charles Dickens used to write, and we like those a lot. But we also read everything else we can get our hands on. The libraries are all operating on strictly reduced hours, along with the post offices and banks. And assistance centers are more concerned with handing out clothes, food, and water than literature. Still, we manage. I've been reading about container gardening, how to build a greenhouse, how to make a composting toilet, how to hook up solar panels, and how to store food by drying and canning. Everything we might need to know about how to survive this apocalypse that the people in charge are refusing to admit we're in.

My sneakers skid on the brush, sending pebbles down to scatter in front of me. By the time I get to the pavement, I'm ready to run again. I cross the highway, leap the guardrail, and head into the trees on the other side. No path here, either, except the one I've worn for myself over the past few months. The woods are quiet except for the shuffle of squirrels in the piles of leaves and the soft chirp of birds overhead. The sun's high, casting shadows through the branches, and I turn my face up toward the brightness to try to soak it in.

That's why, even though I know better, I'm not paying attention to where I'm running. That's why my foot catches on a fallen log and I pitch forward, hands out to catch myself. At the last minute, I remember I can't afford to break my wrist, and I tuck and roll, hitting the ground with my shoulder first. I'm on my hands and knees a few seconds after that, breathing hard, my fingers digging in the dirt and my hair hanging in my face.

That's why I don't see the cheerleader until she's got me by the ponytail.

She yanks me up so hard, stars swim in my eyes, and I bite my tongue, making it squirt bitter, metal-tasting blood. I try grabbing at her as she pulls me to my feet, but she's behind me and I can't quite reach her until I duck and twist around. Pain flares along my scalp, and I grunt as I grab her wrists, trying to unlock her fingers from my hair.

I know she's a cheerleader by her blue-and-gray pleated

skirt, which is all I can see. That, and her long, bare legs, torn by brambles, bruised by who-knows-what. She wears socks with pom-poms on the back and pricey sneakers, and everything's covered in thick black mud. She stinks so bad, I choke and gag from it, doubling over. She comes with me, over my shoulder, flipping onto her back. She hits the ground so hard, her head bounces. I hear the sharp rattle of her teeth.

I let go of her wrists and step away, but not fast enough. She's fast and strong and really pissed off. She digs her fingernails into my ankle, clinging and gouging even as I backpedal. I have no choice but to kick her in the side. My foot connects with a solid *thunk*, which twists my guts— it doesn't matter that I know she won't stop unless I knock her out. It doesn't matter that, probably only a few months ago, this girl was more worried about matching her nail polish to her lipstick, and now she's scrabbling on the ground, grunting like a hog and trying her best to beat the crap out of me.

Oh, God. Her eyes. They're furious and blank at the same time, nothing behind them but rage, no sign of the girl who once lent me a tampon in gym class. We'd had a few classes together and traveled in different social circles, but unlike in all the teen movies I'd ever seen, that hadn't made us enemies. She hates me now . . . and why?

Because I'm here.

Because I'm in her way.

Because she's got holes in her brain that make her crazy, and that's why she's out here in the middle of the woods during the day, still dressed like she's on her way to cheer the football team. That's why she's on her hands and knees with her teeth bared, trying to bite me. My foot kicks out again. This time, it connects with her shoulder, sending her backward. Her nails have left stinging slices in my skin, and my own shoulder aches from where I hit the ground, but my heart's beating in triple time and my fists are clenched, ready to punch.

I don't want to kick her again. She's already bleeding from her chin and lip, and I know the bruises all over her face aren't from me, but I don't want to add more to the rainbow of black and green and yellow. She's still pretty under the mud and wounds. I know her name.

"Tess," I say, before I can stop myself. "Stop, please!"

She doesn't stop. She lunges forward again, with her fingers curled like claws, the nails split and broken. A couple of her fingers look broken, too, bent and swollen, but that doesn't stop her from grabbing at me. I duck out of reach and watch her fall forward. She looks up at me, her hair in her face. She's making a low noise from deep in her throat.

It's not a growl, I think. Not a snarl. People don't growl. . . . Except she's also snapping her teeth at me. Gobbets of white, foamy spit are flying.

If she bites me, it won't make me sick. You can't get Contaminated from a bite or a scratch; it's not a contagious disease. You get sick only if you drink the Contaminated protein water. At least that's what they've been telling us for the past few years. But the bite would hurt like hell and probably get infected, because human mouths are, like, a million times dirtier than a dog's mouth. So when Tess leaps forward and tries to sink her teeth into my ankle, I don't even think. I just kick.

My foot connects with her face. The *crack* of her nose breaking is very loud. My stomach twists again as I hop on one foot to regain my balance, still ready to kick again if she keeps coming at me. She doesn't. The kick has sent her back with her hands to her face, blood pouring from her nose. Her mascara has smeared, black smudges ground into the skin around her big blue eyes, blinking at me in confusion and anger.

I've never been a fighter. Sure, there were some girls at school who made fun of me, along with a couple of dozen other girls they didn't think were "cool," but I always managed to ignore them or flip them off with a few sarcastic comebacks. We never got into hair pulling or anything like that. And, yes, my little sister, Opal, has worked my nerves enough to make me want to smack her, but my parents didn't tolerate physical violence.

Somewhere along the way, I've changed.

When Tess looks up at me with blood smearing her fingers, something inside me starts to go dark. She should leave me alone, but she won't. I can see it in the way her eyes narrow all at once, how her body tenses like she's getting ready to jump up. She's going to keep coming after me until one of us goes down and stays down.

"Stop," I say again. Useless. She can't stop. All she is now is aggression and hate and anger. She will keep coming until she is unconscious or dead.

Her mouth moves but nothing like words comes out. Just that same low growl, raspy and hoarse as if she's spent so long screaming, she broke something deep in her throat.

I could run on. I should leave her behind. She'll wander around the woods until the soldiers find her and take her away, lock her up in the hospital where they're keeping all of them, maybe stick a shock collar on her if she's lucky. Maybe do something worse to her if she's not. But what if she finds someone else first? I'm not the only one who runs through these woods. What if she attacks someone else, someone who's not able to defend herself?

My fists go up in front of me. My knees bend a little, my toes digging into the soft earth and finding support. I don't know how to fight; I just know what feels right, and when Tess launches herself toward me, I'm ready for her with a one-two punch that sends her to her knees. I grab a double handful of her hair. My knee connects with her jaw.

It breaks.

I kick her in the stomach while she flails, her fingers skidding along my dirty jeans and catching in the cuffs hard enough to knock me off balance. She's on top of me as soon as I land on my back. Despite the broken jaw, her teeth snap inches from my face. Her breath smells like mint gum and this more than anything makes me hate her. It's been a long, long time since I had a pack of gum.

I'm on top, then she is. We roll in the dirt, with rocks digging into us. Connies might barely feel pain, but I sure do. I grunt when a sharp stone cuts my side, but I don't have time to wince because Tess is wrapping her arms and legs around me as she tries to smash my head into the side of a boulder.

I hit her in the face until her hands fall away and her growls become soft sighs. Blood bubbles from her lips. Her eyes are open but unfocused. She twitches a few times before she goes still.

I have a rock in my fist. It fits my hand just right. A weapon. I could smash it against her again and again until the light in her eyes goes out entirely, and it would probably be better for her than whatever waits. I could make sure she never hurts anyone else again. I could kill her.

I *want* to kill her.

But, in the end, I drop the rock and back away on shaking legs, the air hot and tight in my lungs. I leave her broken and bleeding in the dirt. Tess and the other Connies who've lost their minds to the prion disease eating holes in their brains might not be able to stop themselves from hurting other people.

But I still can.

TWO

THE LINE'S SO LONG, IT TWISTS THROUGH THE metal guardrails that have been set up in the Foodland parking lot and around the back of a couple of army Jeeps and trucks. It goes all the way to the sliver of grass between the parking lot and the road, and that's where I get in it, at the end.

"What's the holdup?" A man who's three or four people ahead of me snags one of the ration-disbursement workers as she passes down the line with an old-fashioned clipboard in her hand.

She frowns at him, distracted, her lips moving as her finger ticks off lines on the paper. "The supply train was delayed. They're unloading it now; the trucks will be here soon."

"We've already been waiting for almost an hour," the man says.

She gives him a look. "Yeah. I know. But I can't make

it get here any sooner, so maybe you need to take a deep breath and chill out."

For a second, it looks like he's going to say something to her, and it looks like she's almost daring him to do it so she can get up in his face. Something in the flash of her eyes and jut of her chin makes him back down, grumbling under his breath. She looks at the rest of the line and counts again, tapping the clipboard, still frowning. Shakes her head.

That can't be good. The trains have been late before, and that usually means bad news, but the way the ration worker looks, it must be *really* bad news. She gives the man who questioned her another glare and stalks off to the tables, set up for people to get checked in, just as the trucks finally pull into the parking lot. The line rouses, people shifting around, but then we all quickly relax. Nothing is going to move fast.

I'll be here for hours. The woods were cool, but here in the open, the springtime air is warm and the sun overhead, blisteringly bright. It splinters into my eyes until, blinking, I press my fingertips to them and wait for the dancing spots to go away. My stomach is empty because I puked up the half a slice of bread I'd had for breakfast while scrubbing my hands clean of Tess's blood in a scummy puddle of water gathered in a drainage ditch. Now I'd sit on the grass while I wait, but the line's advancing just enough that I'll only get a minute or two before I have to move. Better to keep on my feet in case I find out that once I'm down, I can't get back up.

I've smoothed my hair and tried to make sure my face was clean as best I could, but my clothes are still dirty and shabby. I'm sure I reek. I tell myself I don't look much different from most of the other people waiting in line, but it's a lie that doesn't make me feel any better. Everyone else in line is waiting for their government handouts, same as me, but I'm sure these people still live in houses with running water and electricity. They go to work, school, church. They go to the movies because there's hardly ever anything on television, and even though everything in the theater is rereleases of movies that are years old, it's better than sitting at home. None of them, I bet, are squatting in their childhood homes without power, relying on a generator for the barest of necessities and hiding from the roving patrols of soldiers who sweep the streets every few weeks. The patrols are supposed to be looking for uncollared Connies, but they spend a lot of time just driving around, sometimes shooting at stuff for the fun of it.

The woman in front of me looks a little like my mom. Same dark hair in a similar cut. But she smiles and murmurs hello, and the resemblance disappears as fast as a bone can break. My mom smiles a lot, but never at strangers. She has a few words, sometimes even complete sentences, but still communicates mostly through hand gestures—I'm sure it's as frustrating for her as it is for us.

It's been a few months since we got the collar off my mom just minutes before the soldiers would've taken her into custody in one of their sweeps to reclaim all the Connies who had been previously released. They'd taken away Dillon's mom and dad during one of those raids, and we haven't been able to find anything about them since . . . but we know where they went. They took everyone to the Sanitarium. That's what the Voice, the guy who broadcasts the underground radio show, calls the old veterans' hospital. Like it's some place for people in white lace dresses to cough blood into delicate handkerchiefs. And just like the old-time sanitariums, it's a place where people go and don't come back. It's a research facility where they poke you full of needles, cut into your brains, and try to figure out what is going on. That's not the official word, of course. People aren't being stolen away in the middle of the night; they're not being locked up in cages or experimented on. They're simply being "taken care of."

I don't believe it, and a lot of other people don't, either. We can't get the Net, but the government hasn't figured out how to completely block out underground transmissions. The broadcasts that share as much rumor as truth have been reporting about what they do to people who get taken away. The stories are chilling. Horrible conditions. Overcrowding. Experimental therapies. Neglect. Thinking about how my mom could've ended up there makes my stomach sick again.

"You okay?" The woman in front of me puts her hand on my arm, fingers squeezing gently. "You look really pale."

"I'm okay." Shaking my head's a mistake, because it makes the world swim. I lick my lips, thinking of the water bottle that had been in my pack. It broke and emptied during the struggle with Tess. "Just thirsty. Do you have anything to drink?"

The woman tilts her face toward the bright sun, then at me. I can see her taking in my clothes, hair, the dirt I'm sure I missed on my face. When her gaze flickers toward my hands with the broken, filthy nails, I tuck them into the sleeves of my sweatshirt.

She takes a step away from me, her face going hard. "No. Sorry."

I should've known better than to ask. It feels like begging. I straighten my shoulders and try not to think about gulping down a long, cold drink of water. There will be bottled water in my rations. I can drink then.

The line shuffles forward. I'm not the last one anymore. Behind me is an older man holding a little girl by the hand. She's got red hair pulled into curly pigtails. Her clothes are clean but clearly hand-me-downs a few sizes too big. Under one arm she clutches a doll that's seen better days. When she smiles at me, I smile back.

I'm so hungry, I feel like one of those cartoon characters who starts imagining everything as food. Dancing fried eggs and bacon, a giant chocolate bar. I press my hand flat to my stomach and try counting the cracks in the asphalt to keep my mind off the emptiness.

". . . I hear they have peanut butter this week," the woman in front of me is saying to the couple in front of her. "God. I haven't had peanut butter in so long. I'm really craving a peanut butter and jelly sandwich."

The man, who wears a clean and pressed pair of khakis and a white polo shirt with a blue cardigan, cranes his neck to see up toward the front of the line. His wife's blond hair has a good couple of inches of dark roots showing, but it's obvious she's made the effort to style it. Her outfit matches his. Their shoes give them away, though. Both pairs have worn soles, cracked leather, knotted shoelaces. The scuff marks on the toes of hers have been filled in, probably with a Sharpie marker. Those shoes have seen a lot of use they weren't meant for. Their cloth shopping bags, too, tell a story. These people aren't just trying to be "green." They're used to carrying whatever they need with them.

The ground tips a little under my feet, and I close my eyes for a second against a rush of dizziness. The back of my neck is hot, and sweat drips down the line of my spine. So gross. My pits are swamps all of a sudden, but my hands are like ice. I take a step forward to keep my balance.

The woman in front of me twists to stare over her shoulder at me. "Are you *sure* you're okay?"

"Yeah." A gag strangles my answer. I swallow hard again. I've gone from hunger to nausea. You can't run the way I did, fight the way I had to, without your body needing more than a slice of stale white bread and a handful of walnuts.

She flicks an uneasy glance toward the front of the line. There are only two soldiers there, both in full combat uniform, both carrying guns. Two others are at the back of the truck, passing out packages and cartons to the ration-disbursement workers manning the table. Another soldier stands by the front of the truck. Five isn't so many to stand against the what, hundred? hundred fifty? people waiting to get their supplies.

If we all rose up, I think with sudden, fierce clarity, they wouldn't be able to stop us from taking over the trucks. Cleaning them out of everything inside. Months' worth of food instead of a few days'. I could take the truck, drive it away, drive it fast and far—

"You sure?"

I nod, blinking.

She gives me a suspicious glare. "Maybe I should get you some help."

"No!" My shout turns heads and hurts my throat. I clear it. "I mean, no. Thanks. I'm okay. Just hot and tired and thirsty."

She shakes her head. "You look terrible. I'm going to see if someone can help you—"

"NO!" This time, even the soldiers all the way at the front of the line hear me. My hand shoots out, fingers digging into the soft, doughy flesh of her forearm. "No. I'm fine."

I'm hurting her. I can tell by the way she winces and her

eyes widen. For a second, just a second more, I dig a little harder. A little deeper. I can't let her alert the soldiers to me. I can't draw undue attention to myself. But that's what I'm doing now, so I let her go.

She steps away from me, out of the line, rubbing her arm. Now she doesn't look annoyed or pissed off. She looks scared.

"I'm sorry." I sound miserable. "I'm just really hungry and thirsty, and it's so hot. Please don't worry. I'm really okay, I promise."

The man behind me nudges my elbow to hand me a bottle of water. The label is faded, the bottle obviously refilled a bunch of times, but I gulp it gratefully. Some spills down my chin, over my throat, onto my shirt. I wipe it away and drink until the bottle's empty. The little girl is staring at me when I'm finished. She doesn't smile at me this time.

I hand the man the empty bottle. "Thanks."

He smiles at me, but warily. "You're welcome."

The line has shuffled forward a few more feet. I feel better. Not great, but better. The woman in front of me is very carefully avoiding me, which is fine, since I'm embarrassed at how I overreacted. I can't blame her for being freaked out. For all she knows, I could totally be ready to blow.

By the time I get near the head of the line, it's easy to see the shaking heads and frowns. It's not uncommon for the trucks to run out of the "good" stuff—peanut butter today, powdered milk or toilet paper on others. The Voice says it's not that the government doesn't have enough to go around. It's a way of controlling us in the places where more people became Contaminated than in others. The maps they used to show were color-coded. Green for areas of safety. Orange for midlevel Contamination. And the rest of everything, a deep, solid black.

Lebanon, Pennsylvania, is always entirely black.

So are Lancaster, Harrisburg, Reading. All the way to Philly and Baltimore. New York City, too. So many people there. Cities were hit hard by the Contamination. All the people obsessed with easy weight loss, all the rioting they did that hot, hot summer when the world broke apart . . .

Even with the water settling uneasily in my stomach, the world still threatens to spin. I don't want to puke, not in public, but more importantly, I can't afford to. So I breathe and breathe and breathe until the color seeps back into the corners of my vision.

The line moves forward, slow like snails on a treadmill made of molasses, my dad would've said. The thought of him stings, but it's like I can't stop thinking of him, ever. I know he's gone, but . . . I found my mom. So something inside me, some dark and secret part, still holds out the hope that, someday, I'll find him, too.

"If they run out of peanut butter," the woman in front of me mutters, "I might just kill somebody."

Nobody says a word, and she doesn't smile or play it off like a joke. The man behind me, the one who gave me the water, the one with the little girl, shifts his hand inside the flapping hem of his long-sleeved flannel shirt, and I see now why he's wearing it even though the sun is burning overhead. He has a knife on his belt. A big one. His fingers casually pop the snap on the leather holster.

For a moment, our eyes meet.

He looks away first. I give the little girl a smile she doesn't return. I want to say something light to keep us all from falling into a writhing, snarling pack of dogs with each other, but there are no words on my tongue.

Instead, I turn around and face the front of the line. I mind my own business. The man behind me is not going to sink a knife into the base of my skull; he's not going to slice me up; he's not going to kill me just because he can.

I hope.

By the time I get closer to the front, I need to pee. I dance with the urge, back and forth, pressing my fingers into that magic spot below my belly button that is supposed to make the need go away.

The woman sitting behind the table looks worn and tired, her hair pulled back in a bun that does nothing to flatter her. The lines around her eyes and mouth have cut deep, making her look much older than she really is. She doesn't return my smile any more than the little girl did. But she does recognize me before I do her.

"Velvet," Tony's mom says. "I can help you here."

The woman beside her is busy checking off the names

from the ration cards on her list and pays no attention. Tony's mom doesn't smile at me. I guess that might be too much to expect, but she does gesture for me to come forward, even though I'm still three back from the front of the line.

I'm moving before the woman in front of me, the one who wouldn't share her water, can say anything. The cards I hold out are soft and worn at the creases from being folded so many times, and I hand them over. "Thanks."

"Hey!" the woman says. "I was next."

"Two lines," Tony's mom says, without missing a beat. "You were asked to form two lines. She's in this one. You're in that one."

I can tell the woman wants to make a fuss, but with the soldiers there, guns at the ready, she thinks better of it. Tony's mom has always been a pain. It makes her perfect for this job, and I'm glad for it now.

She scans the cards I give her with a plastic laser gun attached to the laptop in front of her. It beeps every time she scans, and she looks at me.

"You have six residents?"

I force a smile. "Yes."

Me. Mom. Opal. Dillon. Mrs. Holly. She and her husband, Gerald, had refused to leave Spring Lake Commons when it was evacuated, and she came to stay with us when Gerald died a few months ago. We had a little ceremony and buried him in their backyard, which was the best we could do. She said he'd have wanted it that way, to be planted in his own garden. She refused to report it because she said we'd need his rations to stock up for winter . . . or for when they'd stop handing out food. Mrs. Holly came here from Holland when she was a little girl, just before the rest of her family ended up dying in a concentration camp. She says her parents risked everything to keep her and her sisters from having to hide the way we are now, and she's way too old to starve to death. I'm not sure that camping out in a house gone "off the grid" is comparable to being Anne Frank, but I'm not going to argue with Mrs. Holly.

Tony's mom scans the cards again and studies the computer screen. "Opal's still eligible for the children's initiative services, right?"

Opal's birthday was a month ago, but she's only eleven. When she turns thirteen, she'll no longer be eligible for things like extra soy milk and vegan cheese. Or peanut butter, I think as Tony's mom gestures to the workers behind her, who are picking and pulling the different boxes and cartons for everyone in line.

The woman next to me eyes the goods Tony's mom is checking off on her laptop just as the lady behind the table who's helping her says, "Sorry, we're out of peanut butter. We should get more next time."

"*She* got peanut butter." The woman jabs her finger at me.

"She has a card for it," Tony's mom says loudly.

"I do, too!" She waves her card in Tony's mom's face.

"You have a card that says you're entitled to this week's supply distribution. We ran out of peanut butter," Tony's mom says flatly while the other ration-disbursement worker beside her starts to look nervous. "Velvet has a child's card—"

"She's not a child!"

"It's for my sister," I put in, but the woman edges away from me with a scornful sneer.

"Anyone could bring in a card for a child," she spits. "You have how many cards there? Six? Where's everyone else? Why are you the only one doing the pickup? How are you going to carry all that? I bet you're cheating!"

This accusation rings across the parking lot. My stomach sinks. I *am* cheating, but not with Opal's card. "We're allowed to have one person from each household collect for everyone. Because not everyone's capable—"

"Let me see those cards!" Before anyone can stop her, the woman grabs the cards from the table and starts flipping through them. She holds up one triumphantly. "These people don't even have the same last names!"

"They're my grandparents. My mom's parents." I reach for the cards, but she dances out of reach.

"And this one?" She flips Dillon's card in my face, but too fast for me to grab.

"He's . . . my husband." The word still tastes funny, sort of terrible, like licking a battery.

Tony's mom lets out a surprised snort. "Husband?"

"Those cards are all legitimate." I force my voice to remain firm, not shaking. I look at everyone who's staring at me, including the soldiers, in the eye. I start shoving the cans, all with plain white labels and black lettering, into my backpack. It's a big one, meant for hiking and camping, and I can put a lot in it. "We're allowed to combine households, and I'm allowed to pick up the rations for anyone in my household who's incapable of doing it. It's the law!"

The woman who's been giving me such a hard time narrows her eyes. She looks at me. Then at the small pile of rations I haven't had time to shove into my backpack.

Slowly, deliberately she grabs the tiny jar of peanut butter and jerks her chin at me like she's daring me to protest.

"You can't do that!" cries the lady who was helping her. Tony's mom stands up. "Put that back."

I don't say anything as I sweep the rest of my rations into the pack and zip it closed, then sling it over my shoulders. The weight is enough to make me feel as though I might tumble over backward until I snap the waist strap around my stomach to help distribute the load. The heat in my throat and cheeks is back, the sweat in my armpits, my shaking-ice hands. Something in my face must scare the thief, because she pulls the jar close to her chest as she backs up. She bumps into the couple who was in front of her. They didn't get any peanut butter, either.

"No," the woman says. "I was told I'd get peanut butter this week, and I want it."

"Me, too!" shouts someone from the back of the line. "I want peanut butter!"

Other shouts rise. People are really mad about the peanut butter. I'd let her have the stupid jar, except that sometimes peanut butter is all we can get my mom to eat. Opal, too, though that's just because she's a brat now and then.

Besides, it's ours.

I grab it from her hands so fast, all she can do is let out a surprised cry. With my other hand, I shove her hard enough to knock her backward. She stumbles and goes down on her butt. She's lost a shoe.

All at once, the crowd is moving. Someone jostles me from behind, and the little girl's doll hits the pavement at my feet. Staggering with the weight of my pack, I bend to pick it up and press it into her hands, her tears and open mouth reminding me so much of Opal when she was little that I want to grab and squeeze her, tight. Instead, I find myself pulling her against me, out of the way of a couple of big guys in trucker caps and dirty jeans, who've begun shoving their way toward the table.

One knee pressed into the pavement, the pack like a turtle's shell on my back, I try to shield her from the wave of angry people who'd been waiting so patiently in line just minutes ago. They shove and push and kick. Her doll goes flying. A big boot crushes my fingers. Someone tries to rip the pack from my shoulders, but it's secured too tightly around my waist, and he lets go when another person punches him in the face to get to the table.

I can't see the old man she was with, but I scoop up the little girl as best I can and try to get out of the mob surging toward the table. Tony's mom is shouting, waving her hands. Her coworker has disappeared. Someone shoves the table over, and that's when the first soldier steps forward.

He's a young kid, not much older than Dillon, and though he carries a gun, he doesn't seem ready to use it. "Hey! Settle down!"

Only minutes ago, I was thinking about how the crowd could easily overpower these few soldiers, and now it's happening. The scary thing is, so far as I can tell, none of these people are Contaminated.

They're just pissed off.

Shouting, shoving, grabbing. Some push past the soldiers to get at the food stacked behind the table. Others head for the truck. The well-dressed couple who were ahead of me have moved out of the way, but the woman sidles around the side of the knocked-over table and starts shoving packets of instant soup and stuff into her bag.

Everything's out of control. People are screaming about peanut butter and freedom. I hear the far-off wail of sirens getting closer. The old man grabs the little girl away from me, his face twisted and angry. She doesn't have her doll.

"I gave you water!" he spits.

It's an accusation, and I can't do anything about it but back away. I don't run. That would make it look as though I'm fleeing. It would attract attention. Instead, I walk slowly toward the sidewalk in front of the strip mall, toward the office-supply store that has been closed for months and then the outpatient surgical center that's been turned into a walk-in testing clinic for Contamination. I don't want to get anywhere close to that place; I'm afraid of it like it's something in a fairy story, as if trees with grabbing hands will reach for me and drag me inside. Through the glass, I can see the goggle-faced people looking out at the mayhem in the parking lot, and I pick up the pace just enough to get around the corner before anyone can open the door.

Behind me, sirens. A police car speeds past, lights flashing. I keep going. Over the field and past the Tractor Supply, the bank, beyond the half-finished and abandoned shopping complex that had once been rumored to be the future home of a megabookstore. There's an empty cell phone store in it now, and nothing else. Then down the hill and across the gas station parking lot.

I usually have time to repack the backpack after picking up the rations to make sure everything fits in the best way. Even the smallest edge of a box that feels like nothing can become excruciating after a mile or so. I stumble a little on the concrete before I decide I need to sit and take a break.

I find a spot on the grass between the parking lot and the highway, and shrug out of my pack. I'd like to let myself fall onto my back and stare at the bright blue sky and the burning golden disc of the sun, but I want to get home.

There are only a few cars in the lot, fewer people inside the gas station's convenience store. With an eye out for anyone acting suspicious, I pull out cans and boxes, and lay them on the grass in a pile so I can rearrange. Something sticky coats my fingers—syrup. Some things have broken. I would like to break just then, thinking of the ruin inside the pack. Punctured cans, torn boxes, stuff leaking. This food has to last us until the next ration pickup in two weeks, and, when I think about what happened in the parking lot today, maybe longer than that.

The syrup has soaked through the pack and into the front zipper pocket, inside which I find an old baseball cap. It was my dad's. He wore it for yard work and for hikes, and I clutch it to me suddenly, without caring about the goo on it. I can wash the hat at home, and for now I set it on the edge of the curb to keep it out of the way while I refill the pack.

When the car pulls up beside me, I turn, startled and wary. There are people who will take what I have, who won't hesitate to snatch my pack and drive away with it. Worse, people wouldn't hesitate for a single second before taking me, too. But the older woman in the BMW doesn't look like she's going to try and take my battered cans of tofu pork and beans or kidnap me.

She smiles at me kindly and tosses a folded dollar bill

out the window of her car, toward my dad's upturned hat. Without a word, she rolls up the window and drives slowly away. I look after her, confused for a moment before I realize how I must look. If I thought asking for water felt like begging before, now I really understand how it feels. Raggedy clothes, a pack full of food, a hat . . .

There were homeless before the Contamination, and there are plenty of people who lost their homes in the time since, but you don't ever see anyone living on the streets anymore. Anyone who tries is rounded up, tested for Contamination. Sent to the Sanitarium. According to the Voice, everyone tests positive, whether they are or not. Nobody's homeless, but there are plenty of beggars. Raggedy men and women dancing or playing music for coins. Some with children in tow and signs that read PLEASE HELP. Some with nothing but the looks on their faces. I don't know how successful they are—nobody seems to have much of anything extra anymore. What we all get from the government is supposed to be enough.

My mom would be so ashamed if I went begging, especially with a pack full of food. There are people who have nothing, absolutely nothing, and in comparison, we are rich. So it's in me to snatch up the dollar and run after the woman's car to give it back to her. Yet when I start to, when I see it's not a one-dollar bill, but a twenty, I don't run after her. I smooth it in my hands and look across the parking lot to the convenience store, where they still sell things that are never included in the government rations. Sure, the selection is small and the prices make everything a luxury, not a mere treat. But I have twenty dollars in my fist, and I know just what I'm going to spend it on.

If that makes me a beggar, I think as I finish loading my pack and putting it back on, then that's what I am.

THREE

OPAL SQUEALS AND DANCES WHEN I HAND her the pack of gum and the candy bar. For Mrs. Holly, I've brought some artificial sweetener packets—she's diabetic and usually has to do without any kind of sweetener for her tea. I hand Dillon some "beef" jerky—it's made of tofu, of course, since meat products are so highly regulated that now everyone's become vegan by default. He takes it with a slow groan of pleasure that makes me laugh.

"You're welcome."

"Where'd you get this stuff? That's not government rations." He holds me close, and I don't protest, even though to be honest, he stinks of oil and smoke and other messy stuff he has to deal with in his job on the garbage truck. He stinks, but then again, I'm sure I do, too. Funny how we used to all be so obsessed with deodorant and soap and body spray, and now it's good enough if we brush our teeth with the nasty, gritty government ration toothpaste.

"Can I eat it now?" Opal, still dancing, waves the candy in front of me.

"After dinner. Save it for dessert," I tell her.

Opal, crestfallen, scuffs her foot on the floor and looks for confirmation from our mom, who's sitting quietly as she usually is, in the rocking chair. Opal huffs out a breath, but whatever she sees on Mom's face convinces her it's not worth an argument. "Fine. But can I chew the gum now, at least?"

I've already gone through a piece myself, chewing until long after the flavor faded and my jaws hurt. "Sure."

"Where?" Dillon asks quietly in the kitchen while we unload my pack together. "Did you steal it?"

"No." I'd rather tell him I stole it than that a stranger gave me money that I spent on junk . . . though, honestly, there isn't much else to spend it on. Our currency has become the vegetables we're trying to grow in the poor soil of the yard and the scarves and socks my mom and Mrs. Holly knit from salvaged yarn. "A lady gave me money in the gas station parking lot."

"For what?"

I laugh, but keep my voice low. I don't want my mom to hear. Or Opal, who won't be able to keep her mouth shut. "For looking like a beggar."

Dillon frowns and shakes his head. "You should be more careful. Next time, I'm going to go—"

"You know you couldn't." He has to work. Not for the

money; that's barely enough to make it worth his efforts. But because all people between eighteen and sixty have to sign up for assignments in the local utilities.

People still eat and drink and poop and throw stuff away—people who are living in town, and not out here the way we are, still demand electricity, even if it's sporadic and there are enforced brownouts and curfews to save energy. The trouble is, there are more people using up the resources than there are people to provide them. Dillon's been on the garbage detail for the past few months. He likes it because, despite the way the world has turned, lots of people are still wasteful and throw away so much good stuff.

Yesterday, he brought home a bagful of sweaters and old jeans that Mom and Mrs. Holly will take apart to use. Today, I brought home candy and gum and artificial sweetener. When you look at it that way, it's not hard to see who's the better provider.

"It's dangerous out there." Dillon reaches to pull me close again, and I let him.

I should tell him what happened at the ration station, but he'll worry even more. And he can't miss work. You can lose your ration card for that. Or worse.

"Hey! Can we have mac and cheese and beanie weenies for dinner?" Opal nudges against us, pushing us apart.

Dillon and I exchange a glance. "With a vegetable," I tell her. "And you have to promise to eat it."

In the kitchen, I pull out a can of green beans and toss

it to Dillon, who opens it and pours the slimy, soft beans into a saucepan we'll heat over the small fire in the fire pit outside. Our generator runs on gasoline, and we use it only for a few hours when it gets dark, to give us lights and some hot water. That's one thing I forgot to get today, even though I was at the station. A gallon or so of gas. It's all you can really buy anymore. No more than five gallons at a time, unless you have paperwork. But you can still buy the red gas containers, and I buy and fill them whenever I can, keeping them in the shed.

My dad would've said that's dangerous, but what else are we supposed to do? Someday, we won't be able to get any. Right now everything we get, we put half away for the winter.

We live like pioneers in a house filled with electronics gone dusty. We hoe and weed and build up compost heaps in the yard, and fight the deer and squirrels and birds to keep them from eating our crops. We wash our clothes in pails of water because the washer and dryer take too much electricity to run, even if we do have enough water to use. It's not so bad, really.

While living in the crappy apartment in the days after the last wave, when Opal and I didn't know if we'd ever find our mom, we had "more," but it felt like so much less. Now, at least, we're a family, and if we have to work harder for everything we get . . . well, my mom always used to say, "You appreciate what you have to work for more than what you don't."

She'd say it again, I think, if she was able to say much at all, but even though we got the collar off her, Mom is mostly still silent. She understands what we say, especially if we speak slowly and are very, very clear about what we mean. She communicates just fine, mainly with hand gestures. But she hardly ever talks, except at night when she dreams. Sometimes, she wakes us up with her screaming.

Dinner is, as Opal requested, macaroni and cheese and beanie weenies, all from cans. The green beans, which I tried to spice up with a little soy sauce and some garlic and olive oil, aren't terrible, but you'd think we were asking her to gulp down live spiders by the way she wriggles and gags. I frown, tired and frustrated and still thinking about the showdown at the ration station. I've been half expecting a knock on the door any minute. The police. Or worse, the army. Coming to take me away for the part I played in it.

"C'mon, Opal. You have to eat your veggies." Dillon's so much better at getting her to do whatever she needs to do than I am. I lose my patience with Opal, but he's never had a younger sibling. For him, it's still sort of a novelty.

"And your vitamin." I hold out the bottle.

Because Opal's under thirteen, she's issued the government vitamins that are supposed to give her 100 percent of her daily requirements, including vitamin C. It took an epidemic of rickets and other vitamin deficiencies for the pills to start showing up in the ration shipments. The government might once have declared ketchup a vegetable, but at least in this brave new world of post-Contamination insanity, they're trying to keep the kids healthy.

"I hate it!" Opal cries.

Mrs. Holly tut-tuts, which makes Opal look at least a little ashamed. "It's good for you, dolly."

Mom says nothing, but fixes Opal with a look that leaves no interpretation necessary. With a put-upon sigh, Opal eats a few bites of beans and washes down her vitamin with a giant swig from the glass of reconstituted soy milk I made earlier. Along with any kind of beef and even most chicken products, cow milk has become rare. The Contaminated protein water that started everything off was supposed to be animal-protein free, but it got infected with what seems to have been a chemically altered organic protein. You couldn't pay me to eat a real cheeseburger, and most everyone else seems to feel the same way.

After dinner, Mrs. Holly helps Opal with her schoolwork—we gave up the pretense of her going to any sort of school last year, and have been homeschooling her ever since. Everyone else in this house is more patient with Opal than I am. They work on math problems far more useful than any I ever learned in school. Instead of lame story problems about two trains meeting, Mrs. Holly quizzes Opal on converting measurements and figuring out how much square footage of garden plots a certain number of seeds need. That sort of thing. Mom works on a pair of soft, thick socks she's knitting from the yarn she pulled from an old baby blanket.

And I go upstairs to finally, at last, take a shower.

Between the sound of the water pounding all around me and the rasping cough of the generator outside the bathroom window, I don't hear Dillon open the bedroom door. So when I come out of the bathroom, after a shower that was way too short and not nearly hot enough for my taste, I jump, startled when he says softly from behind me, "Hey."

"Hey." I'm still not used to this. Sharing a house with him, much less a bathroom and a bedroom, even though we've set up two twin beds instead of the king-sized bed that had been my parents'. It's certainly not the way I'd ever imagined my life when I pictured it. At least not at seventeen.

Dillon's riffling through the dresser to get something, his back to me and giving me the privacy he knows I still need. We might be husband and wife on paper—that's so I can be covered under his health benefits, the ones he gets from his forced service as a garbage collector. Opal will be taken care of, too, when she's no longer covered under the children's initiative, and also my mom, because they're my family and now his. But words on paper are only that. Words.

We share a bedroom because he can't share with Mom or Opal or Mrs. Holly. We tried having Mom share, but she keeps anyone who sleeps near her awake all night with her mutters and sighs. Mrs. Holly would share a room with whoever we ask her to—she's just grateful we've become her family so she doesn't have to live all alone in the big house she used to share with Gerald. But Opal is such a messy kid that it's not fair to subject Mrs. Holly to the dangers of tripping over every single possession Opal owns. Everything is always all over the floor. And I could share with Opal, but we'd end up killing each other sooner rather than later.

So Dillon and I are roomies, which feels weird and awkward, like we're shacking up right under my mom's nose. In my parents' house. Except that we went and got ourselves married for the sake of dental care. My mom didn't even have to sign her consent, since I'm an adult now in the eyes of the law.

It doesn't quite feel that way, though. It still feels odd, even if we do have separate beds. Sometimes I think about Tony. Once upon a time, I'd imagined what it would be like to marry him, and I'm not at all sorry about never getting the chance. But I know Tony wouldn't be as understanding as Dillon has been about my reluctance to turn the words that have made him my husband into the more physical reality of it. Tony would've been all over me, all the time, but Dillon's not like that.

He kisses and hugs me and stuff, but sometimes, I wonder if he's really into me at all.

The towel I have wrapped around me doesn't do anything to cover the bruises and scrapes that showed up when

I washed away the mud. My face miraculously managed to miss most signs of the abuse I earned at the hands of Tess the cheerleader, but the rest of me . . .

"Oh my God." Dillon grabs me by the shoulders, turning me to face him, not letting go, even though I wince at his grip. "Velvet. What the hell happened to you?"

"I just ran into someone in the woods—"

"Who? Who did this?"

Carefully, I shrug out of his grasp and go to my dresser to pull out a pair of pajama bottoms and a T-shirt. I slip the bottoms on without taking off the towel, but then keep my back to him while I let it drop so I can pull on my top. Bending to pick up the towel, I wince again and gasp a little at the stab of pain in my ribs.

"Velvet."

I turn. Dillon takes my wrist and leads me to the mirror on the back of the door. He turns me and lifts the hem of my shirt to reveal a cascade of darkening bruises all the way up and down my back. He's gentle, but I ache. Suddenly, now that I'm letting myself think about it, I hurt everywhere.

He touches the bruises lightly with a fingertip, and our eyes meet in the reflection. I give him a small smile. "Hey. It could've been worse. She didn't bite me. Tried, but didn't."

"What did you do to her?"

I don't want to think about that. My chin goes up. "I fought her off."

"A Connie."

"Yes."

"There are more of them all the time. Turning." Dillon frowns.

"Yeah. So much for the mandatory testing." I tug my shirt down and push past him. I need to check on Opal and Mrs. Holly and Mom before I go to bed. I need to check the locks on the doors—not that they'll keep out anyone determined to get inside. I need to turn off the generator. I need to . . .

"Velvet," Dillon says again. Louder this time. Harder. "What happened today at the ration station?"

My legs are sore from running and kicking, but they should still be strong enough to hold me up, and I mutter a low curse when they betray me. I sink onto the edge of my bed, which is inches from Dillon's. We could reach out in the night and hold hands across the space between them, if we wanted to. We never have, but we could.

"The Voice was talking about it on the radio," he says. "There was a riot? Were you there when it happened?"

Briefly, I describe the woman who wanted peanut butter. I look at him without flinching. "It was ours, Dillon. I couldn't let her just take it."

He sits on his bed. Our knees touch. He reaches for my hands, linking our fingers together. "You can't go by yourself anymore. The woods are too dangerous. And if there are going to be riots—"

I squeeze his hands. "Hey. Stop. You know that's unrealistic. You have to work. In another six months, so will I. And then what will happen to Opal and Mom?"

"Mrs. Holly will be here. And that has nothing to do with you waiting for me to go with you—"

"And what happens when they pull me aside for testing at the checkpoint, just because the soldier in charge of things is bored that day? You know how much more likely it is for that to happen there than at the pickup location itself."

Dillon doesn't answer.

"We need to stock up," I tell him sharply. "I can't miss a ration delivery. We can't let the vegetables in the garden die or go to waste. We need to be harvesting and drying and canning and hoarding, Dillon. Because when I turn eighteen, they're going to assign me to some job that means I have to leave the house for hours a day, just like you do now, and there won't be anyone here to do everything—"

I'm crying, and I hate it, but Dillon enfolds me in his arms. He kisses and hugs me every day, but it's been a long time since he held me like this. I melt into him. He strokes my hair. He rocks me a little, back and forth, and I want to let him soothe me, but all at once everything seems so hopeless that there is no solace, not even in his arms.

"You don't have to do all this yourself, Velvet. I'm here. I'm a part of this family now. You have to start letting me help you."

I say nothing.

Dillon kisses the side of my face. He hesitates. Then kisses my cheek. Lower. He finds my mouth, and even though he kisses me all the time, it hasn't been like this for a long time, either. He breaks it before more than a few seconds have passed, and pushes away, leaving me blinking and confused.

"I'll go turn off the genny. Make sure Opal's tucked in. Check on your mom and Mrs. Holly. You," Dillon says, mock sternly with a shake of his finger, "get into bed and sleep. You need it. You're going to be in a lot more pain tomorrow. Did you take anything?"

"A couple of aspirin." A couple is all we have, and I lied; I took one. It's hard to get more.

"You need ice for those bruises. And some ibuprofen or something."

We're both silent at that. Like pioneers, we keep our perishables cool in the basement because we don't want to use the energy to run the fridge. We haven't had ice in months. Well. Since winter. And we have a small bottle of aspirin that came a few weeks ago in the rations, but I don't want to use it unless we really have to.

"I'm all right."

"I'll take care of things. Go to sleep," he whispers after a moment, when I slip my legs under the sheet and curl against my pillow.

But I can't sleep. Not for a long time. Everything hurts

so much that I can't get comfortable. I doze a little, but that's almost worse than not sleeping at all. The lights go out when he turns off the generator, and the silence helps, but even after he comes to bed and the soft, regular hush of his sleeping breaths should lull me into dreams, I stay awake.

Eventually, I can't stand it anymore. I get out of bed, quietly as I can, though Dillon's exhausted from working so hard all day and probably wouldn't wake up unless I banged a gong in his ear. From Opal's room comes the soft whistle of her nighttime breathing—she's got a constant cold or allergies or something that makes her snore. The room at the end of the hall glimmers with the flicker of candlelight. Mrs. Holly is almost always the last of us to go to sleep. She says it's because she's old enough to feel how close she is to sleeping forever. Mrs. Holly can be kind of depressing sometimes.

In my mom's room, the one that used to be mine, I find her tucked into her big bed. It takes up most of the room, but she uses only one small piece of it. With a shudder, I remember how I used to have to tie her up at night to keep her from wandering. The shock collar that was supposed to keep her under control had almost killed her.

Mercy Mode, they call it.

I call it murder.

"Mom?"

She blinks her eyes open and holds out a hand for me to

crawl into bed next to her. I'm too old for cuddling, but we hold hands and lie side by side, staring into the darkness. I can distinguish the night sound of everyone's breathing, and Mom's is raspy and hoarse, the way her voice is.

"I miss you," I tell her, knowing she won't say anything. "And Daddy."

Beside me, she turns and strokes a hand down my hair. "Hmmm."

I tell her about the Connie in the woods and the riot at the ration station. About how the woman had tried to take our peanut butter and how I'd knocked her to the ground. My fists clench and open while I talk. I can still feel the thud of flesh against my knuckles. My hands are bruised and aching, just like all the rest of me, but they feel good, too. As if they remember how it had felt to defend myself, to punch and slap and pinch, as if that's supposed to feel good. I know it's not, and ashamed, I look at her.

"I liked it," I whisper. "When she fell on her butt, I wanted to laugh. I wanted her to hurt and be scared, Mom. Because she was trying to hurt us, maybe not with her fists, but by stealing what was ours. And we needed that peanut butter. It's ours. We deserve it."

"Shhh," my mother says. Her fingers tangle in my hair, pulling, but not on purpose. She's clumsy, that's all. The Contamination changed her, but what they did to her brains before they released her into the kennels . . . that's what broke her.

I want to cling to her and cry, have her comfort me the way she did when I was little. The way she still does for Opal when she has a tantrum. Instead, I curl up next to her and listen to her tuneless, singsong hum of random lullabies until she drifts into sleep.

Downstairs in the kitchen, I fill a glass with cool water and sip it slowly. The longer I'm still, the stiffer I get. Moving helps. Looking out the window over the sink, I see movement in the trees. We don't have much of a backyard: just a deck that meets the slope of a hill into the woods. My dad had built a set of pretty wooden stairs, painted red, from the deck and up the hill to a flatter patch where we'd put a fire ring and a hammock, both gone now. Squirrels and chipmunks like to run up and down those stairs, which are splintery and faded. They don't run in the dark, though.

Slowly, I put down my glass on the counter with a clink that sounds very loud. Slowly, slowly, I turn and find the wooden block that holds the knives. They're all very sharp. My dad bought them for my mom one year for her birthday; I thought it was a dumb present, but she'd kissed him and said it was perfect.

I pull out the longest, biggest knife. They're supposed to be weighted just right, balanced to make chopping and slicing easier, and I let it almost dangle from my fingertips as I go to what used to be a sliding glass door before our next-door neighbor Craig slammed his head into it over and over again a few years ago. Dillon and I added hinges to the plywood covering the broken space so that we can use it as a door. It was one of the first projects we did once he moved in. The hinges squeak when I push open the wood, and I tense—without being able to see through any glass, I could be opening the door to anything.

The deck is mossy and slick under my bare toes. Ivy that's supposed to landscape the slope has grown up in a lot of the cracks between the boards, but that's better than the insistent creep of the raspberry bushes, which are slowly overtaking the entire yard. I love raspberries, but hate the spiny, prickly vines. I step on one now and hop, cursing while I bite my tongue. There are prickers still stuck in the sole of my foot, but it's too dark to get them out now.

Limping, I hold the knife a little tighter. I could've grabbed a flashlight from the drawer—we use it sparingly, careful with the batteries. Like with everything else, we have to be aware of using things up and not being able to replace them. Besides, there's a half-moon tonight, and my eyes have adjusted.

In the dark, a Connie will stumble and trip and be made at least a little more helpless than I will be.

More movement catches the corner of my eye. Something jerks and twitches in the trees just beyond the steps. The woods are full of deer, turkeys, raccoons. Opal swore she saw a coyote once, but I'm sure it was one of the mangy dogs that now run in packs. We have feral cats by the dozen. But animals are silent and know how to move through the woods without making a commotion. Even deer slip quietly along their regular paths, running and crashing through the trees only when they're startled. Humans are the ones who don't know how to be quiet in the woods. We haven't had any Connies since we moved back here, but I'm always ready.

Knife in hand, I go up the steps, wishing I'd taken the time to put on some shoes. Even a pair of flip-flops would be better than this—my foot already hurts from the prickers, and now a splinter from the steps digs deep in the meat of my sole.

My foot crunches on leaves and sticks, the sound like a gunshot in the otherwise silent night. I freeze. Ahead of me in the low-slung bushes that have sprung up around an old rabbit hutch, something is rustling. I tense. My fingers sweat. The knife slips. With a raspy growl, I lunge toward the bushes, determined to chase away whoever's in there getting ready to bust through our windows and try to get inside.

I stumble forward, catching myself at the last minute before I can slice myself open. The bushes part, and the source of the noise leaps out. It's not a Connie.

It's a chicken.

FOUR

"I'M GOING TO NAME HER BOKKY. BECAUSE she says, 'bok, bok, bok.'" Opal, with the chicken on her lap, pets the red feathers and giggles when the hen pecks at her palm. "She's hungry."

Opal had been more excited than at Christmas when she woke this morning to find the red hen I'd captured last night. I'd locked the hen in the laundry room until I could figure out where else to keep her. I didn't want her getting eaten by something. She was lucky she had made it in the woods as long as she had.

"Feed her some bugs from your hair," I tease. "She'll like that."

Opal makes a face, but it's hard to insult her when she could have a headful of bugs and not care. I don't remember ever being such a gross little kid, especially not at her age. Heck, at twelve, I'd started getting my period and shaving my legs. . . . That sudden thought sobers me. What will I do when that happens to Opal?

"Chickens like grain. But not rice." Mrs. Holly shakes a gnarled finger. "That's not good for them. Velvet, maybe you can get some feed the next time you and Dillon go into town. It will be too heavy for you to carry on your own."

And it will cost money. No government rations for chicken feed. We all stare at the hen, which seems to be sleeping.

"She's in pretty good shape for living wild in the woods." Dillon's dressed for work. Heavy work pants and boots, long-sleeved shirt. He carries his thick gloves in one hand. His hair's still wet from the shower he took. I don't know how he can stand it. We have plenty of water, but unless the generator's running, it's no better than lukewarm.

"Where'd she come from, Velvet?" Opal pets the soft feathers. "Will she lay eggs?"

"I'm sure. I hope so." Suddenly, my mouth waters. It's kind of ridiculous to salivate at the thought of scrambled eggs. Chocolate? A cheeseburger, tainted memories aside? Sure. But eggs? Who gets worked up about that?

Dillon shakes his head. "Sorry, kiddo, we don't have a rooster."

I give him a sideways look while Mrs. Holly laughs a little. Mom, who's busy organizing the silverware drawer, a task she does again and again and again, looks over her shoulder and smiles.

"What? You need both, right? To make eggs." Dillon frowns.

"You only need a rooster if you want chicks," I tell him.

His brow furrows. He doesn't always have it easy, being the only dude in a house full of women. I don't mean to laugh at him, but I can't help it. He looks so cute that I lean to kiss him.

"Hens will lay eggs so long as they're fed and watered," Mrs. Holly says. "If we take care of this girl, we should be able to get an egg a day from her."

It doesn't sound like a lot, but when you haven't had any in forever . . . nothing but powdered vegan egg substitute . . . My stomach grumbles. Dillon blushes. He's figured it out. I find him so totally endearing just then.

"Gotta get to work. Velvet, do you need me to get anything in town?"

"Chicken feed? I don't know how much it will cost, but you should be able to get some from the Tractor Supply." Lots of other businesses have gone under. Businesses selling things most people don't need or can't afford anymore, like office supplies or manicures or fancy furniture. But Lebanon's a rural area, and even people who weren't farmers before have picked up the habit of homesteading the way we have. "Do you have any cash?"

"Yeah."

At the door, I kiss him good-bye. So domestic. So sweet.

In the bright morning sunshine, I can see a hint of stubble on his chin and shadows under his eyes.

Dillon worries as much as I do. Maybe more, because while I have the luxury of my mom and sister beside me, his parents are both gone. I hug him hard, because even if I'm too young to be married, too young to know about forever, I'm not too young to know how it feels to miss someone so much, it makes you feel like you can't make it another minute.

"Have a good day." It's what my mom always said to my dad when he was on his way out the door.

"You, too." Dillon pauses, looking past me, though everyone else is in the kitchen. His troubled gaze meets mine. "Be careful today."

"You, too." I think we both know that every time he goes out, there's a chance he won't come back. All it takes is being in the wrong place at the right time.

I watch him walk down the driveway to get his truck, parked in the spot in the trees that we cleared to keep it hidden from the passing patrols. The big tree that fell across the driveway is still there—we thought about cutting it apart, even though it's kind of a pain for Dillon to have to park his truck at the bottom instead of closer to the house. But that tree also makes it impossible for any other vehicles to get up the driveway, which means it's just enough of a pain for the patrols that they've mostly left us alone. I wave. Behind me, Opal nudges me with the chicken in her arms. I look at my little sister and touch the chicken's smooth beak. Her bright, dark eyes don't blink as she tilts her head to stare at me.

"We should find out if she has any sisters."

Opal beams up at me. "Oh, do you think she does?"

I'm not sure, but I hope so.

FIVE

I HAVE NO IDEA HOW FAR A CHICKEN CAN wander, but it can't be that far. Can it? I have no idea how to judge anything about a chicken's health any more than I know about its roaming range, but Bokky is fat and bright eyed and not skittish, so that makes me think she must've been taken care of pretty well, at least until recently. There are plenty of farms around, but I'm willing to bet this chicken came from someplace closer.

Opal and I take our bikes. The streets are pitted and buckled, and the tenacious raspberry bushes have started encroaching on the asphalt. My foot still hurts this morning, even after I soaked it and tried to pull out all the tiny splinters, but with an adhesive bandage and an extra-thick pair of socks, it's feeling better.

At the bottom of our driveway, we pause. Opal's grown so much taller that her bike, with its white-and-pink tassels hanging from the handlebars, is too small for her. The hems of her jeans hit her a few inches above her ankles, something I notice just now. Her pants are too short, but her hair's too long.

"Take a picture; it'll last longer," Opal says smartly, and if it wouldn't be weird and also sort of gross, since she hasn't taken a bath in days, I'd hug her.

"Which direction?" To the left is a big hill we'll have to push our bikes up, but will be easier to coast down at the end, when we might be tired. To the right, the road goes down, which will be great to start, but much harder on the return trip.

Opal doesn't think about that. She jerks a thumb to the right. "Down."

"Up," I tell her. "That's toward the back of the neighborhood, and don't you think if anyone was keeping chickens toward the front gate, I'd have noticed when I passed?"

"Do you notice everything?" Opal can be a bit of a brat, and she's too smart for her own good, but she has a point.

"Of course not. But I'd probably notice if someone's living in any of those houses, and I haven't seen any signs of it."

"Maybe they're hiding." Opal shrugs and pushes her bike along with her feet, not pedaling. She heads left, though, so at least we don't have to argue about it.

"Maybe."

"*We* do," she points out.

We don't hide, exactly. Not really. It's more like we lay low. The generator makes enough noise to attract attention, as do the lights we use for a few hours at night. The police come through every so often, scouting for trouble, but they know who we are and they leave us alone, even though Spring Lake Commons was evacuated, and technically, we aren't supposed to be living here. The soldiers are the ones we have to watch out for, because they're mostly young, with lots of time and not a whole lot to do except ride around looking for reasons to make people miserable.

"I bet it's the lady with all the pets." I point ahead to the rising road. The house I mean is just beyond the old bus stop where once I'd waited with my backpack and books and my friends in a life I'd been stupid to think was lame. "Remember her?"

"She was mean." Opal frowns as she puts her feet on the pedals and starts up the hill.

I haven't been down this part of the street since before the Contamination, but I'm clearly in much better shape than I was back then, because the hill that used to make me huff and puff is easy to ride up now. Even for Opal, and I was sure she'd complain about it. At the top, I look back toward our driveway. I feel a little bad about leaving Mom and Mrs. Holly alone in a way I don't when Opal's there. Dumb, I know, since she's a kid and they're adults, but . . . Mom isn't herself and Mrs. Holly is old and not as "spry," as she calls it.

"Come on, Velvet!" Opal's impatient. She waves a hand toward the long, curving street lined with trees and driveways.

This part of the street is flat enough that we can see almost the whole length to where it makes a T at the back end of the neighborhood. And I stop, grabbing at Opal's shirt to keep her from pedaling away from me. There are two cars in the middle of the street, about half a mile from us. Two wrecked cars.

The pet lady's house is only two driveways ahead of us, with still half the distance beyond that before we'd even get close enough to see anything inside those cars, but they *are* between us and the next intersection. Still, I gesture at Opal to hush. I don't know why. Just that the sight of those cars makes my stomach churn.

Opal puts a hand on her cocked hip and gives me an exasperated look. "Chickens? Hello?"

"Right." I push off on my bike, heading for the driveway of the house all the neighborhood kids had been fascinated by, even as they'd learned to stay clear.

The pet lady had loved animals. Kids, not so much. The school even had to move the official bus stop because of how many times she complained about kids standing on the edge of her property while waiting for the bus. Not that any of us ever so much as put a toe on her lawn, because she'd come hurtling out the front door, yelling at anyone who did. We never stopped there during magazine sales fundraising time, nor for Girl Scout cookies, nor for Christmas caroling, nor for trick-or-treating. Rumor had it that she owned a potbellied pig she kept in the fenced backyard, and although that exotic pet seemed worth at least a peek, nobody had been brave enough to try it.

"She has a pit bull trained to bite you in the butt," Opal says solemnly as we pause at the foot of the drive.

"Mom said that's not true."

She gives me a dark look. "Peter Miller said he saw it once."

"Peter Miller never saw anything," I tell her, hoping that was true.

Closer to the house, we both hesitate again. The yard's overgrown with the same weeds and brush as ours, but there's something about this house that feels empty. I listen for the sound of a growling pit bull or anything else, but there's nothing but the rustle of leaves and the far-off chirping of birds.

I ring the bell, anyway. We wait for a minute or so. Opal presses her ear to the door, listening. She rings the bell again and again before I can stop her.

"Nobody's home," she says confidently, and twists the door handle.

"Wait! You can't just . . ."

But she can just, can't she? Nobody's lived in this house

for a long time. Probably years. Inside the foyer, a small table is overturned, and dead leaves skitter across the tiles in front of our cautious feet, but coats still hang from the rack and none of the glass looks broken. You'd think I'd have lost the habit of reaching for the light switch, but I do it, anyway. The lights don't turn on, but the big overhead windows let in enough sunshine so that we really don't need anything extra.

Opal makes a face. "It stinks in here."

It does. Bad. Like cat pee and dog fur and poop, but really old. Mostly it just smells like damp and mold. I rub the sleeves of my sweatshirt.

"C'mon, let's go out back. She wouldn't keep chickens in the house." I move toward what I hope is the kitchen, and Opal follows.

It's creepy, stalking through a stranger's house, even if we're sure she's not home and hasn't been for probably at least two years. We pass a living room, shadowy and dark, the curtains drawn. The carpet looks thick and soft, but the smell coming from that room is worse than by the front door, and when I peek inside, I see that something has made a mess of the overstuffed couch, which used to be covered by what looks like a sheet. Something big enough to tear the cushions apart and scatter the stuffing.

"Pit bull," Opal says darkly, inching closer to me. She actually takes my hand.

I can't stop myself from cringing a little when we pass

the open staircase and bridge hallway above. Something could be lurking up there, waiting to jump down on us. . . . I push Opal along faster as I crane my neck to keep an eye overhead. I imagine the glint of eyes watching us, or maybe it's not imagination. Either way, we hustle through an arched doorway into a bright kitchen that would be cheery if it didn't reek like a zoo. The lower cupboards have been clawed to splinters. Muddy paw prints paint all the countertops. The fridge hangs open, the shelves and drawers covered in the remains of food spoiled so long ago that they, at least, don't stink.

Opal covers her mouth and nose. "Yuck."

"She definitely had pets. Wow." I look around. There are six or seven food and water bowls, all empty and overturned, scattered around the tile floor. A couple of big plastic bins that must've once held pet food are on their sides, punctured and clawed.

Opal studies them, crouching, then looks at me with a frown. "I bet they left and didn't take their pets along. And they got hungry."

We're both silent at that, thinking of our old dog, Jody. You could hardly leave her for a few hours without having to worry she'd get into the garbage or something else. She liked to dig into my mom's dirty laundry and eat my dad's socks, too. She'd been long dead by the time Opal and I had to leave our house to be placed in the government-assisted housing we'd been in while I looked for our mom. But when I think of leaving Jody behind, starving so that she had to claw her way into the cupboards just to find something to eat . . .

"I thought she loved them." Opal sounds bewildered and sad, like she might start to cry.

I know how she feels. "Just because someone has a lot of something doesn't mean they love it. Some people like to collect stuff."

"Even animals?" She sounds horrified and disgusted.

"Yeah. I guess. I heard Dad say to Mom once that the pet lady was an animal hoarder."

Opal pokes one of the bins with her toe. Behind her is a set of sliding glass doors inset with a pet door big enough to let a pit bull in and out. Hell, big enough to let Opal in and out. The rubber flap is ragged and splashed with mud.

"Maybe they got out and ran away when they couldn't get any more food," she says.

Still, I'm sad enough to cry a little myself when I think of how scared and hungry the dogs—more than one, by the looks of it—must've been. Cats, too. Even that poor pig. I don't remember what they told people to do with their animals when we were all evacuated from the neighborhood, but I'm sure the pet lady thought she'd come back.

I don't want to think about why she never did.

We find the pig outside. At least what's left of it. There's no way to tell how it died, just that its skeleton is mostly all in one place, close to a small doghouse off the deck. The only way we can tell it was a pig is by the hoofs.

Opal is silent for a minute or so, then begins to snuffle. "Peter Miller said the pig's name was Wilbur."

"Of course it was." I pat her on the shoulder.

"And those"—she points at the feet—"are called trotters."

I have no idea if that's true, but I turn her gently away from the sight of the pig's remains. The rest of the yard has been dug up so much, it's more holes than grass, but it might've always been that way. We look for chickens, but the yard is empty. Not even a coop to show that once the pet lady might've had some.

"Maybe Bokky was the only one she had," Opal says.

"Maybe." But the chicken looked too fat and healthy to have been scratching out an existence on her own—that's what I think. "C'mon. Let's ride a little farther. We might find something."

It's a relief to get out of that stinky house and into the fresh air. The bright sun overhead feels good after the shadows inside. Opal and I get on our bikes and push off on the cracked asphalt, pedaling for a few feet before she stops.

She's looking at the two cars ahead of us. "Velvet, I don't wanna go past there."

"It's a wreck, that's all. Someone was going too fast, I guess. It's fine. We have to go past them," I tell her, "in order to get to the next houses. And, hey—remember the pond?"

Opal gives me a narrow-eyed look. "Yes."

"We can check it out. See the fish. We haven't done that in a long time."

We don't live in a traditional neighborhood with mani-cured, postage-stamp lawns. Most of the houses have several acres of land, all wooded. The house I'm thinking about is set on what my dad said was one of the biggest plots in the neighborhood. The original owners had dammed up and diverted a few of the springs and streams running across their property to make a couple of ponds big enough to hold fish and frogs. Giant, beautiful koi with flowing tails and bulging eyes. We were all fascinated by the ponds and the tadpoles in them every spring. Sometimes after din-ner, my mom and dad would give us each a plastic baggy full of stale bread crumbs and we'd all walk up there. My parents would chat with the people who lived there while we fed the fish and splashed our toes in the edge of the water.

"It'll be fun," I say.

Opal perks up at that, though she gives the cars a wary glare. "They're creepy."

They *are* creepy; I have to agree with her about that. "We'll ride fast."

And we try, but I can't stop myself from looking in as I ride past. I slow without wanting to, letting Opal go ahead.

The glare from the sun makes it hard to see inside the window, which is starred and cracked from the impact of someone's head.

There's a person in the car closest to me.

Long dead, slumped over the steering wheel, face turned away so I can't tell if it's a man or a woman. I lose my balance, a pedal catching the back of my leg and cutting into my skin. Muttering a curse, I hop, my bike wobbling. I keep myself from falling only at the last second by grabbing the car's door handle. The metal's hot enough to sting my palm, and still off balance, I slap my hand flat against the glass of the passenger-side door.

For a long, terrible moment, I'm convinced that dead face is going to turn and give me a gape-jawed grin, lunge toward me. Try to eat my nose off, slurp out my eyes . . .

"Velvet!" Opal cries, sounding affronted and horrified. "What are you doing?"

"Nothing. Keep going. I'm just looking."

"At what?"

"Nothing," I tell her, and push off with one foot, urging my bike to go.

It is nothing. I should care more, but the person in the car's been dead for a long time. Long enough to have turned mostly to bone and dried, rubbery flesh. I'm not going to pull him out and bury him, and he can't do anything to hurt us, so why not leave him alone?

But I look over my shoulder as I ride away, wondering

how the accident happened and who was in the other car; if he'd wandered away or had been uninjured. Wondering if I knew the person slumped over the wheel. Had I sold magazines to him for a school fund-raiser? Had his kids ridden the bus with me? It doesn't matter, I remind myself, pushing the pedals harder to get up the last bit of hill, working my muscles and my lungs, riding as fast as I can in the hot spring sunshine. Dead is dead.

"Keep an eye out for chickens!" I yell at Opal's back.

She's riding so fast, her hair flies out behind her. I pump harder, standing up on the pedals. Racing. She looks sideways at me and her mouth purses in determination. She pedals harder, trying to catch up, and I pretend I'm going full out but I hold back, letting Opal pull ahead.

In another minute, we're laughing and shouting insults at each other to urge each other to go faster, faster, faster! I lean over the handlebars, pumping hard, loving the effort and strain of my muscles. Even the sweat. How long has it been since I rode for fun, instead of the endless slog to town, choking on exhaust and worried I'll get pulled over by soldiers? The road here has flattened out and we coast, heading toward the back of the neighborhood and the house with the pond. All the driveways are overgrown. I imagine I can hear the frogs croaking. I think about dangling my feet in the water, how nice and cool it will be. How pretty the fish will look. I lift my hands, balancing.

Free.

"I'm gonna beat you, Velvet!" Opal shouts, looking over at me.

That's when I see it, a blur of red. Opal, not paying attention, has veered toward the side of the road just beyond the driveway to the house with the ponds. The red thing flutters and flaps, heading right for Opal's front tire. Hard on its heels come three dogs I recognize as part of the pack that roams the neighborhood.

"Watch out!"

Too late, for Opal and the chicken. The bike hits it dead center; the chicken gives an agonized squawk; and Opal flips headfirst over her handlebars. Shouting, I brake hard and leap off my bike, which catches me on the same calf that bore the sting of the pedal earlier. I run, limping to her. The dogs circle, growling and barking, still trying to get at the chicken fluttering slowly on the street. Without think-ing, I grab up a stick from the side of the road and swing it at them.

I don't want to hit the dogs, but I will in order to keep them from biting me or Opal. "Get out of here!"

They might've gone a little wild, but these dogs remem-ber what it is like to live in a warm house with a bed and people who love them. They back off, whining. The big-gest, a golden retriever with hair so filthy and matted, it's not at all golden anymore, darts forward to grab the chicken in its mouth. It backs away, growling at me, then the other dogs inch forward to try for the prize.

I swat again, scattering them into the brush, along with the chicken. Then I turn to my sister. "Opal!"

I take her in my arms, expecting her to cry or maybe even scream, but Opal lolls, too silent. Eyes closed. Mouth open.

She's bleeding.

SIX

"OOOOOW!" OPAL TRIES TO WIGGLE AWAY FROM me, but I hold her still with my free hand as I dab at the scabbing wounds on her knees. Blood trickles down her forehead, painting her cheeks in a feathery pattern.

"Sit still. I need to clean this, Opal." We can't afford an infection, a trip to the doctor, or the ER.

My shaking hands don't make it any easier to work on the cuts, and my patience is gone. My baby sis can be a brat, but she's not stupid. She sees the look on my face and settles down, wincing when I dab the wet cloth again, trying to clear away the worst of the grit and blood before I clean the wounds with the peroxide I found in the medicine cabinet.

We're in the house with the ponds. I didn't think about knocking the way we had at the pet lady's house—with a limp and moaning Opal in my arms, I'd shoved the front door open and taken her upstairs to the master bathroom. That's where my parents kept all the medical supplies, and it was the same in this house. Fortunately, the master bath was bright from the bank of windows overlooking the backyard and the ponds, and also a skylight. I'd settled Opal on the still-fluffy bath mat while I looked for stuff to take care of her cuts, but she roused herself when I started to clean them.

I swipe at the drying blood on her cheek and focus on the slice on her forehead. It's not too deep, but it probably could use a stitch at one end, where the gravel left a small triangular flap of skin. I do my best to smooth it into place as Opal whimpers.

"You'll have a scar," I say.

She brightens at this and gets to her feet to look at herself in the mirror. "Cooooooool."

"Let me put some Band-Aids on it." I wash my hands at the sink, using soap from a dust-covered but half-full dispenser. I dry them on the hand towel and gesture for her to face me.

It takes only another minute or so to get all of Opal's scrapes and slices covered. She admires her reflection again, turning her face side to side, and I shake my head as I watch her. My hands have finally stopped shaking.

Behind us, a shadow flickers in the doorway.

Opal sees it, too, and we both turn. I put out an arm to keep her from leaping forward. Tense, I listen.

"Velvet . . ."

"Shhh."

Something's in the bedroom. I hear the soft, rapid *shush-shush* of breathing, the shuffle of feet on the carpet. I hold my own breath and put a hand over Opal's mouth to keep her from saying anything else.

Connies aren't sneaky. Most can't speak, but that doesn't mean they're quiet. Connies groan and grunt and flail; they stumble and stagger and knock stuff over.

I listen, listen, listen.

Something rattles like jewelry on top of a dresser. Door hinges creak. I hear a heavy thump.

Opal's lips move against my palm, her voice muffled. "What is it . . ."

I look around the bathroom for something to use as a weapon. How stupid I've been, going anywhere without one. It's not like I can head into town with a golf club strapped to my back without getting into a lot of trouble, but why didn't I think about needing something while wandering through the neighborhood?

All I can find is the handle to a mop, tucked in the corner by the toilet. It's the kind with the removable foot you're supposed to cover with special wet cloths. Gripping it, I step down on the foot and break it off, making the end of the handle pointy.

Opal's staring with wide eyes as I heft the handle, then toss it back and forth from hand to hand. It's lightweight, but metal. Once, I stabbed a Connie in the eye with a penknife. A mop handle should work, too.

I gesture for Opal to stay behind me. Instead, my sister grabs a pair of nail scissors I didn't notice from the counter and holds them up. I'm trying to silently argue with her, but she shakes her head, her brow furrowed so hard, it bunches up the bandage. That has to hurt.

"Opal!"

Before I can stop her, she hurtles herself through the doorway, scissors raised, with a battle yell that would shame a Viking. I'm after her in a second, grabbing the back of her shirt to keep her from going too far. The fabric rips—it's an old shirt, one she's almost outgrown, and I'm left with nothing but a scrap of material in my fist as Opal screams and lunges toward . . .

A puppy.

Barking, it stands its ground, even as a puddle spreads out beneath its paws. The poor thing's shivering and shaking, tiny teeth bared. I grab at Opal again before she can stumble forward and stab it by accident.

"Velvet, it's a puppy!"

Earlier, my hands were shaking. Now my heart's pounding. I taste sweat when I lick my upper lip, and my armpits are sour with it. I don't let go of the mop handle, but I do lower it.

Opal turns to me with a wide grin. "Isn't he cute?"

The puppy looks like a German shepherd, or a shepherd mix. It yips and manages a snarl that will be impressive in a few months but now only earns an "aww" from Opal. She reaches for it, but the terrified puppy snaps at her fingers and backs up a step.

Opal follows, and so do I, trying again to snag her to a stop. I didn't chase off a pack of hungry dogs just to have her end up with bitten fingers, anyway. The puppy snarls, backing up again, then begins to whine. She crouches and holds out a hand to the puppy. "Hey. Hey, little guy. Don't be afraid."

"Opal, don't. He might bite you."

"He's just scared." She looks at me over her shoulder. "He's just a baby, Velvet. He's scared and alone. Can we keep him?"

The puppy has allowed Opal to inch closer. It's still trembling but no longer snarling. It sniffs her hand, then gives it a tentative lick. Opal looks at me with big puppy eyes herself.

I'm not sure I want to take on a pet, not with all the other responsibilities. But how can I leave this little guy behind without anyone to take care of it? I think about the pet lady's house. The clawed cupboards. The poor, sad dead pig. This puppy will starve and die in this house alone, and if we let it outside, it'll be destroyed by the pack. Or it'll become part of it, and I don't want that, either.

Opal sees me wavering. "Hooray!"

"But you have to take care of him," I warn. "Feed him, take him out. If he makes a mess in the house, you have to clean it up—"

"Duh." Opal looks annoyed, then turns her attention back to the pup. "C'mere, little sweetie."

The puppy, wiggling its butt, moves closer. Opal pets it gently. It flops onto its back, legs in the air, and wiggles.

"See," my sister says confidently, "he loves me."

In the kitchen, we find a couple of bags of dog food in a cupboard. I look out the back door into the yard. If there are chickens, that's where they must be. Opal's busy petting and cooing over the puppy in her arms. She giggles when it licks her face, and she puts it down to let it run out into the backyard. We find the chicken coop, all right, but something's worked a hole in the wire fence around it. Inside, we find nests filled with hay and the overwhelming stench of chicken poop. We find a lot of feathers. But we don't find any chickens.

The puppy runs around and around, barking, until we go to the back side of the coop. There, huddled in the dirt in a scooped-out hollow beneath the coop, is a bedraggled red chicken. The puppy noses it, but it barely moves.

"Is it dead?" Opal asks.

I bend to look at it. The chicken eyes me, beak half open. It doesn't move when I touch it. "No."

"Is it hurt?"

Carefully, I lift the chicken out of its hiding place. This chicken's been through some trouble. Cradling it against me, I try to check it for injuries and find no blood. "Maybe it's just scared."

"I'd be scared," Opal says matter-of-factly, "if all my friends got eaten up."

"Let's see if we can find some chicken feed."

I look around for a shed, but there isn't one. Aside from the coop, surrounded by the wire fencing, the yard's bare except for a raised bed that must've been a garden. It makes so much sense to do it that way—the soil's so poor here, so full of rocks, that I can't believe I didn't think of it before now. It would work so much better than trying to use clay pots barely big enough for a few herbs. There's nothing planted in the raised bed, only dirt, but when I filter some through my fingers, it's soft and rich. Not like the hard-packed clay we've been fighting to grow things in.

The house has a set of storm doors leading to a basement. The doors are locked with a chain and a padlock. I settle the chicken back into its place in the dirt and leave Opal and the puppy to guard it while I go in the house to see if I can get into the basement that way.

The basement door is also locked with a chain and padlock.

This stops me. Whatever's in the basement must be worth protecting. So. Keys. I check the kitchen drawers and find the usual broken pens and scratch pads, garbage-bag twist ties. There's a place for keys next to the fridge, a smooth wooden plaque with small metal hooks. But no keys.

I check inside the garage door, which is where my dad often hung his keys. Nothing. Inside the coat closet by the front door, I check the pockets of all the coats and all the hooks. I find a purse hung behind a woman's leather jacket. There's money inside.

My parents *did* raise me right. I *do* hesitate before I take it, but there's nearly a hundred dollars in small bills in the wallet, along with a handful of coins. I take it all. It might not make a difference—you can't spend money if there's nothing to buy. But I can't just leave it here when we might need it someday. Besides, the people who owned this house are long gone and won't miss it.

Checking outside through the kitchen window, I see Opal tossing a ball for the now-eager puppy, which goes after it with great galumphing leaps. The formal living room is just beyond the kitchen, and across from it, a smaller room that looks like a den or office. I can see bookshelves through the half-open door.

Books, oh, books. Without the Internet or much TV to entertain us, they're as necessary as food, and I'm through the door without a second thought. I'm so focused on the shelves, stuffed to overflowing with paperbacks and hard-cover titles, that I don't see the man in the armchair until I almost trip over the footstool.

He's dead.

The black plastic garbage bag hides his face, and the mottled gray and green of his hands, which are gripping the arms of the chair, are clue enough he's long gone, though I shout out a startled "Oh, hi!" out of reflex. The smell wafts to me next, something sickly sweet with an undertone of dirty diapers, but I don't think he's been dead long enough to start to fall apart.

Two dead people in a day is too many for me. I want to run screaming from the room, but instead I stare at him for a long, long moment, happy that Opal's outside. She's a smart kid and knows what's up with the world these days, but I still don't think she needs to see this, even if it's obvious that he died by his own choice, in his favorite chair. There's a water glass next to him, and an almost-empty bottle of liquor. A bottle of prescription pills. He's wearing a robe and plaid pajamas too heavy for this time of year and worn slippers . . . it's the slippers that get me, after a minute or so of staring at them.

He chose to die in this room, which must mean it was his comfortable place, where he could sit in his pajamas and read a book. It's wrong for me to be here. Even if the books won't do him any good, I can't take them.

I do, however, know where the keys must be.

I hold my breath as I pat the pockets of his robe. I know that even if he were Contaminated, he's not going to lurch back to life and grab me. The Contaminated aren't the undead, just people who drank protein water that gave them holes in their brains and made them incapable of controlling their rage. But he's still a corpse, maybe not dead long enough to be totally rotten, but long enough to bloat.

He sighs when I press his belly. Now there's a stink that

makes me gag and choke—I swallow back the rising sting in my throat and force myself not to spew. Worse, that noise goes on and on, more than a sigh. It's a low, groaning noise that sounds like he's trying to talk. It's the gas inside him. The pressure of my hands as I dig inside the other pocket, finding the jumble of keys. I'm the one making him wheeze and moan. My hand gets stuck inside his pocket, my fist bigger coming out than going in. I can let go of the keys and get away from him, or I can yank.

When I do, the corpse . . . settles. The stink is rich and thick and enormous now, and all I can see is the bulge of my hand in his pocket, and all I can think is, "He made sure his slippers were on. He made sure his slippers were on," over and over, but as I tug and pull the keys free, the body's feet shift on the floor and one slipper comes off.

Gasping, the keys in my grip, I stumble back. The body slides sideways, head lolling. His hand falls away and his arm knocks into the table, which rattles the bottle and the glass for a moment before the whole table tips over and everything shatters.

I'm not screaming, I'm whistling breaths in and out of my lungs through my clenched teeth. I don't want Opal to hear and come in. I don't want to breathe the air full of dead-guy germs. The world tips and turns as I push myself away from him, but the body moves toward me, shaking and sliding onto the floor, and I jump out of the way just in time, before it can land on me.

I can't move. The keys in my hand are hung on a key ring of plastic with a picture of a smiling couple inside it. It's the guy on the floor in front of me—I know it—though in the picture he's wearing jeans and a T-shirt and a ball cap. He's smiling, his arm around a pretty woman with reddish hair. The names on the back are KEVIN and SANDRA. The sun's shining on them both, and I don't want to see their happiness because I know how terribly it all ended.

Without even a second longing glance at the books, I back out of the room and close the door behind me. At last, I suck in great gulps of stale air. I want to scrub my tongue and the inside of my nose, but I settle for washing my hands in the tiny powder room that's completely dark because there are no windows. I have to keep the door propped open with my foot, because it keeps wanting to swing shut, and I can't deal with being in the darkness right now, even in a room too small to hide any monsters.

In the kitchen, I open the back door and holler for Opal, who's still playing with the dog. "I'm going to see if the feed's in the basement. You stay there!"

She gives me a curious look, probably at the shaky tone of my voice, but she's too busy playing with the puppy to argue. At the kitchen sink, I wash my hands again, then rinse my mouth. I imagine the taste of that death smell still inside me, and for a minute I'm sure I'm going to barf.

It never gets easier, seeing dead bodies.

I saw a flashlight in one of the drawers when I was

looking for the keys. So I take it, then I unlock the door and make it halfway down the stairs before remembering the *Evil Dead*. I'm so stupid. Anything could be down here, ready to grab my ankles and pull me down, ready to swallow my soul. . . .

Freaked out, I leap the last couple of steps to the concrete floor and turn, waving the flashlight, expecting to see the red eyes and bloody mouth of something horrible coming after me. All I see is a tidy basement cast in shadow, but it isn't completely dark, because there are a few windows in wells.

I see at once why he locked the basement door. Shelves and shelves of food and supplies. Cans, jars, bottles, plastic bins, neatly labeled. Camping gear. Jugs of water. Everything's arranged so neatly, it's like being in a grocery store, and for a few seconds, all I can do is stare.

Every time I go into town, I risk getting pulled for a random screening, and I know the consequences of that. They'd be immediate and terrible. With this stuff, I wouldn't have to worry about getting our rations. Or stretching them to last. This is better than the money I pulled from the purse in the closet, because this is food, and I want to hug each and every can of creamed corn.

I can see the stairs leading to the backyard at the basement's far end, and moving toward them, I let my fingers trail along the shelves, cataloging the contents while I imagine the look on Opal's face when she sees it all. I'm not paying attention to anything—just salivating over chocolate (real chocolate chips!)—when I come to the end of the shelving units and into a brighter part of the basement.

The woman was pretty once. I know that because I've seen her on the key ring I have shoved in the pocket of my denim shorts. She hasn't been pretty for a long time.

A dirty quilt is bunched up next to her but provides no comfort, because she crouches directly on the concrete. Her hair has mostly fallen out, leaving big bald patches and wispy strands of some dull color I can't name. She's the color of snow and so thin, the knobs of her spine stick out. So do her shoulder blades and hip bones. She's wearing only a threadbare sleeveless nightgown that does nothing to hide any bit of her.

She's also wearing a collar.

The lights are steady green, which means it's working and she's calm. I stand staring, unable to speak. She rolls her eyes toward me. There's no recognition in her gaze. Barely a flicker of interest. She shifts on the balls of her feet, and I can hear her body creak from where I stand. The woman rubs her fingers on the concrete in front of her, over and over. The tips of them are raw and bleeding, and on a few of them, I can see the bones.

I want to tell her to stop it, but I can't make myself say anything. I stand and stare, frozen, as she rubs and rubs. I want to cry. I want to run, but all I can do is stand there and watch her wear away the skin of her fingertips. She doesn't even flinch. Blood spatters the floor, and I can see by the stains that this isn't something new.

Then she turns her face to me and grins. Most of her teeth are missing, and the ones that remain are gray or black or broken. Her tongue slides out to lick her cracked lips. Her eyes were dull before, but now they're very blue and very bright. She makes a low, grinding noise from deep in her throat and rocks herself back and forth.

She pushes herself to her feet.

Because of how far into the basement I've come, she is now between me and the kitchen stairs. I don't wait. I run toward the backyard stairs, pushing off the concrete like I'm defying gravity. Five steps, six, and I'm there, but I've forgotten something important.

The doors are locked from the outside. The keys in my pocket might open the lock out there, but right now I'm pressed against the slanted metal doors, crouching on the top step. I see her shadow before I see her. Then her bare, dirty feet. Pale legs. The torn hem of her nightgown and her thighs, covered in bruises.

Then she ducks, still grinning, to get inside the stair-well, and I can't hold back the screams. They rise up and up, stealing my breath. From outside, Opal cries my name. She pounds on the metal doors, and the ringing is loud and fills my head. She's pulling on the chains, but she can't open them. Can't get the doors open.

I'm trapped.

The woman tilts her head curiously and moves forward, teeth bared in that horrible grin. The bloody bones of her fingers stretch toward me. The lights on her collar glow steady green. She's still making that awful noise, and I realize it's . . . laughter?

"Opal! Stop yelling and banging!"

"Are you okay?"

"I'm . . . I'm fine, I just got startled. . . . I'll be out in a few minutes. . . ."

Opal babbles something else while the puppy barks and scratches at the metal doors. The woman below me comes closer, no longer laughing. Drool gathers in a corner of her mouth and slips down her jaw. It drips.

Oh, God, she stinks. Blood and body odor, the stench of rotten teeth. She wipes her bloody fingers on her nightgown, smearing it with fresh stains. Closer, inching closer.

"Stop." I try to keep my voice calm.

This is different from the cheerleader in the woods, when I was already running, already pumped up. That girl was Contaminated but uncollared. The Connie in front of me is not supposed to be able to get aggressive because the collar around her neck is meant to keep her subdued. But she's scarier than that cheerleader, and my heart is trip-trapping so fast, I feel it all over my body, and I can't breathe.

"Velvet!"

"Opal," I cry desperately. "I'll be right out, I promise!"

"Should I come inside?"

"No! Make sure the chicken's okay!"

The woman in front of me hisses out a sigh. Dark yellow urine slides down her legs and patters on the floor while I cringe away. She looks at it, then at me, her gaze gone blank again. She stands in a puddle of her own filth and doesn't move except to put a mutilated hand to her head and pluck at the few remaining hairs.

Now I understand why the man upstairs killed himself, but I don't pity him. Anger fuels me, gets me to move. This was someone he loved, and I know how terrible it must've been for him to watch her become this, a thing more than a person. But he left her to fend for herself, locked in a basement, while he took his own life to escape.

I have to help her.

"Hey," I say softly, reaching a hand the way, earlier, Opal had reached toward the frightened puppy. "Shhh, shhh."

I don't want to touch her, not really. I want to do almost anything but that. I force myself to move closer, slow and calm. In order to get out of the stairwell, I have to move close enough past her that she could easily grab and attack me. She doesn't, but I tense every muscle until I'm back in the basement and can stand upright.

I have an idea, and pulling the keys out of my pocket, I look at the back of the key ring. "Hey. Sandra. Sandy?"

She doesn't move. I try again, touching her shoulder. "Sandra?"

Her head rolls on her shoulders as she looks at me. Shuffling, she turns. Beneath my hand, her bones feel sharp enough to cut.

"I'm going to take you out of here, okay? I'm going to take you someplace safe." Even as I say it, the words sound like lies. I can't take this woman home. That's insanity. But how can I leave her here?

I let my hand drift down her bony arm to her wrist, so narrow, I can entirely circle it with my fingers. I pull gently. Sandra takes a step toward me. Step by step, I lead her past the shelves of food, past her dirty nest, toward the stairs to the kitchen. But she won't go any farther.

She pulls back, grunting. The lights on her collar flash, first blinking green. Then yellow. Then briefly red. I stop pulling her. I know what red means. Mercy Mode. I can't force her to come with me, not without triggering her collar to blast her brain with continuous electric shocks.

"Velvet?"

Crap, it's Opal at the top of the stairs. Before I can tell her not to, she's coming down them with the puppy scampering ahead of her. She stops at the bottom and gasps. The puppy runs at us, tumbling over its own paws and landing at Sandra's feet.

Sandra looks at it. Slowly, she reaches a hand. Her mouth twists into a smile, and her lips move, shaping words I can't make out. The puppy sniffs at her and sneezes, then lies down and puts its nose between its front paws.

"Sandra?"

She looks at me, blinking. Her collar lights glow a steady green. I look at Opal, who's wide-eyed but hasn't run.

"We need to help her," I say.

"She looks bad, Velvet!"

I know Sandra can't understand us, but I still shush Opal with a gesture. Opal sidles a little closer. Sandra doesn't look at either one of us. Her attention's on the puppy at her feet. Drool drips onto the concrete, spattering near the puppy's head, and it looks up with a whine and rolls onto its back, exposing its belly.

"It was her puppy," Opal says.

"Yes. I'm sure it was."

"He's not afraid of her."

"No." I shake my head, watching the puppy butt its head against Sandra's bloody fingers.

"Can you take the collar off her? Like you did with Mama?"

"No." The collars need a special key, which I don't have. I'd unlocked my mom's collar using a straightened paper clip, but that had been after months of seeing her gradually recover despite the collar. Of believing with my whole heart that my mother would never hurt us. I have no idea how violent Sandra had been before they found her and fitted her with a StayCalm collar, but the way she's brutalized her own body isn't a good sign. "And she doesn't want to come upstairs."

Opal looks around the basement with a wrinkled nose. "Gross. Why not?"

"Maybe this is all she knows or remembers." I gesture at the shelves of food and supplies. "And we need to get Dillon to come with the truck. We should take this stuff. Look at it all."

Opal was also raised right by our parents, and she hesitates for a second. "You mean, steal it?"

"There's nobody here to use it." I don't tell her about the man upstairs, but she nods, anyway.

"We could leave a note. Tell them if they come back that we can pay them back."

My heart squeezes with love for that kid. "Yeah. We could. But first, we need to figure out how to get Sandra back to our house."

"How'd you know her name?" Opal inches closer, eyeing Sandra, who is crouching next to the dog. She croons to it under her breath, something tuneless and awful.

I show her the keys and the picture on the front, the names on the back. "How's the chicken?"

"I think it died," Opal says matter-of-factly. "It kept breathing really fast and funny, and when I looked under its wing, there was blood. Something bit it."

I'd have expected her to be more upset by this, but this is the world we live in now. "Crap."

"It's not any worse than being run over by a bike," Opal says with a small, sad sigh and a frown.

I squeeze her arm. "You didn't mean to."

"It's still dead," she says, and there's no argument from me.

Sandra's not petting the puppy, but it's obvious she knows it and it knows her. This gives me an idea. I hook my fingers in the puppy's collar and tug it upright.

"Opal, take the puppy. I'll take Sandra. Maybe she'll follow the dog."

"Velvet . . ." She keeps her distance. "Do we have to take her?"

I straighten. "We can't leave her here."

"Could we just come back and make sure she's okay?" Opal whispers.

I'd rather do that, too, but . . . "She can't take care of herself. Mama wouldn't want us to leave her here alone. She'll die, Opal. She'll die."

Opal's lower lip quivers, but she nods and grabs for the puppy's collar. "Come on, boy!"

Together, we lead puppy and person up the basement stairs into the kitchen, where Sandra balks again. My muscles are tense and aching, and it's so much hotter up here that I pause for a drink of water. I should try to pack a bag for her, at least. Some clothes. Personal items, not that she'd notice. But all I want to do now is get home. I'll bring Dillon and the truck back later to load it full of the stuff in the basement. I can get Sandra's things then.

Opal finds a leash hanging by the back door and hooks

it through the puppy's collar. There's another leash beside the one she took, and I take it down, looking over Sandra's collar. There's no hook to attach a leash, but there's room between the collar and her neck for me to loop the thin strap of leather and hook it to itself.

"Is that going to work?" Opal looks skeptical. The puppy dances on the end of its leash. Sandra doesn't move.

"It might. She needs shoes, at least. Hold on." In the front closet, I find a pair of flats. She doesn't resist when I lift each foot and slip on the shoes, but when I'm finished, I have to wash my hands out of shivering disgust at how dirty her feet are.

Outside, the sun burns on the tops of our heads, making me wish I had a hat. The puppy lunges, chasing a butterfly, and Opal laughs as she runs with it. Sandra, on the other hand, cowers and bats at her face.

This isn't going to be easy.

Sandra can't ride a bike. She can't walk any faster than a shuffle, and she balks every few feet unless the puppy's in front of her. By the time we get to the end of her driveway, I'm already exhausted. My stomach growls. I think longingly of the basement full of foods I haven't tasted in so long. Crackers and cookies and potato chips. I should've taken at least a few things. Water, especially.

"I'm hot." Opal, pushing her bike with the puppy's leash wrapped around one fist, makes a face.

"Me, too. We'll be home soon." We've barely made it to the next driveway. It's going to take forever.

Opal looks at Sandra with a frown. "Where's the guy?"

"What guy?"

"The one with her in the picture."

I hesitate, then shrug. Lying's not always the wrong thing to do. "Who knows?"

We walk. And walk. And walk. I try to keep Sandra in the shade but also out of the weeds on the side of the road, and that's almost impossible. The third time I drop my bike trying to get her to keep moving, I mutter a bunch of words my mom would've grounded me for saying. I drag it to the side of the road.

"Leave the bikes. We can come back for them."

Opal nods and puts hers down next to mine. "Hey, Velvet. I bet we could find a bike that would fit me better, anyway. In one of these houses. I bet we could find a lot of stuff."

We could. There are about a hundred houses in this neighborhood, and even if most of them don't have the stockpiles the last one does and even if a few of them have people living in them, I'm sure we could scavenge all kinds of things we need. I can't believe I didn't think about it before, but I guess there's a little bit of a leap between squatting in your own house and looting your neighbors'. Still, it makes total sense, whether or not we leave IOUs. . . . There are reasons people aren't coming back to these empty houses, and one of them's at the end of my leash.

We've just crested the small hill, giving us sight of the two wrecked cars, when I hear the low rumble of an engine. I know at once what it is. I've heard it before. Too loud to be a car, which means it's an army truck. Probably more than one. Moving slowly but steadily, making a sweep of the neighborhood. Looking for Connies.

"Come on." I jerk the leash too hard, and Sandra stumbles.

I grip her by the elbow, trying to help her, but she hisses and flinches. She snaps with what's left of her teeth and rakes at me with her bone-tipped fingers. I don't let go. I can't let her go.

They're coming.

"Opal. Take the dog into the woods. Hide!"

I'm not positive they'll take us if they find us, but they *will* take Sandra, and if we're with her, I'm not sure what they'll do. Something bad, for sure. I pull again on the leash at the same time I grab at the front of her nightgown. The fabric tears, and I let go before I rip it off completely.

"Sandra," I say in a low, urgent voice, trying to keep calm. The lights on her collar are blinking. "Please, listen to me. We have to hide. The soldiers—"

Something triggers her then. With a snarl scarier than anything that came out of the puppy, Sandra batters me with feeble fists. She's so weak, I have no trouble holding her off, but the problem is that she won't stop. Not out of fear, not from pain. It must hurt her terribly when she batters at me with her raw fingers, but she doesn't even flinch. She won't stop because she can't control herself, and I can't quite bring myself to punch or kick her even though she's coming at me with snapping jaws and clawing fingers.

"Velvet!"

"Hide," I tell my sister.

Opal ducks into a thicket of trees, fading into the shadows. Anyone looking hard could see her, but I hope the patrol won't be looking hard. Connies don't hide. They come after you, even if you're an armed soldier in a truck.

I yank on the leash. Sandra stumbles again. This time, she goes to her knees. Her collar is blinking yellow. The rumble is louder, closer. She rolls, kicking and screaming, swiping at me. Her shoes come off. Her dirty toes snag my shins, and I jump back. I don't want her to cut me—who knows what kind of infection I'd get from those toenails.

I don't have a choice. Leaving her in the middle of the street, I dive into the weeds at the side of the road as the truck clears the hill. Shaking, Opal clings to the whining, struggling puppy. I clamp my hands over its jaw, hard as I can. It fights me, scratching, then calms when it can't get away. I'm hurting it, but I can't help that now.

The truck moves past the wreckage of the two cars without stopping. The soldiers probably checked it out before. Just past the wreck, the truck screeches to a stop, inches from Sandra. She's on her hands and knees now.

A soldier hanging from the back jumps off. "Got one! Hey, this one's collared. Holy shit, lookit this, a leash."

He yanks her to her feet without any scrap of gentleness. Sandra bats at him, but there's nothing she can do. He pulls the leather taut, lifting her onto her tiptoes. The collar blinks, blinks, blinks.

More soldiers pour out of the truck. Most of them are laughing, nudging each other, and pointing at Sandra. One hangs back, his expression blank. He looks like he's still in high school.

They circle her. Poking. Prodding. One tears the rest of her nightgown down the front, and it flaps open. She doesn't even try to hold it closed, but she lashes out with fists and feet and teeth.

She staggers.

"Watch out," one of the soldiers says, dancing back. "She'll getcha!"

I want to run out and stop them, but instead I hold the squirming puppy still and pray none of the soldiers looks around. I nudge Opal to get her to look away. She's crying, fat, silent tears sliding down her cheeks. She buries her face in the weeds and dead leaves.

Sandra's collar beeps. I catch a flash of steady red glare from it; my stomach twists and I swallow thick, copper-tasting spit. The soldiers poke and laugh until she goes back to her knees. Then to her side, twitching and jerking. A low, steady grunt filters from her. She writhes in the gravel, and none of them does anything to help her.

They watch her die.

When it's over, one nudges her with his toe, then gestures at another two to grab her and put her in the back of the truck. One alone could've lifted her, I'm sure; there's so little to her. But one grabs her feet, and the other slips his hands beneath her armpits. They toss her in the open back of the truck like she's a sack of garbage. I hate them.

The one who didn't laugh or take part has been scanning the side of the road. His gaze meets mine. I know he sees me. The recognition is instant and clear. In the next moment, his eyes glide away and he shouts to the others.

"C'mon, let's finish this up!"

The soldiers get in the truck and drive away, leaving behind the stink of their exhaust and the fading sound of their laughter. I let go of the puppy, which whimpers and scuttles away from me to the protection of Opal's arms. Opal sits, her face dirty and tear streaked. I sit, too, and turn and spit over and over until I've cleared the taste of blood from my mouth.

"Why?" Opal asks, but I have no answer. Her next question is what gets me to my feet, suddenly frantic. "What if they took Mama?"

SEVEN

WHEN OPAL AND I COME THROUGH THE FRONT door, we find Mrs. Holly in the living room, knitting away like there's not a thing wrong in the world. At least that's what you might think if you didn't notice that she's just moving the needles back and forth, not actually doing anything with the yarn. She looks up, relief clear on her face, and puts aside the knitting. There's a streak of what looks like blood on the edge of her nose, like it came down from her eye and she wiped it away, but missed some. At the sight, everything inside me turns cold, even though I'm still sweating.

"Thank God it's you, girls. I thought it was the soldiers come back again." She shakes her head and mutters something that I don't need to speak Dutch to understand. The puppy sniffs everything, including Mrs. Holly, who laughs in surprise and bends to pet him. "Oh, where did you find this little love bug?"

"In one of the houses. We found chickens, too, but they were all dead." Opal frowns. "Instead of Bokky, we should call our chicken Lucky."

I want to ask Mrs. Holly what happened to her eye, but not in front of Opal. I flop onto the couch. "Where's my mom?"

Her mouth goes tight. "She's safe."

I sit upright. "Safe?"

"They would've taken her," Mrs. Holly says, "if they'd found her."

"But . . . she's not collared!" Frantic, I jump up.

She shakes her head again. "Now they are testing. They come here, banging on the door, saying they have the right to enter. They have kits with them. Test kits, you know. They say they are going to test us all."

My shaking legs don't want to hold me up. It's what I've been afraid of since they started the random screenings. "Where is she?"

Mrs. Holly pushes herself to her feet. She points at the basement door. A vivid image of Sandra crouching on the concrete hits me like a hammer. Our basement is finished, but even so . . .

"She's in the closet under the stairs. I was outside in the garden when I heard their trucks coming. I knew. I just knew." Mrs. Holly's voice shakes. "I made her go inside and hide. And I was right, Velvet. They had the test kits. They came in."

She touches the inside corner of her eye, where now I can see a purpling bruise. "They used a thin needle. They say they can test everyone this way, much faster than before. No need to take anyone into a center to be hooked to machines. They can do it wherever they like."

"Mama!" Opal's at the head of the basement stairs. She gives me an accusing look. "I'm going to find her."

Together, we go into the basement, which is darker than the one where we found Sandra. But we have battery-operated lanterns set up in different places, and using one, we open the accordion door to the closet beneath the stairs. This closet is full of odds and ends we haven't used since moving back here. Old camping cots and sleeping bags, spare towels and sheets in plastic garbage bags that my mom used for us when we were sick enough to be on the couch instead of in bed, or for sleepovers.

One of my favorite movies, when I was a kid, was *E.T. the Extra-Terrestrial*. Finding my mom in the closet reminds me of the scene in which E.T. is hiding among stuffed animals. Mom's covered up with blankets and towels, sitting patiently in the dark, but she pushes her way out when Opal calls for her.

Incredibly, she laughs as she struggles to get to her feet. She enfolds us, hugging hard. She strokes Opal's hair and makes a face at the dirt.

She doesn't have to talk to make herself understood. When my mom gets upstairs with us into the light, she makes a face at Opal's dirty skin and clothes, and sends her off to get washed up. Opal grumbles, but goes. My mom turns to me next, taking my face in her hands and turning it from side to side.

She hugs me close, patting my back over and over again. I cling to her, wishing I could tell her about the soldiers and Sandra, the man in the den, and be sure she understood. Then I decide it doesn't matter if she knows what I'm saying, only that she listens to me say it. With Opal upstairs and Mrs. Holly puttering in the kitchen, I sit with my mom on the couch and tell her everything.

She holds my hands through the entire conversation. She doesn't let go. And I know that even if she can't answer me, my mom always knows how to make me feel better.

EIGHT

THE BRACELET DILLON IS WEARING REMINDS me of the ones we used to get when we went to the water park. Plastic, with holes punched in it to fit any size wrist. This one's bright green, and whoever put it on him made it a little too tight. I try to soothe the angry red line on his skin around the edge of the plastic, but there's not much I can do about it or about the dark bruising on the inside of his eye socket. It's not as bad as Mrs. Holly's. Maybe the person who did Dillon's test had a gentler hand.

"I'll get a new one the next time they test," he assures me. We're tucked up in his single bed, our legs entwined. He smells faintly of soap and his hair's damp. He got the last of the hot water tonight, but he deserved it.

"How often are they going to do that?"

"I don't know. I hope not a lot. It hurts, even with the stuff they spray into your nose first to numb it." Dillon yawns, then turns, stretching, to get the battery-powered radio from the nightstand. He settles it between us and turns the volume on low, since everyone else has gone to sleep.

"It sounds horrible."

"It wasn't so bad." He pauses. "But they took some people after the test. Ralph from the truck. Good guy. Never heard him even raise his voice. He tested positive. They just put him in zip-tie cuffs and in the back of their truck."

I'm silent at that. What can I say? Dillon adjusts the station until it comes in clear.

"Hey, hey, hey, all you good gentles, ho." The Voice sometimes likes to talk in a "Renaissance Faire accent," which is proof to me that he's not the terrorist the government would like us to believe he is; he's just a nerd with a ham radio. "What's the good word out there in the black zone?

"Yes, you know it." The Voice switches into a normal tone, not so flip. "Black zone. That's what they call us. The maps they don't show on the TV anymore, the ones that used to show us the worst-hit zones. Remember those? Well, we're in one of the biggest, folks, and they call us black zones. 'Cuz we're all dead one way or another. Eventually, we're dead."

Dillon pulls me closer, and I bury my face in the clean-soap-and-skin scent of him.

"You think you're safe because you're still okay? Don't get too comfy. They have the portable tests now: they can stick a needle in your eye socket and take out a teeny-weeny piece of your brain, find out within thirty seconds if you've got something nasty getting ready to eat holes in your gray matter. And if you do? Say good-bye; they're hauling people away without so much as a chance to grab a toothbrush and a change of underwear. If you're lucky, they'll take you on over to the Sanitarium, where at least, I hear, you get three squares and a cot. I mean, you'll maybe have to fight a couple of hundred other drooling Connies for that grilled cheese, and the beds are full of bugs, but it's for science, kids! All for science. Of course, I hear they're taking anyone they want on over there, trying to figure out what's going on that makes you turn, 'cuz it doesn't matter if you're showing any symptoms; you could become a Connie at any second. That's what the government believes, and here's something you don't know, kids, that they don't want you to know. You might be Contaminated without ever having had one single sip of ThinPro."

"What—?"

"Shhh," I say. "Listen."

"Yep, yep, yep, that's right, boys and girls, my fellow black-zone comrades. The poison has spread, and someone knows how, but I don't. Not yet. I'll keep on it, though, never fear, the Voice is here. . . . But I'm not here, not now, not nohow . . . gotta run, kids, the devil's at the door. . . ."

The radio blats with static, and Dillon turns it off. He puts it back on the nightstand before turning to pull me closer into his arms. We stay that way without talking for a minute or so before I pull away to look at the plastic bracelet.

Earlier, I'd told him about the house, the dead guy. Sandra. Mrs. Holly hiding my mom. Now I touch the plastic on his wrist and wonder what this is going to mean.

"They tested everyone," Dillon says. "It wasn't random. We all had to get the test and the bracelets. And it wasn't at a checkpoint. They came into the office to do it."

Dillon has a great smile that lights up his whole face. I miss it. He hasn't smiled like that for a while. He misses his mom and dad, and worries about them, I know. He worries about us here at home when he's at work, and I worry about him when he's not here. Everything is worry and sadness lately. It exhausts me.

"Maybe you shouldn't go to work tomorrow. Or again," I say. "We should stay out of town. . . ."

"Velvet, I have to go to work, or we lose our benefits." Dillon takes my face in his hands and kisses me.

I like the kiss, but not the reason for it. He's trying to quiet me, but I push away and sit up with my legs over the edge of the bed. "I drank the ThinPro. Not a lot. But enough, right? All it takes is a sip, we know that from before, and the Voice just said—"

"The Voice says a lot of things." Dillon sits up behind me, pulls me back against him. Tucks his chin into the curve of my shoulder. "You're fine. You're going to be okay."

I think of the cheerleader I put on the ground. How easily I'd done it. How much I'd . . . liked it.

I know he's trying to calm me, but it's not working. My mind's whirling. I can't stop thinking of Sandra. The collar hadn't kept her from turning violent, but had it really been her fault when the soldiers taunted her into it? They'd killed her as surely as if they'd put a gun to her head.

But my mom wasn't like that. With the collar, she'd shown signs of recovering, and without it, she should've died or turned into a raging Connie, but she hadn't. I lean against Dillon, finally softening.

I think about when things first started to go down, how he picked me up and took me to the grocery store so we could stock up. It was a good thing he did, because what we bought that day had lasted us until the new ration cards were handed out. "We need to be ready, though. For winter. For everything. I think we should start stockpiling stuff even more. Stripping out the houses around us. Fortifying this house. We should've done it before now."

"Yeah. But it felt . . ." Dillon shrugs. "Wrong."

It doesn't feel more right now, but it does feel necessary. "Me and Opal can start tomorrow. The closest houses first."

"I can help." He looks determined.

"You have to work."

Dillon shakes his head. "For what? Medical benefits we'll never be able to use? Ration cards we can't redeem?"

"No. So you can keep an eye on what's going on in

town. And find out what happened to your mom and dad."
I touch his arm, and he pulls me close for a hug.

"Okay. But I'll help when I get home. And on my day
off . . ."

"Dillon." I squeeze him. "We'll figure it out. I can handle it."

He grins. "I know you can. You can handle anything."

"Even if we only took all the food and supplies from the
house where I found Sandra, we wouldn't have to go into
town for a long, long time. At least not until things start to
get better."

"Velvet, do you really think things are going to get any
better?"

I twist to look at his face. Dillon pushes my hair off my
forehead, and I remember how it felt the first time he kissed
me. It still feels that way, even if we are in this weird legal
marriage thing that doesn't make me feel at all like a wife.
I let him kiss me, but it doesn't make everything all better.
It's not magic.

"Do you think they're going to get worse?" I ask.

Dillon's expression tells me everything. "It can always
get worse. Can't it?"

He kisses me then. Again and again. And we let ourselves get lost for a while in the kissing, but later, when I'm
trying to sleep, I can't stop thinking about what he said.

Listening to the soft sound of his breath, I stare at the
ceiling for a while. Then I get out of bed and make my

rounds. It's silly to check the windows and doors when the people who'd want to get in wouldn't care if anything was locked, but my mom always used to do it and now I do it instead. I check on the puppy curled at the foot of Opal's bed. Then Opal, who sprawls with her mouth open, her hair stuck to her forehead with sweat. I crack the window for her, thinking with longing about air-conditioning and electric fans. Down the hall, I peek in on Mrs. Holly, who's silent and motionless in her bed. Then my mom. Always my mom, who hardly ever sleeps anymore.

She's sleeping now, though. Her windows are all wide open, and I wonder if she did that herself. She surprises us all the time with what she's capable of doing.

I think about the soldiers and what they did to Sandra. I think about the man I found in his den. And I know what Dillon said is true.

It can always get worse.

NINE

"IT'S YOUR TURN!"

"No, it's your turn!"

We push and shove, wrestling, though I'm a lot bigger, and Mom and Dad will yell at me if Opal gets hurt. Which she does, the baby brat, in a minute. She bumps her elbow on the chair and starts yelling. I'm gonna get in trouble, but I don't care because it *is* her turn.

"It's your turn," I tell her. "I did it yesterday!"

"Mama!"

"Check the chore chart," Mom says from the laundry room. She shows up in the doorway with a basket loaded with towels and stuff. "One of you, do the dishwasher. One of you, feed the dog and make sure she has fresh water. Both of you, gather the trash."

Opal and I stare at each other, both of us frowning. Opal crosses her arms and kicks her foot against the chair. This stubs her toe, and she hops up and down, hollering.

"Settle the kettle," Dad says from the living room. He's putting together a bookcase from Ikea for my room. He told me it's supposed to be easy because it comes with all the tools you need, but he's been saying a lot of bad words.

"Velvet, it's your turn," Opal whispers really loud.

I don't want to empty the dishwasher. I know it's not my turn. I know it's Opal's turn, because yesterday, while she watched cartoons on Daddy's computer, I emptied the dishwasher and I put a sticker on the chore chart. I could prove it to her. I could point it right out, and she'd have to do it for two days in a row because I did.

But suddenly, I don't really care so much. If she wants to be a baby booger brain about it, she can. I'll unload the dishwasher, because I'd rather do that than open the stinky can of dog food and put it in the bowl, and then rinse the other one and put clean water in it. Jody slobbers all over everything and gets her fur all over it, and when you're trying to feed her, she sometimes bumps into you so hard that everything spills. And she steps on your feet with her dirty paws, and I just got new white sneakers.

"I'll do the dishwasher, Opal." Sugar wouldn't melt in my mouth, my mom would say.

Opal doesn't even look suspicious. She just wiggles and laughs. I bet she thinks she's getting the best of me, but guess what: ten minutes later, when I'm finished with the dishwasher and she's covered in dog slobber, I'm the one who's laughing.

"Yeah, Dexter, I'd like that chore chart back." I sigh. The puppy sniffs my foot and then whines at the back door to go out, so I open it for him. At least he's housebroken.

The memory isn't a bad one. It is less about the dishwasher than about the time when we all were a family, and that's what makes me sad as I rinse the dishes and put them in the drying rack. My dad built me that bookcase, and it's still in my room. But my dad's gone. The towels my mom was folding that day are probably still in the linen closet, but my mom's not the same as she was back then.

Everything's different, and it shouldn't surprise or upset me anymore, but right now it does.

I don't have time to mope, though. Opal's pounding down the stairs, taking the last two at the same time with a leap, one hand on the railing to keep herself from falling. She thunders through the living room.

"Jeez, elephant feet. Settle the . . . kettle," I finish, thinking of my dad. I tell her to brush her teeth and wash her face. To at least try to comb a few of the tangles from her hair. "And eat some breakfast. We have a lot to do today."

Opal rolls her eyes. "Like what?"

I lay it out for her. "So we're going to go through each house, room by room, and get anything we need."

"It will feel like we're stealing." She looks around the kitchen with a guilty expression.

"You're the one who thought of it. Don't worry, it will

be okay." I want to reassure her, because I understand how she feels. It *will* feel like stealing. It will also feel like salvation. "We'll only take from the empty houses. And we don't have a choice, Opal." I don't want to scare her, but I need her to understand how important it is. "Dress in long pants and long sleeves, too."

"But it's hot!"

"Yeah, and we don't know what we're going to be dealing with in any of these houses. There could be . . . stuff."

Opal perks up. "Gross stuff?"

"Maybe." I eye her. "Maybe you should stay home."

"No! No, Velvet, I want to go!" She hops out of her chair, dancing in an agony of not wanting to be denied.

"It's going to be hot and sweaty, and yeah. Maybe gross." I keep my smile hidden.

Opal nods. "Like the dead pig."

"Or worse, Opal." I'm not smiling now. I'm serious. "You have to promise to listen to me. Do what I say. We have to be careful, because there could be—"

"Connies. I know." Her expression darkens.

"Or other things," I say gently. "There could be regular people."

Opal frowns. She's grown so much taller over the past few months that pretty soon she'll be looking me in the eyes. Her hair's still too long, and her pants not long enough.

"We'll have to find you some new clothes," I say.

"Hooray!" She jumps up and down.

For a second, I think she's being a brat, but then I see that she's really happy. That makes me happy, too. The thought of robbing houses to get her some new jeans suddenly seems more like an adventure and less like desperate necessity.

"Mom," I call up the stairs.

Mrs. Holly comes to the railing. "Your mother's still sleeping, Velvet. What do you want?"

I frown. "Still sleeping? It's late already."

Well, it feels late. Honestly, without clocks, it's hard to tell anymore. Mrs. Holly puts a finger to her lips.

"Yes. Shhh."

"I'm gonna get dressed." Opal pushes past me to head upstairs, leaving me with the dishes that I put in the sink with barely a longing glance at the dishwasher.

The puppy, which has been growing even faster than Opal, scratches at the back door to be let in. Then he tries to follow us when Opal comes downstairs and we head for the front door. "Dexter, stay."

"Can't he come with us? He'd be good protection." Opal bends to give him some love.

"He can stay here. Protect Mom and Mrs. Holly," I tell her, thinking of how annoying it will be to have to keep an eye on the dog as well as my kid sister.

Opal frowns. "But . . ."

"He barks at anyone who comes by. They need him here more than we do," I remind her, and she reluctantly agrees.

"I'll keep him." Mrs. Holly hooks a finger through

Dexter's collar, and he sits obediently. "You girls be careful."

Opal does a little dance, fingers bopping from side to side as she sings. "We're gonna get. Stuff to eat. We're gonna get. Stuff to wear. We're gonna get—"

"You're gonna get. A kick in the pants," I sing back.

"Velvet. Stop. Teasing."

Surprised, I turn to see my mom standing halfway down the stairs. She looks tired, like she didn't sleep at all. The circles under her eyes are dark as bruises, and her hair's a tangled mess. She smiles, though, and holds out a piece of paper.

Opal and I share a look. I take the scrap of paper, on which she's scrawled . . . a list? "What's this?"

"We need."

I scan it. Her handwriting is unrecognizable, a toddler's scrawl. I can sort of make out a few words. *Soap. Candles.* But . . . "Mom, you wrote this?"

"We need," she says, "these things."

I don't want to make her feel bad by getting too excited, but this is the most she's done in a long time. For the first time in a while, hope leaps up inside my heart. I look at the paper, but can't make out anything except a few letters here and there. I hug her hard and say into her ear, "I'll see what I can do."

TEN

SANDRA'S HOUSE, WITH ITS OVERFLOWING
basement, is the obvious place to start, because while there's
Kevin to deal with, at least I already know about him. I can
make sure to avoid that room, at least until I can take Dillon
with me so we can take care of Kevin's body. It wouldn't
be the first time we've buried someone together. For today,
with just me and Opal and our bikes, I have the old bike
cart and the canvas shopping bags my mom had collected
over the years. She never remembered to take them into the
grocery store with her and always ended up having to buy a
few more, so we have about fifty. I also have my backpack,
and Opal has hers. It's not the truck, but we'll manage.

"How come we have to go so far away?" Opal stands up
to pedal.

"We already know what's in Sandra's basement; we
might as well start there. Plus, we should have a system. If
we start toward the back and work our way forward, we can

make sure to get all the houses. Like at trick-or-treat time, remember?"

Opal laughs. "Yeah, that house back there always had the full-sized candy bars, remember?"

"But that other one gave out toothbrushes—" We both look at each other and say at the same time, "Let's not go to that house!"

"They probably have all kinds of, like, dental floss and stuff." Opal makes a face as she pedals, letting her bike weave slowly back and forth in front of mine as we head for the hill.

I snort softly. "Good dental hygiene's important."

"So's candy," Opal says. "And I'd rather find a bunch of that!"

Me, too, that's the truth. It feels like ages since I got the treats from the convenience store. My mouth waters for the taste of chocolate and caramel.

"Hey, Velvet, can we stop at the ponds first?"

We park our bikes in front of the garage and go around the back. Opal dangles her feet into the water, looking at the fish. She tosses them cracker crumbs from her pocket, and I don't scold her about wasting food, because feeding the fish is fun for her. It's a normal thing to do, and we need normal.

"Velvet, could we eat those fish?"

I'd thought of it before, of course, but it surprises me that Opal has.

She looks at me. "I mean, if we start to run out of food, and we can't get more from town. If we don't find a lot of stuff in these houses, I mean. Could we? If we had to."

I wonder how much she's overheard. Or guessed. I shrug, looking into the murky green water. "Yes. I think we could."

"I hope we don't have to."

"Me, too."

She gives me a serious, solemn look, the corners of her mouth turned way down. "I'm scared, Velvet."

I sit next to her at once, slipping off my shoes to let my toes dip into the water. "About what?"

She shrugs, reluctant. I wait, giving her time. I tip my face to the hot spring sun and wish we could sit there forever without ever having to talk about the things that make us afraid.

"You're gonna laugh at me," she says finally.

"No. I won't. I promise."

Opal gives me a sideways look. "I miss school."

A bubble of laughter does try to slip out of me but I hold it back. "Your friends?"

"Yes. But also . . . school. What if I just never learn anything?"

She's so sincere, so serious that my laughter fades. I put an arm around her shoulders and squeeze her close to me. We've fallen off with her lessons, that's true enough. It hadn't seemed to matter. Not with the rest of the world falling to pieces. Now I'm sorry I didn't think about how it might make her feel.

"We can go back to doing homework, if you want."

She makes a face. "Ugh."

"Opal, there's going to be a lot of stuff for you to learn. And the best teacher is life, right?"

"That's what Daddy used to say." She sniffles.

"Yeah." We sit in silence for another few minutes. Fish swim beneath our feet, occasionally nibbling at our toes.

"I'm scared about Mama, too. That they're going to take her away, and this time, we won't get her back. And I miss Daddy."

"Me, too."

"When I was in school, Jenna Simmons said her dad got killed right in the beginning. She didn't see it, but her older brother did. He said the police used a knitting needle in his eye, but whoever did it messed up, and he died instead of just getting lobby . . . lobby . . ."

"Lobotomized. Yeah. Lots of people did." That's one of the things I wish I didn't know.

Opal gives me wide eyes. "Do you think that's what happened to Daddy?"

I should say yes, but something different slips out of me, and as soon as I say it, I know it's the truth. "No, I don't."

"It would be better if we knew for sure," Opal says.

"Yes."

"Like when we were waiting to see if you were going to find Mama in the kennels. That was hard."

I squeeze her again. "Yeah. It was."

"I'm scared they're going to take her away again. And you away. And then who will I have?" Opal bursts into tears, raw and horrible.

I hold her close, stroking her hair and rocking her the way our mom always did for us when we were little. It's not the same, I know, but Opal clings to me as she cries and cries. I cry, too, but silently, so she doesn't know.

"Nobody's going to take us away."

"You promise?" She looks at me with wet, red eyes, her nose dripping snot.

It's wrong to promise something you can't be sure of, but I nod, anyway. "Yes. I promise. Now c'mon. Let's go get loaded up. I want to get back before the afternoon."

Opal wipes her eyes and seems more cheerful when we leave the ponds behind. We go into the garage to start, wrenching open the door, which doesn't want to open at first because it's connected to an electric door opener. I have to yank the chain attaching it at the top, but then we roll it open. I picked the garage because I think there will be tools.

Tools can be weapons.

Once light floods the garage, though, an idea hits me so strong between the eyes, I can't believe I never thought of it before. "The car!"

Opal's busy looking at the bikes hanging on the rack, but looks over her shoulder at me. "Huh?"

"There's a car here." I actually slap my forehead, that's how dumb I feel. "Opal, we don't have to ride back and forth on our bikes or wait for Dillon to get home. We can use this car! Load it up, drive it back and forth."

She laughs. "You don't have your driver's license."

"Does that matter?" I snort laughter. "I'll only be in the neighborhood. We'll just have to be careful to avoid any patrols or anything."

Opal looks at the car, a blue two-door Mustang. "It's kind of fancy."

I think of the photo of Sandra and her husband from the key ring. How happy they'd looked, the wind blowing their hair, the ocean behind them. If they had kids, they'd have been adults by now. I touch the Mustang. It's the kind of car my dad said he'd get someday, when we were out of college. His midlife crisis, my mom would reply, but laughing, like she knew our dad would never go through one of those.

"But it's here. And I'm sure there are other cars in the neighborhood, too. Maybe even another pickup truck. A newer one." Dillon loves his truck because it had been his dad's, but it's old and kind of falling apart. He worries about its breaking down.

"All right, well, let's get cracking." Opal puts her hands on her hips, and I'm reminded suddenly that even though she can be ten kinds of pain in the butt, I love that kid.

"We want tools," I tell her. "Hammers, screwdrivers, saws. Also, any nails, screws, stuff like that. Let's start loading up. I'm going to see if it starts."

I have the keys on the ring. One of them fits the Mustang, which roars to life, filling the garage with noise and a blurt of stinky exhaust that has Opal running outside, waving the air in front of her nose. I turn off the ignition, something light bubbling inside me. This simple thing will change so much.

We clean out the garage of anything that seems useful. Boxes of nails and all kinds of fasteners. Tools. Rolls of duct tape.

It's hot, sweaty work, and I wish we could listen to music while we do it. Sometimes, I miss music more than anything. Hip-hop beats, funky pop songs. The classic rock my parents liked to torture us with. I liked the Doors, hated the Who. I'd never have admitted it, but I loved Black Sabbath and Judas Priest and Metallica, too.

That's what I sing now: "Enter Sandman." The words surge up and out of me. Pretty soon, Opal and I are yelling the words and jumping around the garage, playing our air guitars. She busts out a pretty good air drum solo that has me cracking up. We don't get all the words right, but it doesn't matter.

It's the best I've felt in a long time. We sing other songs, too. Some fast, some slow, sometimes we mash them up together in our own sort of remix. The hours pass; we help ourselves to water from the kitchen sink and dig around in the basement for cans of fruit and boxes of crackers.

We've filled the trunk and backseat of the Mustang with just about everything I can think of that would be useful from the garage. There's no more room, and the afternoon has worn on enough that Dillon will be home soon. I'd like to wash up and get some dinner started before he does . . . and, laughing, I shake my head at the domesticity of that. Of my life.

"What's so funny?" Opal slurps juice from a can, tipping it upside down to get the last sweet drops.

"Just thinking about Dillon. How maybe I should get an apron or something to wear for when he comes home." I roll my eyes.

Opal makes a face. "Mom never wore an apron."

"Mom had a job that wasn't just taking care of the house and us."

Opal's brows go up. "So do you! You take care of everything! And you used to have a job, Velvet. And you'll have to get one when you turn eighteen, too." She thinks about this for a moment, frowning. "Yuck. I don't want to have to be a garbage collector."

"You might not have to be. That's a long time off." I ruffle her hair, which she hates and ducks away from. "And there are other jobs. You don't have to be a sanitation engineer. You could drive a delivery truck or work in the sewage plant."

"Ewww!" Opal wiggles around.

We both laugh, but it's true. Those are the sorts of jobs everyone's being forced to take on. It sobers me up kind of fast. I'll be eighteen in a few months. Things could be really different by then.

"Put your seat belt on," I tell her when we get in the Mustang. I turn the key, making sure my foot's on the brake. I never got my license, but that doesn't mean I never had any lessons.

But I never drove a car like this. It's so easy to go fast, even in our neighborhood, with its twisting, turning roads. We roll down the windows and scream, singing again. I avoid the street with the wrecked cars, going another way home, but when we pass the street I need to turn on to in order to get to our house, I keep going.

I drive and drive, fast and slow, getting the feel of the car. The power of it. The speed. I understand now why someone would want a car like this, why it's so much fun. We drive until I think to check the gas gauge and see it dipping to a quarter tank, but I'm not that worried.

We have an entire neighborhood to plunder, after all. There will be more gas. There will be more food. Clothes. Tools. More of everything. And we will gather it all, I think, before the winter comes.

We'll make ourselves a fortress.

ELEVEN

WE MAKE IT HOME BEFORE DILLON, AND I TELL
Opal to figure out what to make for dinner. I want to check
on my mom. Mrs. Holly said she was sleeping again. I find
her still in bed, her eyes closed.

"Mom?" She doesn't move. "Mama?"

Her bed, the one she shared with my dad, takes up a lot
more room in my bedroom, but she keeps everything a lot
neater than I ever did, so there's no trouble reaching her. I
sit on the edge of the bed and wait for her to wake, but all
I get is the soft in-out of her breathing.

"Mom?"

I touch her forehead, checking for fever. It's cool. She
murmurs at my touch and shifts a little. Her fingers twitch.
The soft word slipping from her lips sounds a lot like my
dad's name.

If she's dreaming of him, should I wake her?

Instead, I sit and watch her face move through a range

of emotions she rarely shows when she's awake. She's come a long, long way from the blankness she showed the first few weeks she was home, but there's always something a little . . . slower . . . with her. A little off. Once, Mrs. Holly had said, "It's like watching a television set warm up." I wasn't sure what she'd meant until she explained that TVs used to not turn on and off as automatically as they do now, that it used to take a minute or so for the picture to show up on the screen, and that it would sometimes be faint at first. Like a ghost image, before becoming clear. That's exactly how it was.

Watching my mom now is like scanning through a recorded show to skip the commercials. Sorrow, confusion, glee, anger all flicker across her face. The expressions make her a stranger, and I don't want to watch anymore.

"She's getting worse, not better, Velvet." Mrs. Holly catches me outside of my room.

She wears her white hair long enough to pull into a small, wispy ponytail on top of her head, because she used to get it permed in tight curls close to her head and now there's no way to keep doing that. She showed me pictures in the album she brought with her from her house, one of the few things she took. She used to have pretty, dark hair. She used to look like a movie star. Now she's tiny, her shoulders hunched, her face wrinkled. But her eyes sparkle.

"She's fine." I want it to be true.

Mrs. Holly looks past me for a moment. "She's spending

too much time inside her head, honey. She's like a boy I knew in elementary school . . . he . . . Well. Never mind."

"He what?"

She shakes her head. "It doesn't matter, dolly. What matters is that we take good care of her, right?"

"Are you scared of her, Mrs. Holly?" We both keep our voices down, though my mom shows no sign of waking up. I realize I spend way too much time talking in whispers to keep other people from overhearing.

Mrs. Holly hesitates. "No. Your mother, she's not like that."

"Because you know she had the collar on," I say in a low voice. "They did stuff to her before they released her to the kennel. But before that, we don't know if she ever . . . made trouble."

"I'm not afraid of her. I'm afraid for her." Mrs. Holly looks sad. "She's failing, Velvet. That's all I'm trying to say."

I lean against the wall. I don't want to hear this. Mrs. Holly touches my arm gently.

"The boy I went to school with lived on a farm. And one day, he got kicked in the head by a horse. Laid him out cold, and his parents didn't find him for a few hours. He was unconscious when they took him to the hospital, but eventually, he woke up. But he wasn't ever quite right after that. He forgot things, for one. And sometimes, he would get angry. Violent." Mrs. Holly pats my arm as though that will make this story easier to hear. "Not so much different from these poor people who got Contaminated. Something wrong in their brains, yes?"

"Holes. The Contaminated protein water had twisted prions in it, and it made holes in their brains. It's irreversible." That's what they tell us, anyway.

"Yes. Well, this poor boy had something damaged in his brain. Later on, he couldn't go to school any longer. He couldn't keep up. And though he looked fine on the outside, he wasn't the same as he'd been before. Do you see what I'm saying?"

"I already know she's not the same. She'll never be the same. But she's not like they say they are. Or like she's supposed to be. My mom's different," I whisper fiercely.

Mrs. Holly nods, but looks again over my shoulder to where my mom still lies sleeping. "The boy started to get smaller. That's the only way to describe it, dolly. He stopped laughing or joking. And he stopped the rages, too. He spent a lot more time inside his own head. Sleeping. Or sitting, staring. And finally, after a while, he simply stopped doing anything."

We both look at my mom then.

"You think that's what's happening to her?" I ask.

Mrs. Holly hesitates. Then nods. "I think so, Velvet. I hope I'm wrong. But we need to be ready, you know. In case she's getting ready to leave us."

It would be better for my mom to fade away the way

Mrs. Holly says than for her to become dangerous and violent. Better for her. Better for us.

"How was your shopping expedition?" Mrs. Holly asks with a smile.

She's trying to change the subject, and I know it but let her. "Good. We got a car, too."

"A car?" Her eyebrows fly up. "What on earth?"

"Makes better sense than riding our bikes back and forth. I bet we're going to find a lot of things we weren't thinking about before. We need to get as much as we can before winter." I shrug.

"Yes. That makes sense. Although it won't matter," Mrs. Holly says darkly, "if they come to take us all away."

TWELVE

FOR A WHILE, THERE'S QUIET. SPRING BECOMES summer, which drags on, hot and hotter. Dillon goes to work every day on the garbage truck, and he brings home fewer cool items. People have stopped throwing useful things away. Mrs. Holly and my mom work in the garden, using the raised beds I put together after seeing them in the backyard of Sandra's house. Opal and I scavenge the neighborhood, going house by house, finding a routine. Honestly, I love it. The more stuff we find, the less anxious I feel about the coming winter. About everything. It's like every time I add a row of cans or cartons to our supplies, I'm a little less worried about the future.

The regular radio plays only old songs with occasional government updates reminding us about curfews and rationing, how the soldiers are here to protect us . . . though there's not supposed to be anything to protect us from. So every night, we listen to the Voice broadcasting from a new location, telling us more and more about the most current wave of Contamination and what we're not supposed to know. That's mostly everything.

Opal tries to train Dexter to sit and fetch and roll over, but all he learns is how to beg. It's funny to watch him protect the chicken, though. The one we now call Lucky. Dillon and I built her a pen out of an old rabbit hutch and a dog kennel to keep her safe, and she gives us an egg every day. Sometimes we save them for a few days so we can have them together, or bake a cake or brownies from the mixes I took from Sandra's basement. Hers was the first house we cleaned out, taking all the food, supplies, and tools. All the useful things . . . but not all the books. So every few days, when I need to get away from the house and the never-ending chores that were bad enough when we had electricity to run the washer and dryer and vacuum, I ride my bike to Sandra's house and fill my backpack with books. Sometimes I run, just for the sake of it, to work my muscles in a different way, and because it gives me an excuse to be gone longer.

Sometimes, I sit in the room with all the books and read for an hour in the quiet, and pretend life is the way it used to be.

Dillon and I took care of Kevin and burned the chair he was in. I took another from the living room to use as I sit by the window and lose myself in fiction. I selfishly like having the time all to myself, in a place where I don't have to worry about cooking or cleaning or making sure Opal brushes her teeth. Where I'm simply Velvet, who doesn't have to take care of anyone but herself.

Today, I run. Empty backpack over my shoulders, bouncing with every step. The sun's hot overhead, but I stick to the shade of the trees, crisscrossing the street as necessary to keep out of the overgrown weeds. I don't give the car wreck a second glance anymore. By the time I get to the house, I'm sweating and thirsty, but I don't go inside yet.

I drink from the water bottle I brought along, and go around the back to the ponds. The smaller one has dried up a lot from the heat and lack of rain, but the bigger one is still deep and dark green. Fish swim up to nibble at my shadow. I don't want to imagine being hungry enough to eat goldfish or frogs, even if they are a delicacy in France or wherever.

Still, I like to watch the fish. Slipping off my sneakers and socks, I sit on the edge of the small bridge and let my feet dangle in the water. I listen to the sounds of the birds and trickle of water from the overflow pipe underneath the bridge. Behind me, the stream moves too slow and shallow to make any noise.

I sit with my eyes closed. Relaxing. The sun filters through the trees, keeping away most of the heat so what does hit my face feels good. I lie back on the bridge's warm wood and listen to the trickle of water beneath it. I could stay here forever.

I doze and dream about the Fourth of July. Hot dogs, hamburgers, grilled chicken . . . I fill my plate and eat and eat, but I'm still hungry. I'm with Dillon, his arm around me. We sit next to my parents on a plaid blanket on the edge of Mt. Gretna Lake and watch the fireworks.

Bam, pop, bang!

I startle awake, feeling sticky and hot and sort of achy from the sun. The fireworks sound is not from the dream. That's real. I hear it again, the rat-a-tat of firecrackers.

No. Gunfire. Someone's shooting.

Even before the Contamination, we were used to occasional gunfire. This neighborhood backs up on Pennsylvania State Game Lands, and in hunting season we often heard the bang and crack of shotguns. Since then, there's been some shooting closer than the game lands, because while most of the neighborhood is empty, there are a few other people and some of them apparently are hungry enough to risk eating venison.

This is different, though. No single, echoing bang. I sit up, cocking my head. This is a string of shooting.

Turning, I try to figure out where it's coming from. The opposite direction from my house, which is good. I drink the rest of my water, gone warm from the sun, and put my socks and shoes back on. I set my backpack against the side of the bridge as I leap to the other side, toward the back of the yard, where it meets the trees.

This house is at the very back edge of the neighborhood,

pressing against the game lands and, beyond that, connecting with the highway heading toward Ephrata. That's the road I cross when I head into town, because it helps me avoid the checkpoints, but I'm a few miles away from my normal path. I push through the tangle of raspberry bushes and weeds, and into the thicket of forest beyond the yard.

It's cooler in here, which feels good. I pick my way over fallen trees and around big boulders. I keep my eyes open for random Connies or worse, non-Contaminated people without good manners or morals. I'm wearing shorts and a T-shirt, and my worn sneakers slip on dead leaves and gravel. I keep listening, hard as I can, and have now picked up the faint sound of shouts. The rev of engines. I smell the stink of exhaust and something else, sharp and stinging.

But when I look around the forest, I see nothing. I'm not close enough to the highway, and now I'm far enough away from the neighborhood roads that even if there are soldiers patrolling them again, I shouldn't be able to hear or smell them. Again, the rat-a-tat comes, and the noise of it twists something inside me, tight like a fist.

I run.

I shouldn't be able to go this fast, not with so many obstacles, but something pushes me. I jump a giant boulder and come down on the other side, off balance enough to stumble, but I catch myself. I push off again, bounding. Branches break beneath my shoes. Leaves crunch. I run fast, ducking around trees and rocks and, once, a startled pair of does that turn to stare after me without even running themselves.

The road's ahead, a clearing in the trees, and I slow down. I should be breathing harder. I should be sweating more. Instead, my eyes are wide, mouth dry. My muscles burn and tingle, but not too badly. I crouch and duck to keep myself hidden as I scoot closer to the edge of the hill overlooking the highway.

But now, instead of a two-lane highway stretching scenically through a long sweep of forest, all I see is concrete barriers with army trucks behind them. And soldiers with guns. I see a bunch of cars, one tipped on its side, the others on the edge of the road with their doors hanging open.

And I see people.

Some are in a sprawling pile surrounded by a spreading puddle of red, and I clap a hand over my mouth to hold back a cry. There are others standing in front of the soldiers with their hands on their heads. A man. A woman. Two small children, younger than Opal, stand beside them, but their hands hang at their sides. I can see their collars from here.

As I watch, a soldier tugs the kids away from the mother, who erupts at once, going after him with flailing fists and feet and screams. Another soldier doesn't hesitate; he hits her on the head with the butt of his gun. She goes down. The man goes after the soldier taking the kids, and he's down in another minute.

The soldier puts the silent, unprotesting kids in a truck with a canvas cover on the back. There's shouting. There's that smell, that terrible, awful smell. But there's no more shooting, and I'm so glad for that.

This isn't a normal checkpoint. They're not telling people to turn around. They're shooting them or putting them in trucks.

From below, I hear the rev and roar of a motor. When I peek through my fingers, I see a tractor-trailer bearing down on the concrete barriers and army trucks. The road's so flat here, the truck's in full view, even if it's at least a mile away; and it's going so fast, it will be here in half a minute.

The soldiers shout and scramble. Some to the sides of the concrete barriers. Some to the trucks, which they pull out of the way as much as they can. I've lost track of which one the kids were put into, but I'm hoping it's the one backing into the small park-and-ride lot, far off the road. That tractor trailer is coming fast, no signs of slowing. It's going to hit those barriers and anything behind them at top speed.

I stand, fists clenched, and whisper, "Go." I have no idea who's driving the truck, or why the soldiers are trying to keep people from leaving by this road, but I want it to get through. "Go, go, go!"

Just before the tractor-trailer reaches the barriers, two soldiers throw out something metal that glitters in the sun.

It hits the asphalt a few feet behind the barriers. It's sharp, whatever it is. Glinting blades of metal attached to some sort of wire mesh.

Oh, no.

The truck doesn't even brake. It hits the concrete barriers at probably eighty miles an hour. The concrete explodes, and the truck bucks but keeps going. It would've made it into the roadblock, too, if not for the razor-strip thing the soldiers threw down. The truck rolls over it, and all of the tires on the cab blow in rapid succession. The truck skews, back end swerving. The other tires explode. The cab shudders, and the driver lays on the horn in one long, horrifying bleat as the trailer rocks. It twists, flipping, and takes the cab halfway with it before separating. The cab hits one of the army trucks parked to the side. The trailer keeps going, taking out another couple of trucks, and comes to a skewed stop with the doors of the back end swinging open. In a minute, people start spilling out of it, pushing and shoving over each other, hitting the ground. Some get up. Some don't.

The sound of the crash is immense, and I cover my ears. That doesn't block out the soft *whump* of an explosion from one of the trucks. It doesn't block the sound of screams.

Then I'm not thinking about anything else; I'm running again. Down the hill, leaping the guardrail. The heat is intense and searing, so fierce, I squint against it, but I'm looking for the truck that has those kids in the back. I don't care about the soldiers. I don't care about the driver of the truck.

I can't let those kids burn.

They're collared. They won't scream. They probably won't fight. The pain of being burned alive won't register with them the way it would with non-Contaminated people, but that doesn't mean they deserve to be incinerated. I'm going to find them.

The soldiers are shouting and running. So are the people from the back of the tractor-trailer. A few of them go at each other, swinging and punching. Others mill around with blank faces, some with arms or legs jutting at odd and broken angles. Most of them are bloody. I don't see collars on any of them. Nobody pays attention to me when I push past them. The first truck is tipped on its side, the canvas-covered back flapping open. It's empty. I swerve around it, running for the next one.

The heat slaps me back. Fire everywhere. I can't breathe, can't think, can't do anything but run for the second truck, the one parked at a slant in the ditch, the one the tractor-trailer didn't hit.

The kids are in the back. I hold out my hands, but they don't move. They don't look hurt or scared; they just look blank. I haul myself into the back of the truck, scraping my shins on the bumper.

"Come on," I say, gesturing. "Come on now."

Too slow, the little girl moves. Blinking, she shifts her

weight from one foot to the other. The boy behind her looks a few years older, and his expression is dead, unmoving. The lights on their collars glow a steady green.

I can't wait for them to move. I grab the girl by the sleeve, and she recoils with a grimace. The boy's attention drifts to me. His mouth twists. They're both much smaller than me, so I grab them both and yank backward, pulling them with me. Then they struggle. Then they fight.

"Don't be scared, I'm trying to help you!" It's a stupid thing to say. They're not scared. They're angry at being grabbed.

They fight, but I'm stronger. I turn, pushing them both toward the back of the truck. I jump down, but the kids won't follow me or jump into my arms. They stand staring, without moving.

The soldiers are still running around, the fire is still burning, and if I don't do something soon, someone else is going to come and take them. Or we'll all blow up. I grab the boy first, snagging the hems of his jeans and pulling. He resists, but I tug him off balance until he falls. I catch him, just barely, and put him on the ground. The girl's next. She's smaller and lighter and doesn't resist as much.

I think I see a glimmer of something in her eyes when I catch her. Maybe something like understanding, but it's so fleeting and there's no time to find out more. We have to get away from the fire.

I pick them both up, staggering under the weight. One

under each arm. I stumble forward, toward the ditch, the woods. I can't make it up the hill, but I can get them out of the way—before the tractor-trailer cab explodes in another soft *whump* of flame. Something like a giant fist punches us forward. We go to our knees.

I see their mother, blood running down her face. She's screaming; I can see that by her open mouth and frantic eyes. But all I can hear is a dull, thick roar. She limps toward me, hands outstretched, but the kids don't run to her any more than they did to me. I push them, though, trying to get us up on our feet.

Their mom looks hysterical as she grabs them. For a second, I think she's going to punch me in the face, but something registers in her gaze—I'm not a soldier. Her mouth moves, but I'm still deaf from the explosion. Shaking my head, I help her get the kids up. She takes the boy, I take the girl. Together, we run away from the wreckage, toward a car with all the doors hanging open.

I don't know if it's her car, but she tosses the boy into the backseat, so I do the same with the girl. The woman slams the doors shut and gets in the driver's seat—the keys dangle from the ignition, so at least there's that. She gestures at me, but I back up, shaking my head. I can't go with her.

She slams the driver's door and guns the engine. I jump back as the tires grind the gravel. I run toward the hill into the woods, but it's too late; we've drawn too much attention.

A soldier jumps in front of me, his face covered with soot and a burn on one cheek. If he has a gun, I don't see it, but I know his face. He's the young one from the patrols, the one from the day they killed Sandra.

I shove hard on his chest and he stumbles back. Before I can get past him, he grabs my sleeve, which tears as I pull away. The car the woman's driving is pealing out, but she gets only a few feet before someone shoots the tires. The trunk. Glass shatters.

The soldier grabbing me lets go when the gunfire starts. I wait for bullets to shred me or flaming metal to land on me, but we're standing so far to the side of the road that we seem to be out of range. I dig my fingers and toes into the hill, much steeper here than where I came down. Rocks tumble and patter, but still all I can hear is the muffled roar.

I wait for him to grab me again, but the soldier only watches as I climb the hill on my hands and knees, digging my fingers into the ground to push myself along. I get to the top, again waiting for him to pull a gun or for someone else to, but nobody seems to be paying attention to me. The soldier pushes his hands toward me.

Run! I can't hear him, but I see that's what he's yelling. Go! I use that as my chance to scramble into the trees.

"I didn't save them.

"I didn't save them."

That's all I can think as I stagger through the trees and keep going, even when every muscle wants to shut down and become as solid as the rock I finally trip over. I land with my cheek against the cool, hard ground. Leaves and rocks poke into me, but I can't move. I try to catch my breath, and suck up dust. Coughing, choking, I roll onto my side and listen for the sound of soldiers coming after me. I can't hear anything but my own heartbeat.

"Get up, Velvet," I think. "Get up and run." But I'm so tired, I can't move.

All I can do is let the darkness sweep over me.

THIRTEEN

I WAKE UP WITH THE TASTE OF DIRT IN MY mouth, and for the first minute or so, before I can pry my eyes open, I'm convinced I'm dead. A minute after that, when I try to move, I wish I were. Groaning, I roll off the rock poking me in the small of my back. My arms and legs move, but I can't get up until I force my muscles to work. Then I push myself to my feet.

It's dark, which means it's late. Which means I've been gone for hours. I try to run, but my body will only let me walk. I'm lucky I don't have to crawl.

I orient myself in the darkness. A glow in the sky has to be the lights of Lancaster, which is south of my development, and I head in that direction. I pick my way over rocks and fallen trees, taking my time whether I want to or not. I can't go any faster.

If I miss the backyards of the houses that edge the game lands I'm in, I will eventually hit the cleared land around the power lines and be able to follow the trail that leads to an access to my street. The neighborhood kids all used to play along the stream back there, and even if it's overgrown, the well-worn path will still be there. But fortunately, I don't go that far—I hear the soft throb of the frogs croaking in the pond at Sandra's house, and I follow my ears until I stumble out into her backyard.

It's not much lighter, but out of the trees, I have no trouble figuring out where I'm going. I pick up my backpack on the way into the house, where I run the water in the sink and gulp down what feels like a gallon of cold, spring-fed water until the taste of grit and smoke is washed away.

My stomach clenches and I hunch over the sink, but everything stays put. I wash my face, splashing the water onto my neck and chest and arms, too. Everyone will be worried about me, but I still have a mile or so to walk before I make it home.

I can't stop thinking about what I saw.

I don't know how much longer it takes before I finally stagger over the downed tree at the end of my driveway and up the hill to my front door. The glow of lantern light from inside guides me. When I open the front door, the *whoosh* of a golf club passing an inch past my face stops me.

"Dillon, it's me!"

"Velvet!"

His hug hurts all my aching muscles, but I melt into it, anyway. Dillon's fingers tangle in my hair, tipping my face to his. Then he's kissing me, and that hurts, too, but I don't mind.

"Where were you? What happened?"

Behind him, the shadow of my mother separates from the others. She comes toward me faster than I've seen her move since I found her in a cage. Her hug is gentler than Dillon's but still presses all my aches and pains. She shakes her head, over and over, her mouth working to form words I'm sort of glad she can't say.

"I need something to eat," I tell them both. "And a bath."

"Is Velvet home?" Opal's sleepy voice echoes from upstairs.

My mom and Dillon share a look.

"Yeah. Go back to sleep, kid." Dillon's voice is steady, even if his face is worried.

"But I want—"

My mother huffs low, her brows knitting. She pats my shoulder and goes up the stairs. I hear the faint sound of Opal's protests, then the click of her door shutting.

Dillon kisses me again. Softer this time. Lingering. He pushes the hair off my forehead, and his gaze searches mine, but I'm not sure he finds what he's looking for because he doesn't look relieved.

"Food," I tell him. "And I'll tell you everything."

In the kitchen, lit by a pair of guttering candles set into a candelabra my parents got for their wedding and we used to only use on Halloween, Dillon makes me some vegetable soup on the camp stove we took from Sandra's house. It's heated by small propane bottles we also took from her basement, and it's so much easier to cook on, it's almost like having a real stove again.

I devour the soup, slurping and gulping so fast, I burn my tongue, but I can't care. I haven't eaten for hours, and it feels like days. I drain the bowl of every bit of soupy goodness and sit back with a sigh. Then a long belch I try to cover with the back of my hand.

My mom, coming into the kitchen at the tail end of it, shakes her head. She sits in the chair across from me and reaches for my hands. I let her take them. She squeezes them, then lifts them into the light, showing off the dirt under my nails. The scrapes and wounds on my knuckles. I have a few scalded red patches on the backs of my hands, and a blister has already formed and popped. She shakes her head, sighing, and gets up to go to the sink, where she runs water over a dishcloth and brings it back to start dabbing at the dirt.

"Mom, I'm going to take a bath. It's okay."

She gives me a stern look, so I let her keep going, even though it hurts when she scrapes at the sore spots. Dillon pushes a full glass of water toward me, with one for himself, and sits next to me. I drink half the glass while he watches.

"Soldiers," I say finally. "There was a roadblock on Route 322. But not a checkpoint—I mean, they weren't letting anyone through. They were . . ."

I stop, wishing I hadn't eaten the soup so fast. Every-thing's sloshing inside me. I swallow hard. My mom looks up from the task of cleaning my hand, and puts it gently on the table. Dillon puts a hand on my shoulder.

"They were shooting people." The moment I say it out loud, it becomes real all over again.

Dillon doesn't look surprised. "The Voice has been reporting that they're closing borders all over the place. Iso-lating us. He says they're making them closer and closer, trying to keep people from traveling, cutting off access even from one town to the next. But he didn't say anything about them shooting people."

"They had trucks lined up and concrete barriers, block-ing off the road for all the cars. I don't know if the people in the cars were trying to run or what, but they shot them all." I draw in a hitching, choking breath, but keep my voice down so there's no chance Opal can overhear. "There were two people with two kids in collars."

I shudder and go silent.

My mom's gentle squeeze of my fingers makes me look up. Her eyes glisten with tears. They told us she'd never be normal again, that because she was Contaminated, she would always be angry and aggressive and unstable, that without the collar keeping her calm, she'd be dangerous. But she isn't. She's not the same as she was before, but she isn't any of what they said she'd be. She's still my mom.

I look at Dillon. "A tractor-trailer tried to crash through

the barriers, so someone must know what's going on. I mean, it looked planned. It came racing toward the road-block at, like, eighty miles an hour. It would've made it through, too, but they threw out these metal, razor-strip things that blew the tires. The truck crashed and caught on fire. And the kids were in the back of one of the army trucks. I had to get them out, Dillon."

He pushes back from the table to pace, one hand raking through his hair so that it stands on end. "Velvet . . ."

"I had to. I couldn't let them just burn up!"

He looks at me. "They saw you?"

"Yes." I think of the soldier who'd tried to stop me but then let me go. I think it might've been the same one who saw me that day when Opal and I were hiding in the weeds.

"You don't think they'll be looking for you?"

I lift my chin. "What should I have done? Just watched? Let it happen?"

My mom murmurs something wordless. She pats my hand. I can see she wants to say something, but all she can do is shake her head. I go around the table to hug her.

"I'm okay, Mom." To Dillon, I say, "They were all so busy running around, they couldn't have paid much attention to me. And even if they did, what can they do?"

"They could recognize you when you go into town." He scowls. "They could come through the neighborhood again, looking for you. You think they won't figure out that you had to come from close by?"

"They're coming through the neighborhood again, anyway," I point out. "The patrols are getting more and more frequent."

We both stay silent for a few seconds, thinking about that.

"They have testing stations set up in town, by the ration station. I had to get tested today again before they'd let me pick up our stuff," Dillon says.

"Oh . . ."

"I'm okay, obviously. They didn't take me. But they'd take you, Velvet. And you wouldn't come back."

I can't answer that. Dillon thinks I'm Contaminated? No question about it, just solid acceptance. I shake my head, stunned into silence, silent as my mom. She pats me again and gets up from the table to wash out the dishcloth.

"I'm going to take a shower," I say without looking at him. "Was the generator running earlier?"

"Yes. Velvet . . ."

I don't answer, I just walk away. Upstairs, I shower quickly in lukewarm water that turns cold before I'm ready to get out. Everything aches, but at least I'm clean. I pull on my pajamas and slide into bed.

After a while, Dillon comes in. He slips into bed behind me, holding me against him. I want to cry, not because he thinks I'm a Connie, but because I'm worried he's right.

He kisses the back of my head. "I'm sorry I said that."

I turn in his arms to face him. In this narrow single bed,

there's not much room for two. "But it's true. I drank the water. I could be . . ."

"Shhh." He kisses my mouth.

We kiss for a long time after that. When he finally stops, we break apart, breathing hard. I touch his face with my fingertips.

"We should think about leaving." I don't know where the idea came from, but suddenly it's all I can think about.

"Where do you want to go? Where can we go?"

"Out of the black zone. The Voice says there are places where the Contamination didn't hit so hard, right?"

Dillon nods. "Yeah."

"Where? How do we find out? We can go there." I say it with more confidence than I feel. I think about what I saw today. "Right now they're just blocking the roads. What happens if they start to put up fences?"

He is quiet for a minute. "I can't go anywhere, Velvet."

"What are you talking about? We could pack bags. Supplies . . ." I think of Mrs. Holly, knowing she wouldn't be able to hike very far. My mom probably couldn't, either. But, despairing, I keep talking. "There has to be a place to go, a way to get there. Right?"

"I can't leave without my parents." Dillon's voice is flat. Hard, but sad.

My heart aches for him. I was stupid, and selfish. I kiss him, not able to say anything that could make it better. Of course he can't just pick up and go without finding out what happened to his mom and dad, even if it's only to learn they're . . . but I don't want to think about that.

"We'll find them. We can go to the Sanitarium, can't we? Don't they have visitation? Something? There have to be records." It's a desperate thought, but we are both a little desperate.

"Mario, who works on the truck with me, says that before he was on my route, he handled the pickups for the hospital. He said they have sections for Connies and also for others . . ." Dillon pauses. ". . . non-Contaminated. But they're doing stuff to all of them in there, he's sure of it."

I think on this, wishing I didn't find it so easy to believe. "Like before, in the second and third waves?"

They killed them in the first wave. Lobotomized them and took them away in the second wave. Ran tests and experiments before releasing them into the kennels to wait to be claimed. But that was only Connies. Not regular people.

"He wasn't sure. He got transferred. Says he never saw anything on the inside, just people being unloaded from trucks and buses, and taken inside. Uncollared, but in hand-cuffs and stuff."

"If your parents are in there, we could find out."

"Stop," Dillon says then. "It's impossible. I mean, they're taking people away and nobody's stopping them, Velvet. What makes you think we can just walk in there and ask to find her? Or my dad? Or anyone?"

His voice breaks, and I'm not sure what comfort I can offer, but I hold him, anyway. He barely lets me, fighting his tears and swiping at his eyes until they're dry again. We're silent together, and I wonder if he's thinking that I can't understand how he feels, since I have my mom, at least.

"They can't keep doing all of this. It's not right. It's not legal," I say finally.

Dillon snorts lightly. "Don't you know? They can do whatever they want. And they are."

"Someone should stop them, then."

"Who can stop the government? The army? You've heard the Voice. They're closing us in, blocking us off from all the green zones. You think the people there are going to care? They're safe. They're protected. Who's going to fight for us, especially if it means losing what they have in order to do it?" he asks, and for that I don't have a good answer.

FOURTEEN

"PHILADELPHIA. NEW YORK. PITTSBURGH. Boston. Baltimore. DC." The Voice has been replaced for tonight with the higher-pitched voice of a girl calling herself Raven. The Voice is on the run, she said. In hiding, because the feds are closing in on him. She's listing the cities that have been black-zoned. "Almost the entire East Coast, folks, yes, that's right. Ohio seems to be okay, based on what we can find out, but anything east of the Pennsylvania border is toast. On the West Coast, California's totally gone, obviously. It was the Hollywood virus, am I right?"

Opal looks up from where she's been working on a word-search puzzle. Dexter yawns from his place beside her, then puts his nose back between his paws. "We're in a black zone?"

"Yes." I'm folding laundry and sorting out things that need repairs. Mostly stuff for Dillon, since his clothes get the most wear and tear. We've been raiding closets and dressers as well as pantries, but the whole point of that is to make sure we have enough to last us for a long time—not to toss things when they get worn. So I'm looking for buttons that are missing and holes that can be patched. I feel domestic and housewifely, and I don't really like it. I spent the morning scrubbing all this stuff in a washtub out back, using a legitimate scrubbing board he brought home after finding it in someone's garbage.

This is not the life I'd dreamed of.

"So . . . what does that mean?" Opal bends over the book, with her pencil gripped in her fist, her tongue between her teeth in concentration.

"That there was more Contamination here than in other places, so we're affected more."

"There's still more here, huh?" She gives me a look.

There's no point in lying to her. "Yes. That's why we're on strict rations, so they can help keep it from spreading. All the food's tested and stuff."

"How come it's not working?"

"Because people who were Contaminated already might not know it or show symptoms until later. That's why they're testing people." I sort out a work shirt with a grease stain I couldn't get clean. There's a tear in the sleeve, and my fingertips hurt already, thinking of pushing a sewing needle through the thick fabric.

"That's why you don't go to town anymore." Opal stabs

the book with her pencil, snapping the point. "What time is Dillon going to be home?"

"I don't know." With a sigh, I put aside the work shirt and focus on the rest of the laundry. Even with the scrub board, none of it's very clean. But it's warm from drying in the sun, and I hate to think about what I'll do when winter comes around again.

"What's for dinner?"

"I don't know yet."

"What's Mama doing?"

"Opal," I snap, "I don't know, okay? Go find out!"

Opal sniffs, affronted. "Just asking. I'm bored."

"Finish your word search." I shake a shirt to get the wrinkles out, but why does it matter? When everything's dingy and stained, anyway?

"I did!"

"Then help me fold laundry," I tell her. "Make yourself useful. Maybe it's time you start helping out a little more around here, Opal. I'm tired of doing all of this myself."

Opal's eyes widen, then narrow. Her lower lip pushes out, and she crosses her arms. "I help out. I do lots of stuff."

"You should do more." I straighten, my back aching. "Why don't you make dinner?"

Her eyes get big again. "You mean it?"

I shrug, thinking about what a big deal it was when my parents started letting me use the stove. I was a little older than Opal is now. And, honestly, I'd love it if someone else made dinner sometimes. I don't trust my mom with the stove, and Mrs. Holly says she doesn't trust herself with it. Old fingers, she says.

"What do you want to make?" I ask in the kitchen as we stand in the pantry and look at all the stuff we've collected from Sandra's basement.

"Macaroni and cheese!"

I laugh. "That's not very challenging."

"I wish we could have pizza," Opal says longingly.

Me, too. My mouth waters at the thought of it. Thick, crisp crust. Layers of gooey, real cheese. Tomato sauce. Garlic.

"We could have spaghetti." I touch the boxes of pasta, the jars of sauce. "And a salad from the garden. We could make some garlic bread with those saltines and some olive oil and garlic powder."

Opal sighs. "It's not pizza."

"It's not a poke in the eye with a sharp stick, either." It's something my dad always used to say, and for a moment we stare at each other like we both might burst into tears.

Instead, laughter bubbles up and out of me as I think of him. It's such a silly thing to say, but it was typical of him. I miss my dad so much, but these memories, these good things he gave us, will always stay. Tears sting me, but I laugh and laugh, and after a minute, Opal does, too.

Dillon finds us in hysterics in the pantry, and I can tell by the way he flings himself into the doorway that our shrieking laughter scared him. Opal holds out the box of crackers, her giggles shaking her so hard, the plastic sleeve of saltines rattles inside the cardboard. I'm doubled over, holding my stomach, each round of laughter rising and leading into the next.

"It's not a poke in the eye!" Opal cries.

"With a sharp stick," I add, breathless.

Dillon stares.

"Velvet's letting me make dinner!" Opal giggles.

He visibly relaxes, leaning against the door frame. His face is dirty, and so are his clothes. He doesn't smell so great, either. "What's for dinner?"

"Spaghetti." She holds up the crackers. "And garlic bread."

He looks a little confused, but smiles. "Sounds great. Can't wait; I'm starving."

"Were you able to get some gas for the generator?" I ask as we set the pasta, sauce, and crackers on the kitchen island. We ran out a few days ago. I'd given him the last of the money I found in Sandra's purse this morning, but I knew it wouldn't buy much. Gas is now close to ten dollars a gallon.

Dillon shakes his head, looking solemn. "No. They're not letting anyone pump it into containers anymore. You had to have a license plate ending in an odd number today. Tomorrow's a letter. The day after that, even numbers can get gas."

"Can we get some from the truck? Siphon it?" I eye

Opal, who's busy trying to reach a pot from the rack. She's too short, so I get one down for her. "Fill this with water."

"I only have a quarter tank. I'll need it to get back and forth to work. We'll have to wait a couple days. Sorry," Dillon says at my look of disappointment.

"You need a hot shower more than I do," I tell him.

Opal wrinkles her nose. "Yeah. You stink. Bad."

"Hey." He swats at her, but she dances out of the way, the full pot of water splashing. This makes Dexter bark, and Opal shushes him.

"Hey, both of you. Don't make a mess." I sigh, leaning against the island. It's been three days since we were able to run the generator. Three days without hot water or lights after dark. I want a real bath, not a five-minute splash in cold water, and I'm sure Dillon feels the same way.

"Where's your mom and Mrs. Holly?" He opens the cupboard to pull out a bag of pretzels. The last we have, but there's no point in trying to save them for something special. They'll just go stale. He offers me one, and I take it.

"Upstairs. Mrs. Holly's napping. Mom's . . . sitting." She's been doing that a lot more. Sitting and staring out the window. Sometimes, her hands make the motions of knitting, even when she's not. It makes me nervous.

Dillon knows what I mean. He kisses me while Opal watches. She scowls.

"Gross!"

"You do stink," I say against his mouth.

Dillon laughs and sniffs his pits. "Yeah. Sorry. It was so hot again today. You guys don't know how lucky you are. You come into this neighborhood, and it's, like, ten degrees cooler 'cuz of the trees."

It's sweltering. "I'd still give anything for a hot shower."

Dillon looks serious. "I have an idea. You ladies, finish dinner. I'm going out back."

My brows raise at the "ladies, finish dinner" comment, but he's ducking out the back door before I can say anything about it. I shake my head. Opal snorts softly.

"Boys," she says.

"No kidding."

I show her how to work the stove, which doesn't have an automatic ignition and must be lit with a match. It's a little nerve-wracking, watching her hold the flame so close to the slightly hissing port where the propane comes out, but though the burner flares, at first, a bit higher than normal, Opal does a great job. I let her do the other burner by herself, adjusting the amount of gas and lighting it. Then I show her how to settle the pot of water on one burner, the smaller pot of sauce on the other.

"Garlic bread." I give the crackers a dubious look. "I'm not sure how we can toast them."

If it were winter, we'd do it on the fire, but it's way too hot to light one. At least inside. I smell smoke, though, and look out back to see Dillon fanning a curling column of smoke on a small pile of wood he's set up next to the old swing set.

"Hot bath," he says with a flourish, pointing to the old claw-foot tub my mom used to plant flowers in. He's taken out all the dirt and rinsed it with the hose, which is spitting what I know will be icy water into the tub.

I blink. Then grin. Yep, he's put the washtub full of clean water on top of the fire and set a couple of buckets beside it.

"It'll be great for washing clothes, too," he says. "I know you were complaining how hard it is to get stuff clean. And, Velvet . . ."

I look at him.

"I just wanted to say thanks for washing my clothes." Dillon looks a little shy and totally cute. "I appreciate it."

It makes up for the sidewise comment he made about dinner. "Someone has to do it."

"Yeah, but . . . I know it's hard and not fun."

"Like picking up garbage is?" I laugh and kiss him, taking my time.

He puts his arms around me, holding me close. We stay that way for a minute or two while the tub fills and the water in the washtub starts to steam. His lips press into my hair.

"Maybe I should get you a long apron and one of those head-scarf things, pioneer woman," he says into my ear, in a way that totally makes me shiver. *"Little House in the Big Woods."*

I shiver again, but this time, not from his kisses. I pull away to look at him. "Stuff like this . . . we have to get better at it, Dillon. This homesteading stuff. Don't we?"

He frowns a little, then nods. "Yeah. I think so."

"Do you think we should try to move into town? Be honest." I need him to tell the truth.

Dillon takes a minute to look up at the sky. Blue, with clouds overhead. No planes. I haven't seen a plane fly over us in months, and I used to see the white lines of their passing every few days. He looks at me and shakes his head the tiniest bit.

"We're better off here. Safer, I think." He pauses to clear his throat. "In town, there's no place to . . . hide."

He means my mom. I think he means me, too. I don't want to talk about that anymore, though. Instead, I point at the hot water.

"You go first while I finish helping Opal. Let me go grab you some soap and a towel."

"Wifey," Dillon murmurs, snagging me close for another kiss.

This time, I knuckle him in the bicep until he howls and dances out of reach. "Don't get saucy with me, Béarnaise."

It's another thing my dad used to say, but this time it doesn't make me laugh. I eye him. Dillon looks chastened, then grins.

"Sorry." He doesn't sound sorry. Not quite. "But I like it, Velvet."

I make a face. He looks serious. I roll my eyes.

"I mean it," Dillon says softly. "I know it's not what we'd be doing if things were different. But I like to think that maybe we'd have done it, anyway. Someday."

I'm not sure what to say to that. Things aren't different; they're the way they are. But his words warm me more than the heat coming off the fire. Inside, I check on Opal, who's stirring the spaghetti. She's painted the saltines with olive oil and a sprinkling of garlic powder. Upstairs, Mrs. Holly's stirring in her room, and my mom's sitting by the window in hers with a magazine on her lap.

"Mom?"

She looks up. She's looked at that magazine a hundred times. I guess it doesn't matter. She smiles, her gaze a little distant, and I wonder again what it is she can actually think.

"Dinner soon, okay?"

She nods. In my bathroom, I grab a towel and bar of soap, taking a quick peek out the window to see Dillon stripping down by the tub. Blushing, which is silly, since it's not like I saw anything but his bare back, I take everything out to him. He's just settling into the water when I show up.

"How is it?"

"A little cold. Can you bring another bucket of hot water?"

I hand him the soap and hang the towel on the back of

one of the deck chairs he's pulled close to put his clothes on. I bring him a bucket of hot water, hissing a little as it splashes on the back of my hand. Averting my eyes, I hold it up.

"Watch your feet."

Dillon pulls his knees to his chest. I pour in the hot water, which makes the level in the tub rise and spill over. He settles back with a sigh.

"Perfect."

"I'll go inside and check on dinner. It should be ready soon." The sun's not close to going down, but it has dropped behind the trees, making the deck nice and cool. "We'll eat outside tonight."

Dillon nods. "I'll be done fast."

"Take your time," I tell him. "I intend to, when it's my turn."

Opal's so proud about the dinner she made that I don't care to criticize the fact that she let the pasta boil too long and it's soggy, or that the sauce is a little burned. We set the table on the deck as Dillon, towel wrapped around his waist, goes inside to put on clean clothes. Opal adds a flower in a vase in the center. I pull out the pretty cloth napkins my mom always kept for special occasions—because, why not? Sure, I have to wash them, but the idea doesn't seem like such a burden now that Dillon's rigged up the washtub the way he has.

"Pretty," my mom says when she sees the table.

Opal and I share a glance. Opal takes my mom's hand to lead her to the table. "I made it, Mama."

"Good girl. You're a good girl," my mom says. It's the most words she's spoken for a while, and it seems to tire her.

Mrs. Holly is equally impressed. "Oh, girls. What a nice dinner. Thank you."

It *is* a nice dinner. It almost feels normal, sitting on the deck with my family, eating and laughing. The sun dips lower behind the trees, and the insects start to hum. Dexter perks up at the sound of rustling in the trees and bounds off into the backyard to go after whatever squirrels are settling down for the night.

"I never noticed how quiet it could be without the noise from the highway," Mrs. Holly says as we all lounge with cups of sweet tea and the last of the cookies from one of the packages we scavenged.

I listen. She's right. There always used to be a low, constant murmur coming from the highway that passes the front of the neighborhood. Even though our house is set about halfway toward the back of the development, maybe a mile away from the entrance, we still could hear the traffic. There's nothing now but the rustle of the breeze in the leaves and Lucky's soft nighttime clucking.

"Nice," my mom says.

Mrs. Holly pats her hand. "Yes, Malinda. It's very nice."

"I'll get the dishes, since you and Opal made dinner." Dillon stands and stretches.

I stand, too. "I'm going to heat water for a bath, and you can grab some for the dishes, too."

While they clear the table, I help Dillon with the water.

"Looks like we're going to have to get a better system," Dillon says as we use the hose to fill the washtub again.

The fire's died down to hot coals, but that's okay. I don't want the water to boil, just get hot. I swirl it with my fingers and nod, thinking about the winter ahead. "We could dig a pit and line it with some of the bricks from the pile behind the shed, the ones my dad didn't use for the front walk. Put the metal tub in it. We'll just have to make sure we keep the fire fed and banked, right? That's what they call it?"

"I think so." He laughs gently. "Pioneer woman."

"Pioneer man." We share a grin.

"We can do this, you know, Velvet." Dillon looks serious.

"Make a fire pit?"

He shakes his head, then nods. "Yes. That. But also everything else. We can survive this."

"We make a good team." It's the truth. Dillon works hard to make sure our patchwork family can stay together. "You really think things are going to get worse?"

"Yes. The houses I pass on our route, so many of them are empty. We went past a house last week, and the front door was hanging open. It was still open the next time we passed it. People are being taken away, more and more all the time."

"Or they're running away." I think of the soldiers defending the barrier. "If they can."

Dillon frowns. "Velvet, look. I know you think we should run—"

"No." I shake my head. "I know why you can't. And I think about my mom, Mrs. Holly. Heck, Opal's a trouper, but she's still only eleven. I saw what the soldiers did to the people trying to get past them. And listening to what the Voice and Raven have been saying, I'm not even sure where we'd go. Everything's a black zone around here for a hundred miles."

For a moment, Dillon looks like he means to say something. Instead, he kisses me on the mouth quickly, then takes the bucket inside, leaving me to stare after him, with that warmth spreading through me again. I fill the tub with water from the hose, then add water from the washtub until the temperature's good. The night air's chilly enough that it feels good when the water's a little too hot. I hiss when I get in, then let out a long, happy sigh.

Overhead, the stars are bright and sharp. They've always been visible here, but just as the noise from the highway never seemed loud until we didn't hear it anymore, the same goes for the lights of civilization. They're so much fainter now that the sky seems that much blacker. I don't want to think about why so many lights have gone out, so I settle back into the tub and let the hot water soak away my aches. I soak until the water cools, which is a pretty long time because the claw-foot tub's cast iron and holds the heat. I'm a little dizzy when I get out, and naked, I stand and let the night wind dry me.

Upstairs, I slip into bed, ready for sleep as soon as my head hits the pillow. From his bed, just a couple of feet from mine, Dillon shuffles. His whisper tickles me in the darkness.

"Are you sorry you married me, Velvet?"

"No."

I hear the smile in his voice as he turns onto his side, then the soft huff of his breath as he goes back to sleep. "Good . . ."

I haven't quite managed to fall asleep, when clucking pries my eyes open. Blinking, I shake away the blurred edges of a dream, half convinced I'm imagining it. But, no, there it is again. The rapid rise of Lucky's *bok-bok-bok*, then louder and louder.

I didn't know chickens could scream.

I'm out of bed without a second thought. Dillon catches me at the sliding door in the kitchen, that's how fast I ran down the stairs. He snags my T-shirt, but I'm already pushing open the plywood door and running out onto the deck.

"Velvet, wait!"

My bare feet sting with splinters and the cut of rocks and dead twigs as I run up the stairs and into the trees toward Lucky's pen. Something is rattling the door to the dog kennel. It's not a raccoon or a possum. It's distinctly human shaped.

Dillon's a few steps behind me when I shout and jump toward the figure trying to get at the hysterical hen. "Hey! Stop!"

There's not enough light for me to see more than shadows, but a big one turns to me. A flash of light catches its eyes and what I think must be the gaping wetness of its mouth. It's a man. The dog kennel door isn't open, but the man's fingers are caught in the wire mesh, and he's still shaking it. That's what's making Lucky go crazy, that shaking.

"Velvet, get back!"

Suddenly, there are bouncing lights coming down the hill. Flashlights held by people running through the trees from the road above. Shouts. Black shapes, spreading out, lights flashing. Not regular soldiers—I catch a flash of white letters on black uniforms. Special unit.

"Get in the house now," Dillon says into my ear, pulling me backward. "Get your mom. Find a place to hide. They're after this guy, but they might be looking for others, too."

I don't argue as he puts himself between me and the Connie still struggling with the dog kennel. A beam of light cuts through the trees, highlighting what looks like ragged scrubs and bare, battered feet. A flash of wild red hair and a straggly beard.

Then Dillon's shoving me back again, and I turn tail and run, grateful for the darkness that still shields me. Crashing and shouting follow me as I duck inside the house and race toward the stairs. I nearly run over my mom, who's standing in the kitchen.

"Mom. We have to hide."

She's heading for the back door, but I snag her nightgown.

"Mom, now."

I pull her into the basement, which is pitch-black. I'm sure we're both going to tumble down the stairs and break our necks, but here's a funny thing about learning to live without electricity—you get really good at finding your way around in the dark. We make it to the closet beneath the stairs, where we burrow under the pile of sheets and sleeping bags.

My mom's hand slips into mine and squeezes tight. Footsteps pound on the floor upstairs. I hear voices, not shouting.

After forever has come and gone and come around again, Dillon's voice eases through the darkness. "Velvet. They're gone. You can come out."

Mom and I struggle out of the hiding place. Dillon has a lantern covered with a dishcloth to keep the bright white light from hurting our eyes. Mom pats him gently.

"Gone," she murmurs. "Sleep now."

She's calm. I'm not. I'm ready to jump out of my skin.

Upstairs, she goes silently to bed while I pace in the kitchen, my hands shaking. I go to the sink and splash water on my face, but it doesn't help.

"It's okay," Dillon says. "They only came inside to make sure we were all okay. They weren't actually looking for other Connies. This time, anyway. They got him. You don't have to worry."

I turn to him with my face dripping. My T-shirt's wet. So's my hair. My teeth are chattering, though it's heat that sweeps through me, not a chill. Dillon pulls me close.

I cling to him, my eyes shut tight against the memory of what I saw. The wild hair, the beard, the flash of light on bright blue eyes. It can't be. It can't.

"Dillon," I say. "That Connie . . ."

"Shhh. They got him."

I shake my head, unable to let go of him, but I force myself to look up at him. "No. You don't understand. That Connie in the woods. I think it was my dad."

FIFTEEN

THERE'S NO MORE SLEEP, NOT FOR ME. IN the hooded light from the lantern, Dillon looks solemn. I've made hot tea, though I don't want any. It gives me an excuse to do something, though, so I don't go out of my mind.

"It makes sense. He'd come back here, if he could. To make sure we were okay."

Dillon turns his mug in a circle. The scrape of it against the kitchen island makes me want to scream; I settle for putting a hand on his to keep him from doing it again. He sighs.

"Your dad's been missing since the first wave, right?"

"Yes. But they never found him. I mean, they didn't find lots of people. But that doesn't mean he died. We just assumed he did because he was one of the first, but they didn't kill everyone. They took a lot of people, remember that." I talk too fast, but keep my voice low.

Dillon sighs again. "I know you want to think it was your dad. . . ."

"It was him." I'm convinced of it. My dad's eyes fill my vision when I close mine. How could I mistake them for anyone else's? I think of something else, the way my mom had come into the kitchen, trying to get out the back door. "I think my mom knew it."

"Oh, Velvet. How could she know that?"

I grit my jaw and cross my arms. "I don't know. But I think she did."

Dillon yawns. He has to be up in a few hours for work. He should go to sleep, but I can't.

"It was my dad," I repeat. Stubborn.

"Okay, so it was your dad. Where's he been this whole time? How'd he get out? How'd he find his way back here?"

"I don't know. You know they kept so many of them in the labs. Trying to figure out what was going on. Maybe he got released into a kennel and I didn't . . . I didn't find him. . . ." I draw in a sharp breath, fighting tears. I'd looked for my mom. Never looked for my dad. We'd just assumed he was dead.

"He didn't have a collar."

I hadn't noticed. "That doesn't make sense. My dad would've been Contaminated two years ago. If they'd been keeping him someplace, I'm sure they'd have put him in a collar."

Dillon says nothing, leaving my words to hang between

us. I know it doesn't make sense, but I want so much to believe that it's like a knife in my guts. I swipe at my eyes.

"He definitely didn't have one." Dillon shakes his head. "Look, Velvet, I know you want to believe—"

"If it was *your* dad, wouldn't you?"

He flinches, and I feel bad immediately. "Yeah. Of course I would."

"I'm sorry." I should hug him, but I can't make myself reach for him. We never fight, and this feels like it might be one. Sort of.

He yawns again and scrubs at his face. "It's okay. It's been a long night. And, listen, tomorrow . . . well, later today, I guess, when I get home, we're going to seriously get to work on fortifying the house, okay? Barricading windows and doors. That sort of thing. And making a place for you and your mom to hide. Something safer, where nobody could find you if they come looking. Okay?"

"Okay."

We give each other faint smiles.

In the morning, after Dillon has headed off to work and I'm getting ready to rouse Opal so we can have some breakfast before we head out for another day of scavenging, I check in on my mom. She's still sleeping, curled on her side with her hands clutching something tight to her chest. When I look to see what it is, it's a picture.

Of her and my dad.

SIXTEEN

THE MUSTANG'S NOT THE BEST CAR FOR going back and forth. Fun. Fast. But not that big and not really practical. We find a Chevy Suburban, and I take that instead. Dillon's not willing to give up his dad's pickup, though he admits that if it does break down, he can see the benefit of looking for something else.

"It's like our own private car lot," I tell him as we arrange supplies in rows on the shelves we've set up in the basement, echoing the way it was in Sandra's house. I push that thought away, not wanting to think about what else they'd kept in the basement. We've built a little shelter, way more comfortable and safe than what she had. But I don't want to think about my mom needing to use it. Or me, for that matter. "And shopping mall. And warehouse club. And we don't even need a credit card. . . ."

Dillon gives me a strange look. "You love this."

I pause in arranging the cans of fruit I'm organizing by type. "I don't *love* it."

But there is something exciting about it. Once we got started, Opal and I have become really good scavengers. We can strip out rooms in minutes, taking what we can use and putting aside what we can't. We can clear a house in a day, sometimes one in the morning and one in the afternoon.

Dillon grabs my arm to keep me from taking another handful of cans from the plastic bin I'd packed them in to bring home. He squeezes my bicep. "You're getting strong."

I curl my arm, making the muscle bulge. "Rawr."

In the harsh white light of the LED lantern, his eyes look very bright. His hair's grown long enough to fall into his eyes, and he shakes his head to push it away. All at once, he's so handsome, I can't stand it. I have to kiss him.

"What's that for?" He laughs, kissing me back.

"Because I . . . wanted to," I finish, unable to say more than that. Lame. Oh, so lame.

Cheeks burning, I turn back to pulling out cans of fruit and vegetables and soup, stacking them in order.

"Velvet," Dillon says softly. "Hey."

I don't want to look at him. We've never talked about being in love. We went from dating to being married in what seemed like a snap of our fingers. And even though we'd barely been boyfriend and girlfriend before that, I didn't mind the titles of husband and wife, that legality, because it made sense. It had always felt like a totally practical decision we'd both made when we got the word that they were going to start restricting ration disbursement and health benefits. It hadn't been romantic. We hadn't talked about our feelings. We'd just decided that the benefits made sense. But now . . .

"It's going to be dark soon. We should get this stuff put away," I say.

The work goes fast. And he was right, I think. I do love it. Not just the clearing out of the houses, one by one, which leaves me feeling accomplished and at least like I'm doing something worthwhile for the future. But actually having all the stuff here, lined up like this, as some kind of insurance against the future. Yeah. I do love that.

"It makes me feel better." I take the last of the cans out of the bin and settle them into their correct places, according to what's in them. And alphabetically, for good measure. "When I lived with Opal in the apartment, looking for my mom, trying to go to school and work, I was always worried that we weren't going to have enough. That we were going to run out of food before the next check. Or that I wouldn't be able to keep up with my grades, that Opal would flunk out of school. That I'd never find my mom. So all of this stuff, barricading the windows, making all the safety things really does make me feel better. I do love it. I guess I have a thing for organization."

"That's kind of weird, you know," he says. "The alphabetizing. Weirdo."

I stick out my tongue, because I can tell he's teasing. "Takes one to know one."

We're silly with it. He chases me up the stairs, trying to pinch the backs of my legs. Teenage-boy stuff, but I don't mind it, and we both tumble out into the kitchen with sort of guilty looks on our faces like we're doing something we shouldn't.

I know at once something's wrong. Dexter's whining in the living room, and I hear Opal saying, "Mama," over and over. Mrs. Holly is bent over, just the top of her head visible over the arm of the couch.

"What happened?" I'm at my mom's side in a moment.

She's on the floor, gaze blank, flecks of foam curdled in the corners of her mouth. Her body tenses and releases rapidly, like she's shivering. A low, grunting moan slips out of her, and Opal claps her hands over her ears and scoots away from her.

"How long has she been this way?" I ask Mrs. Holly.

"It just happened." Mrs. Holly lifts my mom's hand, patting it. "Shhh, shhh. Malinda, it's okay."

Dillon brings a damp cloth and kneels beside me. I use it to wipe away the spit. My mom's eyes roll back so far, all we can see is white.

Then everything relaxes. Her eyelids flutter closed. She lets out a soft sigh.

Then she sits up.

"Velvet? Opal?"

"Mama?" Opal launches herself into Mom's lap. "You're okay!"

"Mom . . ."

She hugs Opal tight, looking at me over her shoulder. She's confused, but . . . clear in a way she hasn't been since before the Contamination. She gives me a half smile.

"Opal, ouch, get off me." She shifts Opal to the side and gives her another confused look. "My goodness, you've gotten so big."

We all stare at her. She looks around the room and settles her gaze on Mrs. Holly. "Vera . . . what on earth?"

She doesn't remember anything; that seems clear enough. Her gaze settles on Dillon, and something flickers across her expression. She recoils the tiniest amount, but I notice. I look at him, but he's not doing anything.

"Hello," she says. "Who are you?"

"My name's Dillon. I'm . . ." He gives me a helpless look.

My mom shifts Opal off her lap and puts her fingertips between her eyes, the way she always used to when her head was hurting. Her shoulders rise and fall. She shakes her head a little. Her gaze is somewhat less unfocused when she looks up again.

"I'm so tired," she says. "So very, very tired."

Then her head falls forward, and she's unconscious again.

SEVENTEEN

TUCKED IN ON THE COUCH, MY MOM LOOKS kind of small and younger than she did before, even though, for the first time, I notice long swipes of silver in her dark hair. She has a damp cloth on her forehead, and she's still and silent under the blankets we put on her. She hasn't moved for hours.

I sent Opal to bed when her eyes drooped and she couldn't stay awake. Mrs. Holly went a while ago, too, with apologies I waved away. I don't mind sitting up with my mom. She did it enough for me when I was sick.

Dillon stays with me, though he's finally given in to sleep. He's on the armchair, his feet propped on the footstool. His mouth is open, his head back. He's snoring, which I'd find annoying if I were trying to sleep and cute if I weren't so worried.

My mom doesn't have a fever, but her skin feels tight and hot. She sighs in her sleep and shudders, but it's not the same as the earlier convulsions. It's not like the times her collar triggered her, either. Something else is going on, and I can't figure out what.

But she spoke normally. She was like her normal self. Confused, memory lost—true—but for those few minutes, she knew exactly where she was, and she knew me and Opal.

Hope is such a dangerous thing, but I can't fight it down. It fills me up, fluttering like a bird, seeping into all my cracks and crevices like water, lifting my heart like a bunch of balloons. I've always had the thought in the back of my mind that my mom might come back to us, but this, tonight, is the first time I've seen any real evidence that it might be possible.

Dillon snorts and wakes. "Hey. How is she?"

"Still sleeping." I stifle a yawn with the back of my hand.

He comes over to me and rubs my shoulders, easing aches and pains I didn't know I had. "You should get some sleep. I can stay with her."

"No." I shake my head.

He sits next to me on the floor and takes my hand. "That was weird today, huh?"

"Yes. But good. I think. Don't you think?" I lean against him, glad for his solid warmth, even though it's pretty hot here in the living room.

"I hope so."

I understand his caution, but I want more assurance than

that. "She knew me and Opal. She sounded normal. She looked clear, not blank."

"I just don't want you to get your hopes up, that's all." His fingers squeeze mine.

I don't say anything. My mom shifts and sighs. She mutters. She hums something tuneless.

"Velvet. Velvet. Velvet." Her voice wakes me sometime later, when the sky looks brighter through the windows. "Velvet . . ."

"Mom?" I sit up, scrubbing at my crusty eyes. My muscles ache from sleeping on the floor. Dillon's still beside me, still sleeping.

My mom sits and looks right at me, but she doesn't see me. Her mouth forms the syllables of my name, over and over, but I'm not sure she really knows what she's saying. I put a hand on her arm; the muscles are bunched and solid, and then the shaky, shuddering thing starts again. Her back arches, her spine creaking in a way that makes me wince.

The seizure is worse this time. It goes on and on while I try everything I can think of to keep her from hurting herself. Dillon wakes up, brings me another damp cloth, some water, but there's nothing we can do but watch her helplessly as she fights whatever's making her do all of this.

"She needs a doctor," I cry against him as we watch her struggle.

But we can't take her to a doctor—they will test her for Contamination and find her positive. They will take her away. Dillon holds me tight, then pushes me away with a grim look on his face.

"There's a doctor who doesn't test, who takes care of people like your mom. Or the collared Connies whose families kept them in hiding. I heard about her from one of the guys at work, but it's all real quiet, you know. She's not legit."

"She's not a real doctor?" Frantic, I try to hold my mom still, but she quakes and quivers. At one point, her jaws snap like she's trying to bite me. Dexter whines and tries to butt against her, but I push him away.

"She's a real doctor, but she's not in a practice, I mean, I don't know—" Dillon tries to help me, but there's not much he can do. "She's, like, not working for a hospital or anything. She's not supposed to take care of people. I think she lost her license or something."

All we can do is watch my mom writhe and twist. She calms for a moment, but only long enough for me to think she might be okay. Then she starts again, harder than before.

And horribly, she talks. My name, over and over. Opal's. Heartbreakingly, my dad's, in a softer tone of voice that sounds almost normal. Everything sounds almost normal.

"It's in the pantry, behind the sugar. I want to make something out of that pair of curtains, like Scarlett O'Hara.

Oh, I couldn't possibly eat another bite. Not another bite." Her teeth snap. Nothing she says makes sense, it doesn't go together. Then her words trail off into a string of garbled nonsense.

"We have to take her," I say.

Dillon nods. "Let's get her up. We'll go in the truck."

"Go tell Mrs. Holly. I'll get my mom ready." There's not much to do but wipe her face again. She's wearing her clothes from yesterday, and at least they're not pajamas.

Dillon's able to carry her as far as the driveway, where he has to set her on her feet. Together, we sling her arms over our shoulders and get her down the hill to the truck parked at the bottom. It's a little hard to get her over the tree across the end of the driveway, but Dillon lifts her. She leans against me, but her eyes are open.

"Mom. You have to wake up." I slap her cheeks lightly, and give him a panicked look. "Dillon, how are we going to get her past the checkpoints? How are we going to get her into town?"

Dillon looks grim. "In the back."

I look in the back of his truck, which rattles with various bits and pieces of junk. A tarp, secured with a bungee cord, covers a few bins we used for packing stuff we find in the different houses. One large bin with a lid stands out.

"In there?" I point, stomach sick at the thought. "She'll have to curl up on her side, but she's lost so much weight. . . ."

Dillon climbs into the back of the truck bed and lifts the lid to dump out the contents—a few stray, smashed boxes of crackers. We get my mom up into the back of the pickup, and urge her first to step, foot by foot, into the bin. She'll fit, but the question is, will she let herself be put into it?

"Mom, you have to lie down. Curl up, knees to chest. You have to stay in this bin, okay? You have to stay quiet." I push her shoulder gently.

She starts to shake again as she does what I said to do. She curls on her side, but her body's convulsing against the bin's sides, shaking it. I look at Dillon in a panic.

"This will never work."

"We don't have a choice," he says, and I know he's right.

We cover her with some blankets and towels from another of the bins. I tuck them around her to cushion any spot where her body presses against the plastic. I lower the lid, casting her in shadow. I can't seal it on. I don't worry about her not being able to breathe or anything; the lid's not airtight. But I do worry about putting her in the dark.

"Mama, you're going to be okay. We're taking you to the doctor. I promise you're going to be fine."

My mom blinks up at me. "Velvet? What's going on?"

Relief floods me so hard, I go to my knees beside the bin. "Mom. Can you hear me?"

"Of course I can hear you. . . . Why am I . . . ?" She

struggles to get up but doesn't fight against me when I push her shoulder.

"You've been sick. We need to take you to the doctor in town. But you have to be really quiet. Okay?"

Her gaze is sharp. Focused. She licks her lips with a grimace, like her mouth tastes bad.

"Something's wrong."

"I know, Mom. I know."

She shakes a little, but it's not out of control. I think she's just scared. She curls into the blankets with a sigh.

"It's really important you stay quiet. Even if you hear voices or the truck stops. Or anything. Just stay still."

She nods. I'm not convinced she understands, but there's nothing to do but get in the truck and pray we make it through okay.

Dillon's quiet as he pulls out of the development and heads toward town. We pass the exit for Route 322, which is the road I saw blocked off, where the soldiers were shooting people who tried to get through. There are still barriers closing off the exit. The concrete's pockmarked with what could be weather damage but I know are bullet holes. I look away.

A mile farther is the roadblock. Traffic's light, only one car ahead of us. The soldier who taps on Dillon's window looks tired and bored.

"Purpose for travel?"

"Work. I've got to report in to the sanitation team, and

she"—he jerks his thumb toward me—"is signing up for over-eighteen assignment."

I tense, waiting for him to pull me out, jam a needle in some soft part of me, and dig around in my brains to test me for Contamination. Would it be a relief, in a way, to finally know for sure? But though the soldier gives me a solid, long perusal, I guess I don't look threatening or dangerous, or they just don't care at this checkpoint. He waves us through.

Dillon drives slow and careful, making sure to obey all the traffic signals, though we are now the only car on the road. I stare out the windows at the gas station, the motel, the strip mall. Lots of buildings are boarded up. Grass grows in the parking lots.

I turn to him, stunned. "This all happened in a few months?"

"Yeah." Keeping his gaze on the road, Dillon makes a careful turn down a side street.

We go past the city high school, closed for the summer but looking more alive than any of the other buildings. Someone's hung a banner across the letters of the school name. It used to say LEBANON HIGH SCHOOL. Now it says TESTING FACILITY.

"That's where they take people?"

Dillon nods and makes another turn. We're in a small neighborhood of little brick houses, most of them alike. They look as empty as the other buildings we passed. A lot of them have boards over the windows and doors, with spray-painted symbols on them.

"Emptied," he says quietly. "Places that had people who kept Connies. They took the people out. The government confiscated them. The houses, I mean."

"The people, too."

He gives me a quick look. "Yeah. The people, too."

We pull into a driveway that circles around the back of a brick house with a green roof. It has a separate garage and a large paved area with a basketball hoop that's become only a metal ring with a few ragged shreds of rope hanging from it. A tall fence divides the backyard from the houses on either side. There's a light on in the kitchen, and inside, a shape moves, twitching the curtain.

The back door opens. A tall, thin woman with cropped gray hair is in the doorway. She wears jeans and a man's button-down shirt, sleeves rolled up to her elbows. She comes down the three concrete steps to the truck.

"Can I help you?"

"It's my mom . . ." God, I hope this is the doctor or someone who knows her, not a stranger.

The woman smiles. "Is she sick?"

"Yes." Dillon's already out of the truck, heading for the back. He leaps up into the bed. "She's here."

"Hurry." The woman, the doctor, looks from side to side. "Take her inside."

She leads us to a finished basement, which is cozy and

cool and smells faintly of disinfectant. There's a grouping of battered, out-of-style furniture gathered around an ancient TV set and a bar made out of giant barrels, the top covered with black leather. There's a dartboard and a wagon-wheel table with matching chairs.

"Through here." She pushes on a section of paneling that opens with a squeak to reveal a white-painted room complete with a steel examination table and a cabinet full of medical supplies. "What's her name?"

"Malinda."

My mom has been quiet this whole time. Either she can't speak or she's staying silent because we told her to. Now she looks up.

"Come sit here," the doctor says gently.

I lead her to the table and help her sit. "C'mon, Mom."

"Hi. I'm Ellen." The woman shakes my mom's hand, holding it carefully. She turns it over to examine the palm. She has to straighten out my mom's fingers, which curl stubbornly, to do it. Keeping her gaze on my mom's face, she says to me, "Tell me about what's been going on."

Before I say anything, it starts to happen again. My mom's eyes roll back. Her muscles go tight. Ellen grabs her to keep her from falling off the table, lowering her back. My mom's feet thump against it.

"Shhh," Ellen says. "Here. Hold her down."

Dillon and I do, one on either side. Ellen prepares a hypodermic needle and syringe with some sort of clear fluid, uncapping it with her teeth and then tapping it with her finger before she slides the needle into my mom's arm. It seems to take forever, but eventually, my mom goes still. Her eyes close.

"What did you give her?"

"It's a mild sedative." Ellen carefully puts the used syringe in a red container and then washes her hands at the bar sink behind her. She turns to us, leaning on the counter with her arms crossed. "Where's her collar?"

Dillon and I share a panicked look, but I take a chance. "We took it off her a few months ago during one of the first sweeps. Some soldiers came into the house, looking for collared Connies."

"You had a key?"

I shake my head. "We used a paper clip."

Ellen barks out laughter. "You didn't."

"We did." Dillon squares his shoulders. "My mom had a key, but I wasn't able to get it from her before they took her away."

"Your mom worked in a kennel?" Ellen frowns, not angry, but like she's putting the puzzle pieces together.

"Yeah." Dillon straightens the hem of my mom's shirt, pulling it down where it had ridden up to show her belly.

I burn with love for him because of that kindness.

"Was your mom's name Jean?"

"Yes!" Startled, he raps his knuckles on the table, but my mom doesn't so much as murmur.

"I knew Jean. She was a good woman. I did a lot of work for the kennels in the beginning. They took her away?"

"Yeah. When they started cracking down on everything, they came and got my dad. They took my mom after that. She was fighting the soldiers who came to get him." His voice cracks.

I take his hand, and he looks at me gratefully. "We haven't been able to find out anything about where they took her. Do you know?"

Ellen shakes her head. "No. Your dad, was he collared?"

"No. But he'd been ice-picked."

"Ah." Ellen nods. "Was your mom Contaminated?"

"No. At least . . . I don't think so."

"If they took her away and tested her," she says, "and found out that she was, then she'll be at the research facility."

"The Sanitarium," I say. "And if she wasn't?"

Ellen hesitates. "To be honest with you, she's probably there, no matter how she tested. They've been doing things to people for a long time. Things they . . . shouldn't."

"How do you know this?" Dillon sounds angry, but I know him well enough to know that he's more scared.

"Because I worked there." Ellen scratches her chin for a second or two before looking each of us in the eye. "The things you hear on the radio? That's only half of it, what goes on there. So . . . I'm sorry to tell you this, but I think you need to accept that you'll never see your mother again. I'm sorry."

Dillon lets out a low, soft sigh and stalks away, turning his back to us. "She's dead. My dad, too."

"If they're lucky," Ellen says quietly.

We're silent at that, looking at my mom. Ellen goes to her, testing her pulse with two fingers at her wrist. Lifting her eyelids to look at her pupils with a white light, which doesn't even make her flinch. Ellen smooths my mom's hair for a moment, like she's petting a cat, before she turns back to us.

"This will keep her quiet for a while. But you'll need to give it to her regularly, at least fifteen to twenty minutes before it wears off, so she won't have time to become violent—"

"She's never violent," I interrupt.

Ellen looks dubious. "They're all violent. What's your name?"

"Velvet. This is Dillon." I lift my chin at her tone.

"They're all violent," she says again in a flat voice. "It just depends on how much and when and what they do. But trust me, Velvet. All of the Contamination victims succumb to their rage. All of them."

"My mom's different." Surely she can see that.

Ellen looks at her again. "You say you got the collar off using a paper clip?"

"Yeah. We straightened it, the way you'd do to reset

a computer modem or cell phone," Dillon says, turning to face us. He has himself under control, but his eyes are red.

"That's not supposed to work, you know. That's supposed to trigger the collar into Mercy Mode."

I shrug, knowing I'm giving her a little bit of attitude, but not caring. "Well. It didn't. Obviously."

"Obviously." Ellen looks sad. Then mad. "There could be proper treatment, preventive measures, especially for the people not showing any symptoms, but nobody's bothering with that research anymore. Nobody's working on a cure or a way to reverse the progress."

"You sound like you know what you're talking about," Dillon says.

"I was a researcher. The Sanitarium. Did you know one of the biggest research facilities in the whole country is right here in Lebanon? Hardly anyone does." Her lip curls. "This little brown stain of a town in the middle of farm country. Who'd have thought it? I worked with some of the best researchers in the world, and now here I am, working like some kind of basement butcher. . . ."

She stops herself, though she's breathing hard and is clearly angry. She clears her throat and looks at both of us again. "I can give you a month's worth of the drug. One syringe a day. But after that, honestly I don't know if I'll have any more. I can't just pull up the Web site and place an order, you know what I mean?"

"What if we just give it to her when she starts to have seizures?" I hold my mom's hand. It's cold, and her fingers don't curl around mine. "What if we don't want to keep her doped up constantly?"

"I told you. You have to. Or you'll regret it," Ellen says sharply. "Do you want your mom to hurt you? Do you want to have to hurt her? Because that's what will happen eventually. Sooner rather than later. She's clearly been Contaminated, and the disease has progressed quite far, if it's affecting her motor skills and speech patterns this way."

"But she's getting better!" I cry, hating what she's saying. "Yesterday, she knew me and my sister. She recognized us and spoke to us, and she was normal. Dillon, she was normal, right?"

Dillon nods, but looks wary. "For a little bit. Yeah."

Ellen tips my mom's chin to look at her throat, pressing her fingers there to take her pulse again. Then she turns her face from side to side, peering close to look at the tiny, faint scars where they put the electrodes in. "She's definitely an unusual case. But, Velvet, I don't want you to get your hopes up. There is no known cure for Contamination. No reversal. The only hope we ever had was trying to keep the disease from progressing in people already Contaminated. That was the focus of the research when I was there. I don't know what they're doing now."

Boldly, I stare her down. "How come you're not there

anymore? If you were such a big-shot researcher and all?"

Ellen doesn't look offended. Instead, she gives me a wry smile. "Let's just say they were stepping on my civil liberties."

On the table, my mom lets out a soft snore, then goes silent again.

"How long will she sleep?"

"Another few hours. Then she'll be groggy, but you should be able to get some food into her. I assume she's using adult diapers?"

"She uses the bathroom," I say. "She feeds herself. Dresses herself. She knits socks and works in the garden and sweeps the floor and sings us lullabies!"

Ellen looks surprised. "But . . . you said she'd been collared. It's obvious—"

"It's not obvious at all," I snap. "Dillon, c'mon. Let's get my mom home."

He's helping me lift her to sit, and she's so limp and unresponsive that it's clear there's going to be a problem getting her into the truck. We'll have to carry her. Frustrated tears burn my eyes and throat.

"Hey. Wait a minute." Ellen's touch is gentle on my shoulder as she tries to turn me to face her, but I shrug her off.

I don't want her pity. I don't want her to touch me. I want to get out of here and get my mom home. I slap her hand away hard enough to knock it against the metal table, making it ring.

"Velvet," Dillon says.

I glare, sliding an arm under my mom's shoulders to lift her.

"Maybe we should—"

"I'll do it myself," I tell him. My heart hurts at how skinny she is, light enough that I can lift her upright all by myself. "Mom, c'mon."

Her eyelids flutter. Her mouth works. But she's limp as overcooked spaghetti. The only way I'm going to be able get her out of here is if I sling her over my shoulder, and while I could carry her that way for at least a short distance, I hesitate and let her slump back against the table.

"Is this true?" Ellen asks Dillon. Not me. "She's capable of all that?"

He nods. "Yeah."

"Of course it's true! Why would I lie?" I'm furious now. I move toward Ellen, who backs up a step and puts out a hand to keep me from coming closer.

I've scared her.

Good.

"Velvet, have you been tested?"

I know why she's asking, and I can't stop myself from baring my teeth in what should be a smile but I know looks more like a snarl. "No."

"How have you managed that?"

I hesitate, already having trusted her with enough information to get us into a lot of trouble. "We live out of town."

"How? They've been closing off all the roads, restricting travel. Getting the population into a more dense area." Ellen's brows knit. "They've made testing mandatory now. You know that, right? If you want to get your rations, you need to be tested."

"Yeah. We know. We have supplies. We're okay."

"Is there a reason you don't want to be tested?" she asks sharply, looking at both of us. "Either of you?"

"Because it goes against my civil liberties," Dillon says smoothly.

Ellen laughs. "Well, I hate to break the news to you, kid, but there aren't any civil liberties left, in case you hadn't noticed. Not in the black zones, anyway. It doesn't matter. Sooner or later, everyone will be tested, voluntarily or not. And you know what happens if you come up positive. But you"—she gestures at Dillon—"you've got the bracelet, which means you tested negative. I designed that test, by the way. Before they asked me to leave. It was still in the testing process. I'd intended it to be much less invasive, less damaging."

Dillon winces. "Damaging? It didn't hurt. I got a black eye, but . . ."

"The testing process I wanted would've eliminated even that." She shrugged. "Not that it matters. They rushed it, but it works. Though the false positive rate was too high for what I wanted."

I cringe. "So they're finding people positive who aren't?"

"It's possible." Ellen pauses. "It's also possible that the test is so sensitive that it can detect such low levels of Contamination that the patient would never show symptoms."

"So what difference does that make if they're taking away everyone who tests positive?"

She says nothing at first. Then: "Velvet, what's your last name?"

I don't answer her.

"Where's your father?"

I make an effort to unclench fists I hadn't realized I'd made. "He's . . . gone. He's been gone since the first wave."

"But she thinks she saw him. A running Connie got chased into our backyard—"

"Dillon!"

Ellen studies me. "You think it was your dad?"

"They . . . went back home. A lot of them who were out when it hit them. They made their way back home." I swallow at the memory of the news reports showing the swarms of people raging up and down the streets.

"They did. But that was two years ago. If your dad was part of the first wave, there's a good chance he was killed."

"I know that," I tell her coldly.

She studies me again, eyes narrowed. "Where do you live, exactly?"

I give Dillon a warning look so he doesn't answer. "Outside of town. You don't need to know where."

"But a collared Connie, running? How would he get so far out of town?"

"He didn't have a collar," Dillon says, and I want to punch him so hard.

Ellen looks like she's thinking laboriously. "If he didn't have a collar, then he had to have succumbed to the Contamination more recently. Unless . . ."

"It's time to go." I glare at Dillon, then Ellen. "Thanks for helping my mom. What do we owe you?"

"Nothing."

"The drugs. They're not free." Nothing's free—I'm old enough to know that for sure.

"No. But I didn't pay for them, so I don't charge." Ellen shrugs. "Got to stick it to the man in any way you can. You can stay here with your mom until she wakes up enough, if you want."

"No. We need to get home. And Dillon's missing work." I've just realized that, but I see by his expression that he'd thought of it already.

Ellen rubs at her forehead. "You can use my phone to call in, if you have to. I'm sure you don't have access to one."

Dillon looks at me apologetically. "I should, huh? Call in sick, I guess."

"If you don't show up, maybe they'll fire you," I say.

"If he just doesn't show up, they'll make note of it and he'll be flagged the next time he goes into work. Probably get a retest. Might get detained, because they can." Ellen's voice is hard and blunt. "They're not messing around out there, kids. I'm not sure you understand what's going on, but this isn't about stubbing the toe of your civil liberties. We have no rights here. The government has all the power, and believe me, there's more coming."

I think of the soldiers shooting the people trying to leave town. "I know more than you think."

"Tell her," Dillon says.

Ellen gives me a curious look. I look at my mom, who seems peaceful. "Can we move her to a couch or something, at least?"

We settle her on the sofa in the other part of the basement. Ellen closes the hidden panel door carefully, and directs Dillon to the phone upstairs in her kitchen, where she makes us both glasses of iced tea sweetened with sugar she scrapes from the bottom of the ceramic container on her counter. She sighs, stirring each glass.

"No more sugar. This is the last. They're only disbursing chemical sweeteners now. I guess nobody told the idiots in charge that sugar isn't made with animal products."

We have several five-pound bags of sugar at our house.

Who needs cash, I think, when we've got sugar? I sip the tea. It's not very good.

I describe the scene I witnessed to Ellen. The blockades, the soldiers, the collared kids. The tractor-trailer trying to break through. She leans closer, eyes wide, thoughts clearly racing behind her gaze.

"Damn. They really tried it." She shakes her head and drains her glass, then wipes her mouth with the back of her hand. It's shaking. "The soldiers shot people?"

"Yes." I don't drink more tea. "Who tried what?"

Dillon gets off the phone. "I told them I was puking and had diarrhea."

I make a face. "Gross."

He grins. "Hey. They told me not to come back until I'd been puke and poop free for twenty-four hours. I figure that bought me at least three or four days."

"Who tried what?" I ask again.

"Not everyone was asked to leave when I was. Some of the docs were fully invested in what was going on. Some just knew how to kiss butts better. I keep in touch with a few of them. They were talking about trying to get out of town with some of the research subjects, getting out of the black zone. I'm not part of the planning; they had to keep it supersecret of course. And honestly, I'm surprised they tried."

"Research subjects?" My heart sinks. "They were in the tractor-trailer? The one that blew up?"

Ellen looks stricken, as if it had just occurred to her. "Oh. God. Yes. Possibly. Oh, Velvet, I'm so sorry you had to see that."

"Be sorry for the people in the back of that truck," I say. "Because I'm pretty sure they're all dead."

"They'd have been dead, anyway," she tells me gently. "That's what they do to them when they're finished with the testing."

The three of us sit there in sick silence. Dillon drinks some tea; ice clinks in the glass, and I am envious of Ellen's refrigerator. Her electricity. Her phone.

"But we have real sugar," I think.

"How can this all be happening?" Dillon says in a low voice.

"In the matter of public safety, a lot can happen." Ellen rubs again at her forehead, then her mouth as though to wipe away the taste of her words. "When soldiers with guns outnumber the private citizens, when the population has been decimated by disease and subjugated with fear, all it takes is a handful of people in charge who think they're doing the right thing."

"But it's not the right thing! Taking people away and putting them down like stray pets, that's not right!" I stand and pace. "None of this is okay or right!"

"And you're not the only one who thinks so, Velvet."

I turn to her. "So . . . what do we do? How can we stop this?"

Ellen's mouth twists. "I wish I knew. I wish I could tell you. But all I know is that there are people out there who are trying to stop it."

I want to be one of those people.

Before I realize it, I've gripped the glass in my hand too tight. It shatters, spreading tea all over the table. Ice cubes skitter and fall onto the floor. Pain slices me, and blood wells up on a couple of my fingers.

"Velvet, are you okay?" Dillon reaches for my hand, but Ellen pushes her way in front of him.

"Let me see."

At the sink, she washes the wounds and checks them for splinters of glass, but once the water rinses away the blood, it's clear they're only scratches. She pats them dry with a dish towel and pulls open a drawer to take out a package of adhesive bandages.

"I can do it." I wrap them one by one around my fingers. "Thanks."

"You're angry a lot," she murmurs. "And you're strong. Aren't you?"

"Lots of people are angry, and, yeah, I guess I'm getting stronger." I look at Dillon, who frowns.

"I'd like to test you—"

"For Contamination? No." I back away. "No way."

"I'm not on their side. You can trust me," Ellen says. "Velvet, if you're afraid you're Contaminated—"

"What good would knowing do?" I toss the question at

her. "You said yourself, there's no cure. There's barely any hope, even, about stopping the progression. And anyone who's Contaminated becomes violent and dangerous and loses their mind. Right?"

Ellen says nothing.

A soft sound in the basement doorway has us all turning. It's my mom, looking groggy and unsteady. I go to her quickly, grabbing her arm to keep her from falling backward down the stairs.

"Hi," she says.

Ellen looks startled. "Hi. Malinda, right?"

My mom nods. She yawns. She looks at me with a confused smile. "What's going on?"

"Velvet, I wish you'd let me test you. And your mom."

"No!"

Ellen sighs and goes to another drawer, one she pulls out entirely. Then she reaches into the open hole. She stretches her arm deep into the depths of the cabinet and pulls out a small box, which she opens to reveal a number of colored bracelets like the one Dillon's wearing. "Then, at least, let me give you these. They're from different testing periods. They should be enough to pass you through any sort of roadblocks if they ask to see if you have one, but they're not going to hold up against any real scrutiny. And if they snag you for random, actual testing instead of just checking to see if you already have been tested, they definitely won't. But . . . it will be better than nothing."

"Way better," Dillon says. "Wow. Thanks."

I'm reluctant to take them from her, but my mom holds out her wrist obediently when Ellen picks out a blue bracelet and slips it on, adjusting for the fit. Mine is orange, and she binds it a little too tight. It pinches the skin.

"We should pay you something," Dillon says. "I could bring you some real sugar next time I come into town."

Ellen grins. "That would be great."

In the truck, my mom between us, I say, "You shouldn't have offered her the sugar."

"We have plenty," Dillon says.

"Not if you keep giving it away," I tell him.

I've never seen him look at me the way he does now. Cold and hard and sort of condescending. It makes me feel small.

"She just gave us a month's worth of drugs to help your mom and bracelets that will get us past the soldiers. I think a freaking bag of sugar is worth that, don't you?"

I don't answer, just look out at the boarded-up windows and grass-grown parking lots we pass on the way out of town. I can't explain to him that I don't trust that doctor, no matter how much help she gave us. She used to be one of *them*, wasn't she?

The soldiers don't ask to see our bracelets, but, yeah, knowing we have them makes it way less stressful when they stop us at the roadblock and wave us on. I wait until we've driven a mile before I say, "When do you think they will stop letting you back through?"

Dillon turns into the development, driving slower because there are fallen trees and debris all over the roads here. He gives me a quick glance across my mom, who stares out the front window, barely blinking. "I don't know."

Soon, I think. I shiver like someone dumped ice water down my shirt. With the way everything's changing, it's going to happen soon.

EIGHTEEN

DILLON SPENDS THE NEXT FOUR DAYS AT HOME. It's been nice having him there. We leave Opal behind while we take the pickup truck to scavenge more houses, and though we share a bedroom, there's something better about being alone together. Really alone.

But I can't stop thinking about the way he looked at me the day we took my mom to Ellen's. He wasn't wrong to judge me for being a brat, but I hate that he thinks I was being unreasonable. He must've been thinking about it, too, because as we glean the cupboards in one of the houses toward the back of the neighborhood, he pulls out a bag of sugar shut with a plastic clip.

"I'll take this to Ellen tomorrow when I go back to work."

"Dillon."

He looks at me, sort of furtively and guiltily, like he feels bad for poking me, but not that bad. "What?"

"I'm sorry." I shrug. My parents taught me it was important to own up to things you did wrong, even if you did them for the right reasons. To say you're sorry when you are, and I am, if only because my reaction made him think less of me. "I know we owe her something, and if it's sugar, that's fine. It's just that I don't think she has our best interests at heart. That's all."

"She risks a lot to help people, you know. She risked a lot to help us." He snags my wrist and holds it up, rubbing the red mark the orange bracelet's left on my skin. "You know what would happen if she got caught?"

"The same thing that's happening to people who try to leave the boundaries. Or just the ones who test positive. The same thing that's happening to a lot of people." It sounds harsher than I mean it to. "She tested people, Dillon. Who knows, she might've been one of the ones who ran tests on my mom."

He doesn't answer that, and drops my wrist. I can see he's working up to tell me something, though, and I wait for him to spit it out. I busy myself opening drawers and pulling out broken pens and notepads and rubber bands, setting aside anything that looks like it might be useful.

"It's just that . . . you're hard, sometimes, Velvet."

I don't look at him, though his words sting. I keep my shoulders from hunching, pretending I'm not at all upset by what he said. I dig through someone else's junk and say nothing.

"Most of the time, you're strong and determined and you work hard, and I know it's frustrating for you. Doing all this. And scary. But, sometimes, you're hard, too."

"And you don't like it?"

"No," Dillon says after what feels like a really long time. "I guess I don't."

I don't turn. "I don't know what to say to that."

"You don't have to say anything, I guess. I just wanted to tell you."

"Why?" I cry, finally facing him. "Why would you tell me that? Does it serve a purpose? You want me to be sweet and soft and passive, or what?"

"No," he says, but I cut him off.

"Because that's ridiculous!"

I toss the pens with their missing caps and the broken stubs of pencils to the floor. I kick them, making them roll. I slam the drawer shut hard enough to splinter the cheap wood.

"If I'm hard, it's because I have to be!" I shout.

Dillon reaches for me, but all I see is red, the edges of my vision blurring and wavering. I try to breathe, but the air's so tight and close in this dark, stinking kitchen that reeks of mold and decay that all I can do is cough and choke. I swat away his hands, meaning only to keep him from hugging me, but the back of my hand catches him under the chin and sends him staggering back.

Silence.

Long, painful silence.

Dillon touches his lip, which is swelling a little from where he bit it. His eyes are wide. He backs up from me when I move toward him.

"I didn't mean to," I tell him, but it doesn't matter.

He leaves me there.

I don't run out after him. I wait for the pickup truck to start up and drive away, and then I let myself loose in the kitchen until everything within reach is destroyed.

NINETEEN

LATER, I LIMP HOME WITH MY HANDS BATTERED and bruised. Every part of me aches, but mostly my head hurts. Not like a headache. It's full of my thoughts and fears, all of them pressing against the walls of my skull until I want to scream.

I think Dillon's scared of me.

I want to cry.

I want to break more things.

Instead, I let myself in the front door and go to my bathroom to scrub away the dirt under my fingernails. It's hard. I have plenty of soap but the water from the well is icy cold. I bend at the sink and splash my face again and again.

The smell of something good greets me when I come downstairs, as clean as I can get and wearing fresh clothes at least. The table's set. Opal and Mrs. Holly made a pasta dish with olive oil and veggies from the garden. My mom's already sitting in her spot. Dillon won't look at me.

"Can we play a game after dinner?" Opal says, stabbing her fork into a pile of pasta. "I kind of want to beat your butts at Monopoly."

Dillon laughs, not looking at me. "Good luck with that."

"I think a game would be wonderful," Mrs. Holly says so carefully, I know that Dillon must've said something to her about me. "Lots of fun. Velvet?"

"You all play. I'm going to read." I concentrate on my dinner, scooping mouthfuls of pasta and chewing just enough to keep myself from choking on it. The food's delicious, but I can't appreciate it. My stomach's aching with emptiness, though, so I force myself to eat even though I don't want to.

After dinner, they play Monopoly while I read and my mom sits and stares out the window. She hasn't had any clarity since we brought her back from Ellen's, but she hasn't had any seizures or anything, either. I haven't given her the shots, figuring that despite what Ellen said, we'd only use them when she has trouble.

I wonder if I should shoot myself up with whatever's in them.

I go to bed early, before it's even dark. When I was little and my parents made me go to bed in the summer before night had fallen, I remember pounding my pillow at the injustice of it. Maybe I've always been an angry kid.

I fall asleep so hard, I don't remember the descent into dreams, and I wake up as fiercely.

I smell smoke.

There's a rustling, like paper being crumpled in a fist over and over. And it's hot, worse than the normal summer heat that comes from being upstairs without air-conditioning or even electric fans. When I try to sit up, it's like a fist is holding me down. No, worse, like I'm underwater and I can't get to the surface, and I'm going to drown.

I open my eyes, but they immediately sting. I take in a deep, choking breath that shreds my lungs. I roll out of bed and onto the floor with a thump hard enough to rattle my teeth, and finally, I can breathe. It's just cooler enough here that I can gather my senses.

It's a fire. I can't tell if the house is on fire or if it's in the woods outside, but now I'm awake enough to remember all the things I ever learned about what to do in a fire. I crawl toward Dillon's bed and shake him until he also rolls onto the floor.

We crawl to the bedroom door, but before I can open it, he slams a hand against it to keep it closed. He touches it all over. I remember. He's feeling it to make sure it's not hot. There's less smoke in the hallway, maybe because there aren't open windows here and it's coming in from the outside.

"Opal!" In her room, I pull her from bed. She stumbles, sleepy, following me while Dillon races to wake Mrs. Holly. Dexter, sleeping at the foot of her bed, barks raspily and tumbles after us.

In my mom's room, I find her already awake and sitting up in bed. Her windows are open, so the smoke is thicker in here. She's coughing when I pull her from the bed. In the hall, Opal, Dillon, and Mrs. Holly are already heading downstairs.

The fire's in the backyard. It eats the trees, turning them black with its red and orange and gold mouth. A tree falls as I watch through the windows, and the crash of it makes us all scream. Opal's crying, and Mrs. Holly has her arm around her.

If the house were on fire, we'd run outside. But it's the outside that's on fire, so where do we go? Dillon runs to the kitchen.

"Wet towels," he shouts over the sound of the crackling.

We run the water in the sink, soaking dishcloths and a few beach towels Mrs. Holly brings in from the laundry room. We wrap them around our heads and our shoulders, dripping them down our backs. My mother doesn't move. She stands perfectly still, blinking with the light of the fire lighting up her face.

"Mom! Come on! We have to get out of here!"

No time to grab anything. We push out the front door and into the driveway. There's fire there, too. Pushing from the back of the neighborhood toward the front.

We stumble-run to the bottom of the driveway, into Dillon's truck, all of us crammed into the front seat that doesn't have enough room for five, plus a frightened, squirming dog. The smoke is so thick that when Dillon turns on the lights, it's like they shine onto a stone wall. He drives, too fast for safety.

Animals run ahead of us. The pack of dogs that roams the neighborhood runs in front of us, too. Bounding deer leap across the road, and he nearly hits one before braking to a halt.

Everything's confusing and terrible, but I trust Dillon to get us out safely. And he does, navigating the dark and twisting streets until we get to the highway. And there he comes to another screeching, braking halt.

Because there's a blockade of soldiers and trucks there, waiting for us.

TWENTY

"WHERE ARE YOU TAKING HER?! YOU LET HER go!" I fight against the soldier who has me by the back of my T-shirt.

They've already loaded Mrs. Holly and my mother into a van. Dillon into another. Dexter has fled into the night, and I can only hope he makes it to safety. But now they're trying to take Opal, and I can't let them.

"Let go of me!" I wrench myself free and run after her, but another soldier is in the way.

This one hits me on the head with something hard, and I drop to my knees. Only for a minute, because even though there's pain and the shine of whirling stars, I am desperate to get to my sister. I struggle to my feet, and the look of surprise on the soldier's face is enough to give me the time to go after her.

I don't make it. This time, they tackle me. Force my face into the ground. Gravel cuts my cheeks. Two of them lift me, one with his hands between my shoulder blades, the other's fingers hooked into the waistband of my pajama bottoms. I swing between them like they're going to give me an airplane ride, twirl me around in a circle. Instead, they toss me onto my feet, changing their grip to my upper arms.

"Velvet!" Opal's scream stretches out between us.

Take care of your sister. She's the only one you'll ever have. Look at her, how precious, how sweet. I know she gets into your toys and bothers you, Velvet, but you're the big sister. You have to protect her. Take care of Opal, Velvet. You're the big sister.

I open my mouth and scream. No words. Just fury. Do they let me go? Or do I pull away? I'm on my feet and running toward Opal, who's being shoved into the back of a van. Her arms and legs flail. They put a hand on her head to keep her from hitting it on the door as she struggles.

Their shouts go low and somehow syrupy, like time is stretching out all around us. Someone swipes at me, but I duck him. A hand passes over my hair, fingers snagging, yanking my head back. I keep going. I'm free. I jump over bundles and duffle bags on the ground and come down hard on my ankle, which twists. Pain shoots up my leg, but I ignore it.

Opal reaches for me, but there are people between us and I can't get to her. I shove and punch and kick. I see

Dillon watching with horrified eyes. But I'm trying to get to Opal.

That's when something thick and sour smelling, worse than the smoke, fills my nostrils. A white haze covers me. Gas. They're spraying me.

I'm down.

TWENTY-ONE

WHEN I WAKE UP, I'M IN A HOSPITAL BED. MY wrists are cuffed. My feet, too. I can't move.

My head hurts so bad, I'd gladly cut it off. I'm wearing a hospital gown, I can tell that much. A needle pinches the back of my hand, attached to a tube that runs to a hanging bag of clear liquid.

I'm in the Sanitarium.

I look around, expecting dirty floors and a crowded room, but everything is white and sterile. I'm alone in here. My throat is raw, painful when I swallow. I'm desperate for a glass of water, but I can't call out for one. There's no button for me to press, either. But in a minute, a guy in a pair of brightly colored scrubs bustles into my room. He's older than me but younger than my parents, and he has kind brown eyes and a head of thick, dark hair that looks like it could use a brush.

"Hi. Velvet, right?" His voice is soft.

I croak an answer.

"Thirsty?"

I nod.

The man pours a cup of water from a pitcher next to the bed, and sticks a straw in it. He offers it to me, and I drink greedily. It hits my tongue and the back of my throat, the most delicious thing I've ever tasted. I want more, but it's all gone.

"Let that settle first." He checks everything, including the wrist and ankle cuffs. He doesn't make them looser, but snugs them tight. Then he checks the bag of fluid and the needle in the back of my hand.

"Where am I?"

"You're in the hospital. You were involved in an accident. A fire. You sustained damage to your lungs, but you're going to be just fine."

I remember the fire. I remember running from the house and the drive in Dillon's truck. The soldiers.

"Opal. Where's my sister?"

"She's fine. Try to relax." He pats my arm and does something to the bag of fluid.

In seconds, warmth floods me. I start to feel sleepy. I blink away the tiredness.

"What about my mom? Dillon? Mrs. Holly?"

The man swings toward me, brown eyes wide. He checks the bag again, adjusting some dial. More warmth fills me, but again I shake off the weariness. I have to know what happened to my family.

"They're all fine. You should rest now. You have to be tired."

"I'm not. I want to know where they are, and why am I locked up like this?" I tug at the wrist restraints, which rattle against the metal rails.

The man backs up a step. "They're for your safety."

I think I understand. They're not for my safety, but for his and for whoever else comes in here to take care of me. I yank again.

"Why am I locked up? Is it because I'm Contaminated?"

He starts to burble something that's supposed to sound vague and medical and threatening.

"Am I Contaminated?" I scream it. I yank so hard on my left wrist that the leather buckle gives. Not enough to let me free, but enough to make it noticeably looser.

Without giving me an answer, the man flees. The door locks behind him. I see him look for a few seconds through the window to the hallway, his eyes still wide and scared.

I fall back on the bed, breathing hard. My wrist hurts. My ankle hurts; I remember twisting it. My lungs and throat hurt, too, but that's from whatever gas they dosed me with, I'm sure of it.

The clear fluid drips into me in a steady stream. I count the passing of time by the number of drops. I'm so bored, I want to scream; so thirsty, it's like I've been swallowing sand. My stomach starts to rumble, too.

Worst of all, I have to pee.

I count the hours by how long it takes the bag of fluid to empty, and by how hard it is to stop myself from wetting the bed. I work at the restraints on my wrists, tugging and releasing over and over until finally they're loose enough for me to slip one hand free. The skin on my wrist is raw and bleeding, but the pain is somehow distant.

I take the needle from the port in the back of my hand and unbuckle my other wrist. Then my ankles. I have to pee so bad, I can barely move, and I crouch with my hands pressing my belly as I go into the bathroom. I use the toilet and shake with relief.

There's a woman standing in the room when I come out of the bathroom. She's dressed in a neat black skirt and white shirt, and her blond hair's tucked into a tight French twist. She wears a pair of black patent-leather stiletto pumps with red soles that look totally impractical.

"Hi," I say warily, pausing in the doorway. I rest my weight on one foot to keep the pressure off my sore ankle.

She turns so fast, I know I've scared her, but she puts on a fast face of welcome. "Velvet. Hello. I'm Dr. Donna D'Angelo. You can call me Dr. Donna."

I'm not calling her anything but creepy, that's what I think. I nod stiffly, not moving, though I want to get back into bed, even if I don't want to be locked up again. The room's spinning a little. I can't tell if my stomach's sick, or if I'm so hungry that I'm nauseated.

Dr. Donna must realize she's between me and the bed,

because she steps out of the way with a grand gesture. "Please. Don't let me stop you. I'm sure you're exhausted."

I'm not, really. Aching all over and my head's swimming, but I'm not tired. I stay where I am, trying not to make it obvious that I'm scouting the room for anything I can use as a weapon to get out of here.

"Where am I?"

"Arnaldo told me you'd woken."

"Arnaldo's the guy who came in before? With the scrubs?"

She nods eagerly. "Yes. Arnaldo's one of our best nurses here. He'll take great care of you."

"He said I'm in the hospital because of the fire."

"Yes. You're so fortunate that you were all found so soon." Dr. Donna's red lipstick is so expertly applied, I wonder how she can move her mouth without smearing it. But there's a little on her front teeth when she smiles, and that makes me feel better.

"Uh-huh." I lean in the doorway, wishing for my clothes. This gown is open in the back, and I'm not wearing anything under it.

"He said you were a little . . . agitated."

My brows go up. "You think?"

"I think," she says carefully, "that you must be confused and concerned about what's going on. Anyone would be, in your situation. So why don't you get back into bed, Velvet, and I'll explain everything to you. Okay?"

Her bright smile and the way she tilts her head make me think that Dr. Donna is used to getting her own way. If not by acquiescence, then acquisition, my dad would've said. It's a quote from one of his video games. A blur of motion outside the window gives me a glimpse of what looks like a military uniform.

"If I don't get into bed, will those soldiers out there make me?"

Her smile is wide and probably meant to be calming, but it makes me think of a shark. "Get back into bed, Velvet. I'll have something brought in for you to eat and drink. How's that?"

She might think she's bribing me, but I know a threat when I see it in her eyes. I sidle past her, half expecting her to grab me as I pass, but I make it to the bed okay. I slide under the covers.

"Are you going to lock me up again?"

"Should I?" Dr. Donna gives me a strangely fond but stern look.

"I don't want you to."

"And it seems you're able to get out of the restraints, anyway. Despite being pumped enough sedative to put down an elephant." With another of those ugly, strange grins, Dr. Donna crosses to the empty fluid bag. She pokes it with a red fingernail. She looks at me. "You're a very special girl, Velvet. Do you know that?"

I don't answer her.

Dr. Donna claps her hands together. "It's going to be such a pleasure getting to know you. I feel it. Now you be a good girl and stay in bed. I'll order you something to eat and drink. Bland foods at first, I'm afraid. You've been out for a while; we don't want to shock your system."

"Wait . . . what? Out?" I sit up. "How long?"

Dr. Donna waves dismissively. "Stay in bed. I'll send someone with food for you."

"How long?" I call after her, but she's out the door without answering me.

Of course I get out of bed. Of course there are soldiers posted outside the door. They have guns. I get back into bed.

Arnaldo brings me pudding and oatmeal and milk and offers to feed it to me.

"You're kidding."

"No," he says with a smile I don't want to return. "But believe me, I have other things I'd rather be doing. Some toilets need scrubbing down the hall, that's way more fun."

I give him a grudging half smile, but feed myself. He takes away the dishes and leaves me in bed without restraining me, but there's nothing to do in here. No television. No books, not even a Bible or something in the drawer.

There's no window to the outside world.

There used to be one. The outline's still there. But now it's bricked up. What sort of hospital room has no window? The Sanitarium, that's what kind. I've never been in the hospital before as a patient, but I've visited a few people, and there's never been a room without a window. There are curtains here, which create an illusion, but behind them is only a plain concrete wall and the square of bricks that have replaced the glass.

Limping, I pace the room. There's a bed. A small dresser of flimsy wood, all the drawers empty. A nightstand, its single drawer also empty. Everything smells new, like paint.

In the bathroom, I look at my reflection for the first time. No wonder my head hurts. Both my eyes are black and blue, like I got double punched in the face. I turn side to side, studying the pattern of bruising. I touch it gently and look closer to find the two tiny pinpricks of blood where they must've put the needles in to take samples of my brains.

There's no soap or shampoo in the bathroom, but the water is hot and I shower forever, waiting for it to get cold, but it never does. I lie on the tiles and let it rain down all over me, easing away the aches and pains until it hurts more to be on the hard floor than it feels good to be in the hot water.

Finally, I crawl into bed with my hair soaking and the hospital gown clinging to me. I remember my mom's friend telling her once about her hospital stay, how it was impossible to sleep because the nurses came in every hour or so to check on her, but nobody comes in. If they stare at me through the window in the door, I don't know it. I don't want to know it. I pull the blankets over me and sleep, though my dreams are restless.

When I wake up, Dr. Donna's sitting in the chair next to the bed. How long has she been watching me? I'm totally creeped out. I sit, rubbing my eyes and wincing when I forget to be gentle.

"Oh, good. You're awake. You know, you remind me so much of my daughter. She was your age."

"Was?"

Dr. Donna's smile falters for a second, and she doesn't answer me. She stares, though, her eyes glittering. Then she seems to shake herself out of it. "We need to do a few tests on you—"

"No."

Dr. Donna's next smile is not at all friendly. "Velvet, don't be like that. It's just a few simple—"

"I said no." I sit up higher in the bed, pushing my tangled hair off my face.

"You don't have a choice." Her smile disappears. I like her better when she's not pretending to be my friend. "You can be a good girl or a bad girl. Up to you. But it will be easier for you if you're good."

"It will be easier for you, that's what you mean."

Something flickers in her expression, and she stands. "Fine. We'll see how you feel in a few hours when you're hungry."

She doesn't come back for a whole day.

TWENTY-TWO

ARNALDO HASN'T COME BACK. INSTEAD, A short, burly guy with a shaved head brings me a tray of what looks like vegetarian noodle soup, crusty white bread with margarine, a side of thick-sliced fries and ketchup. Dr. Donna comes in after him.

"Thanks, Cody, but you can go."

Cody gives me a long, hard stare. "You sure? I can stick around in case she gives you any trouble."

"She's not going to give me any trouble. Are you?" Dr. Donna's smile stretches wide across her face and doesn't reach her eyes.

My mouth waters and my stomach clenches with hunger, but I stare her down. I don't make a move for the food, even though she puts it within reach. Cody leaves, but not before giving me another glare.

"It's just a few small tests, Velvet. Then you can eat."

I have no intentions of doing anything this woman

wants, but I put on an innocent face and give the food a longing glance. "What kind of tests?"

"Just a few motor skills tests. That sort of thing."

"What does that have to do with being in a fire?" I hold out my hands, palm up, then down. "I mean, I'm not even burned or anything."

Dr. Donna's eyes narrow. "You were very lucky."

"Where's the rest of my family?" I can't disguise the *boing-going* of my stomach at the smell of the soup.

"They're fine. Dillon and your sister and the older woman—"

"Mrs. Holly."

"All of them have been placed in displacement housing."

"What's that?" I think of the apartment Opal and I were given as Conorphans. At least then we'd been able to take some of our stuff from our house. And we'd known our house was there for us to go back to someday. I think of our house, burned to the ground, everything we ever knew or owned . . . gone.

"Housing for people who've been displaced," she says. "Eat up."

Well, duh. I don't make so much as a twitch of my fingers toward the food. "Are they together?"

"Your sister has been placed in the guardianship of your . . . husband. Yes."

Relief floods me that at least Opal isn't alone. "And my mom?"

"She's being treated for her injuries as well. I'm sure you're aware of your mother's special condition, and how it would require additional treatment."

Thick spit pools in my mouth. I was starving, but now I'm not sure I could eat if she pried open my mouth and poured it full of soup. "What kind of additional treatment?"

Dr. Donna smiles. "Let's get you started on those tests, shall we? And then you can eat."

It might not have occurred to her that the soup will be cold by the time I'm finished with any sort of tests. That tells me a lot about her, that she's so sure of getting what she wants that she doesn't think all the way ahead. And mostly that she thinks I'm stupid, in the way that lots of adults seem to think kids don't have a clue about what's going on. I blink at her slowly.

"What kind of tests did you say they were again?"

"Oh . . . let's see. We'd like to test your motor skills, for one thing. And some others."

I put a hand to my stomach, not having to fake a groan. "I'm sure I'd do much better on the tests with a full stomach. I'm so hungry, I feel faint. I'm sure I couldn't do a good job."

Dr. Donna tilts her head to study me, but I keep my expression as innocent as possible. "Fine. Eat first. You do need your strength. And I'm a fair person."

She might be, but I'm not. I eat the food slowly, savoring it, not gulping even though I'm hungry enough to gobble.

I sop up the last of the broth with the bread and wipe the corners of my mouth with the paper napkin on the tray. Dr. Donna watches me impatiently the whole time, and when I'm finished, she stands.

"All right. Ready?"

I push the tray away and settle back against the pillows. "No."

I see the moment she realizes I've played her. "You little . . ."

I smile. She bites back whatever it was she meant to say. Leaving the tray and everything else behind, Dr. Donna leaves the room, slamming the door behind her.

This time, it's three days before she comes back.

TWENTY-THREE

THREE DAYS IS A LONG TIME TO GO WITHOUT
food. I've had water from the bathroom sink—they didn't
think about that. And the human body can survive much
longer without food if it has something to drink. I'm so
hungry, though, that the moment Dr. Donna opens the
door and the waft of noodle soup hits my nose, I'm ready to
do just about anything she asks.

"Funny, isn't it? How simple it is to get someone to give
you what you want?" She gestures for Arnaldo to put the
tray on the dresser top and waits for him to leave before she
leans against the dresser. He gives me a sympathetic glance
before he goes, and incredibly, a wink. It makes me feel
better, like he's rooting for me.

I've been sitting in the chair by what the curtains want
me to think is a window to the outside. My knees to my
chest. Chin on my knees. I unfold myself carefully, my
muscles stiff and creaking.

"Tell me something first."

She eyes me. "What?"

"You tested me for Contamination. Twice." I touch my eye sockets, one, then the other. "Why?"

"Your results were inconclusive." Today, Dr. Donna's wearing a tight gray skirt with a pale gray shirt, but the black pumps are the same. I can't imagine how she can even walk in them, much less run.

If I get the chance to run, I'm taking it.

"What does that mean?"

"Inconclusive means not leading to a firm conclusion," Dr. Donna says smugly.

I'm so hungry that even if she weren't treating me like I'm stupid, I'd be annoyed. "I know what the word *inconclusive* means. I want to know what it means that my test results are inconclusive."

She gives me a shifty glance. Her mouth thins. "It just means we weren't able to determine if you were Contaminated or not. That's all."

I should be relieved, but I'm angrier now than I was before. "Is that why you want to do tests on me?"

"Yes."

"Why?" I stand. My knees are weak, and I'm so hungry, I'd eat anything. Liver. Bugs. Bowl of lard with a hair in it. Anything.

"Because we've determined that the Contaminated have certain . . . attributes that additional testing can show, if the initial results aren't as focused as we'd like. We can make a diagnosis of Contamination based on certain other results."

"Why do you care so much?" I refuse to look at the food on the tray, though the smell of it's impossible to ignore.

"We need to make sure the Contaminated are taken care of, obviously," Dr. Donna says smoothly. "So we can make sure you're given the proper treatment. That's all. We want you to be well."

"You can't cure Contamination."

She gives me another shifty look. "We're working all the time on trying to figure out a way to prevent Contamination, or to reverse it in people who've already succumbed. So if you come and let us test you now, Velvet, not only will you be contributing to the research that will help other people, you'll be fed and taken care of."

"I want clothes."

"You'll be given clothes."

I don't agree right away, and apparently, Dr. Donna's had enough. She gives some gesture toward the window, and two armed soldiers come in and take me by the elbows, lifting me so my toes barely scrape the floor.

"Take her to the testing room," she says to them. To me, she adds, "Velvet, you bring this on yourself."

Before I have time to ask her what exactly that means, they're dragging me out of the room and down the hall. I don't fight them, not because I don't want to or can't, but because I'm trying to see as much as I can about where I am and where I'm going. We pass closed doors that look identical to mine, but I can't see inside any of them.

The soldiers don't say anything to me on the trip, which includes a ride in the elevator. We go down nine floors to the basement, where they force me to walk in a quickstep through dripping and dimly lit underground tunnels until we get to another elevator. I pay attention in case I have the chance to run for it, the best I can, anyway, with a haze of hunger making everything sort of blurry. I don't get a chance to run.

"This place gives me the creeps," one of the soldiers mutters as he punches the elevator button over and over, though it's already lit up and everyone knows hitting it won't make the elevator come any faster.

The second soldier eyes me. "Think this one's gonna be trouble."

"Hey," I say sharply. "This one can hear you, you know."

After that, neither of them says anything. In the second elevator, one hits the tenth-floor button, but we stop on the seventh floor first. With a muttered curse, the soldier immediately begins to pound the close-door button, but it opens, anyway. Not into a hallway, but into a large ward, lined with beds. Nothing is new or bright or white there; nothing smells of paint. The waft of urine and sweat pours in on us, and before the doors close, I've had a full-on view of the people in those beds. All of them collared, all sitting, staring at nothing. Some milling around. The hum of their muttering sends a chill through me, and when the door finally closes, the soldiers with me both grip my arms even tighter, like I'm going to try to get away.

"What was that?"

But they won't tell me anything. I should've pretended I didn't talk, or at least couldn't hear. The elevator opens on a short hall, then they take me through a set of swinging doors into a large room set up with gym mats and equipment. A rock-climbing wall. Other equipment I don't recognize, set up in what looks like an obstacle course, sort of like the ones they'd had us running in gym class before I left school for good.

A man in a white lab coat, his glasses pushed on top of his head, greets me with a broad, sincere grin. He shakes my hand, and I'm too surprised to resist. "Velvet Ellis! Hello. I'm Dr. Arthur Billings. Thanks so much for joining us."

I blink. Dr. Billings doesn't look at the soldiers, but not as though he's ignoring them. More like he's afraid of them, and that's interesting to me. It makes sense to be afraid of soldiers with guns, but Dr. Donna hadn't looked at them that way. She was totally in charge.

"I didn't have a choice," I say.

The soldiers let go of my elbows, and I stumble forward. The back of my gown flaps open, and I hold it shut with one hand. I turn around, glaring, but neither of the soldiers seems to have noticed.

"If you expect me to run that course wearing this, you're crazy," I tell Dr. Billings flatly.

He laughs. "Oh, no. No. Of course not. Jenny here will fit you with a tracksuit and some sneakers." He frowns for a second. "You don't have your own clothes?"

"I had my own clothes when I got here, but when I woke up, I was wearing this."

He consults a clipboard. "Ah. Yes. You were in a house fire?"

"The entire neighborhood was on fire," I tell him. "What else does that say about me?"

"Let's get you dressed, and we can talk about the testing." Dr. Billings gives me a smile I don't return.

Jenny turns out to be a few years older than me. I think we went to school together. She was a senior when I was a freshman. She's wearing a white lab coat, too, her name on a tag pinned just below the embroidered script that says *Industrial Dynamics*.

"What's that?" I point. "ID?"

"It's the company the government hired to run the tests." Jenny pulls a pair of sweatpants and a T-shirt from a drawer and holds them up to me. "These should fit."

"Underwear?" I can't keep from sounding snide.

She digs around in another drawer and hands me a pair of plain cotton panties and a matching sports bra. Also a pair of white socks. There are a few pairs of sneakers in a small closet, but none of them fits me.

"You can do the testing in your bare feet," Dr. Billings says. "For some of it, we require that, anyway."

"I don't suppose you have a granola bar or something in one of those drawers. I haven't eaten in three days."

Dr. Billings won't meet my eyes. "Well. Yes. Umm, well, that shouldn't actually affect the efficacy of the tests; in fact, it might actually enhance some of your responses. . . ."

I put both hands flat on my belly as it gurgles. "You're serious?"

"If you'd agreed to the tests the first time," he says apologetically, "you wouldn't be so hungry now."

My hands are shaking. He notices, and writes something on the clipboard. When I start to pace, Dr. Billings stands back, out of the way, and gives the soldiers a nervous glance.

"What is it you want me to do?" I ask. "The sooner we get this over with, the sooner you'll let me eat?"

"Yes. But we have to—"

"What. Do. You. Want. Me. To. Do," I say through gritted jaws.

A lot, as it turns out.

When he pulls the thing from the box, at first I'm convinced it's a collar. It's round and black, but there are wires attached to it. They fix it to my head like a headband, with flat pads of soft material at my temples.

"It monitors your brain waves," Dr. Billings says.

"Does it shock me to death if I don't do what you want?"

He looks a little embarrassed. "No. Of course not, Velvet. It's just part of the test."

First, I run the obstacle course, clearing it in a few minutes, which Dr. Billings times with a stopwatch and notes on the clipboard. I have to climb a rope, something I'd never have been able to do even a few months ago, but now is easy enough that I make it all the way to the ceiling and back, barely breaking a sweat, even though it makes me hungrier.

He has me run across gravel in my bare feet. He has me kneel on grains of rice, timing me to see how long before I squirm. I have no idea how good or bad I'm doing, because even though every so often Dr. Billings lets out what seems to be a squeak of joy at something, he won't tell me what anything's supposed to mean.

He lets me take a break after a couple of hours. By that time, I'm seeing double with hunger. The fruit-and-nut bar they give me tastes like dirt, but I gobble it, anyway. Dr. Billings has been scribbling notes the entire time, and he's dancing like he's got ants in his pants. He excuses himself like I'm going to tell him he can't go and leaves me with Jenny.

"What's the deal with all this stuff?" I chew on a second granola bar, not exactly savoring it since it still tastes terrible. But definitely taking my time with it.

"I don't know, I don't ask. I got assigned this job as my over-eighteen thing." Jenny hands me a bottle of water with a plain white label on it. "I don't care what it is; it beats working at the sewage treatment plant, which is where my sister got assigned."

After three days, my stomach was squeezed so empty that even this small amount of food has filled it to bursting, but my hunger's back, twice as fierce. I hate Jenny. I hate Dr. Billings. I hate Dr. Donna, most of all.

Dr. Billings bustles back in. "Ready to get started again?"

"What about all those people I saw? The Connies. Do you run tests on them, too?" I wipe my mouth with the back of my hand.

"That's really not relevant," he says.

Jenny shrugs, though the look on her face tells me she doesn't know anything, and it's because she doesn't want to.

"It's probably relevant to them," I say.

"Hmmm," Dr. Billings says, and makes some more notes.

Then the rock wall.

I stand in front of it, looking up. It tilts up and out near the ceiling, which means that in order to get to the top level, you have to hang almost parallel to the floor. There are padded mats below, along with a pit full of spongy blocks, but even so, it looks hard. And scary.

"Oh, there's no safety rope or spotter," Dr. Billings tells me. "We want to test your reactions to situations as well as your ability to navigate. . . ." He stops himself, as though he's said too much. "Just climb it, Velvet."

It's easier in bare feet. My toes grip, my fingers grasp. The first few feet are easy. After that, my head swims from lack of food. I'm convinced I'm going to fall. If I do it now, it won't hurt so bad.

I go a little higher. Closer to the top. If I fall now, I could break something. Maybe kill myself. So I keep going. Determined now. I won't let them win. And I get to the top, digging my fingernails into the ledge until I can pull myself up to sit with my feet dangling over the edge.

Dr. Billings and Jenny are both staring up at me, mouths open.

Now the only problem is going to be getting down.

TWENTY-FOUR

THIS BECOMES MY LIFE. EARLY TO BED, EARLY to rise. Arnaldo or Cody brings me breakfast and dinner. I like Arnaldo better, because at least he tries to make me laugh. Cody's always trying to catch a glimpse of me when I come out of the shower.

I'm allowed to eat lunch in the cafeteria, always accompanied by someone to and from the room. Never allowed to walk alone. And every morning, the soldiers take me to the other building, where Dr. Billings has something new for me to try. They test me, day after day. I think it's about a week of running the obstacles and climbing the rock wall before they put me in a different room.

White walls. White floor. White ceiling. White tables, white chairs. Mirror on the wall that I'm smart enough to know is really one-way glass.

I make a face at it, sticking out my tongue and waggling

my brows. Dr. Billings laughs. I'd like him if he weren't working for Dr. Donna.

"Okay, Velvet. I'm going to give you a set of manipulatives, and what I need you to do is put them in rainbow color order. I'm going to time you, so don't start until I say to begin. Okay?"

I haven't done this sort of thing since, what, preschool? Kindergarten? But it's not hard work, that's for sure. We spend the morning at it, and I must've done it all right, because Dr. Billings comes in looking very happy.

"Lunch," he says. "I think we can take you to the cafeteria now. If you promise to be a good girl."

"You and Dr. Donna with that good-girl thing. I'm not five." I stand and stretch, working my fingers to loosen them. Fitting blocks into their slots is surprisingly tough on your hands when you do it for four hours in a row without a break.

Dr. Billings looks startled, then speculative. "No. No, you're right. Of course not."

The cafeteria is standard. Tables with chairs, a steam table with trays you slide along a metal rack. I load my plate with tater tots and a tofu dog, extra onions and relish. Chocolate pudding. A dinner roll. Caesar salad. I'm a glutton, stuffing my face while Dr. Billings watches and makes more notes.

"What?" I say, mouth full of food, waving my fork at him. "If I have to sell my soul to you all for food, I might as well eat up, right?"

"Is that what you think you're doing?" Dr. Billings has only a peanut butter sandwich and a cup of coffee on his tray. He drank the coffee but barely ate anything.

I swallow a mouthful of crusty fried potatoey goodness and lick the grease from my lips. "Isn't it?"

"Food motivated you?"

"I was hungry." I shrug, then add, "And if I don't do what you want, will you kill me?"

Dr. Billings chokes on his coffee, face turning red. "Velvet!"

"It's what they've been doing to the Connies since the first wave."

"There were extenuating circumstances." He looks solemn, but doesn't deny it. "Now our goal is to try and help those people."

"But you're keeping me here against my will. This isn't a hospital, where you took me to treat injuries I got in the fire. I didn't have any, anyway." I push the bits of hot dog around in a pool of ketchup, but my appetite is fading.

"Sometimes, what an individual wants has to be put aside for the greater good of all." Dr. Billings sounds like he believes what he says.

"Why me?"

He won't answer me, that's clear enough. He pushes my tray a little closer to me. "Finish your lunch. We have more tests to do."

I see him as Dr. Billings and I stand. He's in the far

corner of the cafeteria, dressed in jeans, and a T-shirt I remember because I bought it for his birthday. I'm sure I'm imagining him, but he turns toward the woman he's sitting with and smiles, and there's no mistaking him, not even after all this time.

"Tony!"

"Velvet—" Dr. Billings starts.

Ignoring Dr. Billings, I get up from the table and head toward my ex-boyfriend. Tony looks up at the sound of his name. That smile gets wider. Somehow, we're in each other's arms before anyone can stop us, and I hold on to him so tight, he huffs out a laughing sigh at my squeeze.

"Hey, Velveeta."

I'm so happy to see him that I don't care he's using that old nickname, or that he cheated on me and let me down and broke my heart. "What are you doing in here?"

Tony's gaze shifts toward the woman he's with, and for a weird, world-tilting second I wonder if they're dating, or something. Then the details fall into place. Her name badge, like the one Dr. Billings wears. Her age, which makes it unlikely she's Tony's girlfriend, though I guess it's not impossible.

"Tony's a day-shift volunteer in our testing facility. Like you." The woman smiles and nods toward Dr. Billings.

"I'm not"—But I cut myself off and lift my chin. Pride. I don't want Tony to know I'm not here by choice—"a day-shift volunteer."

"No," the woman says, and I know she knows exactly what I am. "You're one of our full-timers."

"Cool," Tony says.

He's gotten taller and broader, grown into his features sort of unexpectedly. I see the boy I used to love, but he's in a man's body. There are shadows under his eyes, though, and his cheeks are a little hollow. I look at the tray on his table. He'd filled his twice as much as mine. I think I understand why he's volunteering.

"Well. It's good to see you, Tony. How's your family? I used to see your mom at the ration distribution."

Tony's mouth works, but he doesn't answer.

"Tony, we should be getting back to work," his guardian says smoothly, with a narrow-eyed glare at me.

"Yeah. Hey, Velvet, it was great to see you. You look . . ." That's the old Tony, sweeping me up and down with an appreciative look. ". . . really good. Really, really good."

I won't lie, the compliment warms me. It's not until later, in my room, when I feel like I should be guilty for liking it. I stare at my reflection, wondering what it was about me that Tony saw.

My hair's longer. Thicker. I haven't plucked my eyebrows since before they brought me here, but they're sleek and shaped. My lashes, long and full. My cheeks are hollowed, too, but not from hunger. It's like I've grown into my own features, too. Becoming a woman.

Is that what Tony saw?

Or is it more? The sleekness of my muscles, bulging and flexing? My flat stomach, taut with the faint outline of abs that I trace with my fingertips.

I strip myself naked and try to see all of me in the mirror over the dresser. My body's changed. The parts of me that used to be soft, then just scrawny, have tightened. I don't have a bodybuilder's shape or anything like that. It's subtler than that. But I've definitely changed.

I flex my fingers, making fists.

"Your results were inconclusive," Dr. Donna had said.

I think about the day I'd intimidated Opal's principal when I told him I'd be taking her out of school. And of the day in the woods with the cheerleader, what feels like so long ago. Then later, in line for the rations, how that woman had backed away from me. Afraid.

I touch the twin spots in my eye sockets where they slid the needles in, no longer sore or black and blue. No sign they'd ever tested me at all. Inconclusive, I think.

But that's not true. I feel it in my gut, and the flex of my muscles, and the push and pull of my breath, and the rise and fall of my grief and anger.

I'm Contaminated.

★ ★ ★

"I want to see my mother. I say this after the usual morning drills. "And what about Dillon?"

"Your . . . husband." Dr. Billings laughs a little.

"You think that's funny?"

His smile quickly fades. "It's just that you're so young. To be married."

I put my foot on the chair and stretch my leg, feeling the pull of muscles in my thigh and lower back. "Things are different now."

Dr. Billings usually smiles a lot, but this time, he looks a bit sad. "Yes. Yes, they are."

Then he has me do a whole other round of jumping and running, and he tests my reflexes all over with little rubber hammers, and everything that the wires connected to my head tell him, he writes down.

"Does he know where I am?" I ask. "Why hasn't he tried to see me?"

Dr. Billings shakes his head. "C'mon, Velvet. Let's get these tests over with for the day, shall we?"

"Is Opal all right?" I'm desperate to know, and it must be obvious in my voice, because he looks sympathetic.

He pats my shoulder. "She's fine, I'm sure."

"Why did they all get taken to displacement housing, but not me?"

"You fought" is all Dr. Billings has to say for me to understand.

I'm quiet for the next hour or so while he has me do stupid stuff like jumping jacks. Then he makes me blow into a tube to measure my lung capacity. They feed me lunch from a tray. Fruit. Oatmeal. Nuts. All the portions look carefully measured, and he takes notes on how much I eat and in what order.

"I need to use the bathroom," I say. "Are you going to measure that, too?"

And he does.

By the end of the day, I'm worn out physically and mentally, so glad to hit the sheets of my hard hospital bed that I'm asleep before I remember I didn't brush my teeth.

They get me up again in the morning for more of the same. Breakfast on a tray in my room, the same bland stuff with some tofu bacon strips added, and a glass of orange juice. Greedily, I gulp it. It's been so long since I had fresh orange juice—we'd been drinking powdered orange drink mix, and had run out of it months ago.

When an orderly takes away the tray, the soldiers come in. Not always the same ones. I've been paying attention. They have names sewn onto the fronts of their uniforms, but I call them all Jeff and George, except if they're girls. Then it's George and Martha. Only once was it Martha and Bertha, and mostly it's Jeff and George. The biggest they can find. None of them talks to me.

"Is it because you're not allowed to talk to me? Or what?" I oblige them by holding out my elbows so they can grab them. "Wouldn't it be easier to cuff me or something? I mean, what if I try to get away?"

"Don't try it, and we won't have to cuff you," says the one I've mentally called Jeff.

They take me down the corridor, past all the closed doors, heading for the elevator.

"Am I the only one on this floor?"

No answer.

"Is this a pretty good job? Or do you like other assignments better?"

On my left, George snorts softly, but neither of them replies. The elevator's taking forever to get here. I shift from foot to foot, waiting for one of them to relax his grip on my elbow. Not that I'm planning on running or anything. But you never know what you might do when you're offered an opportunity.

"You like working the roadblocks? Checking people out? I bet you get kind of excited when you get to pull someone out of their cars, right?"

Jeff's fingers tighten on my right elbow. Not hard enough to hurt, but I wiggle it a little to make him think maybe he did. He doesn't look at me. Neither of them does.

"Do you like it when you have to run someone down? You like it when you have to shoot someone because they're trying to get out of town? How about when—"

"It's a job," George snaps, "to keep people safe and protect them. It's a job. We do what we have to."

"Shut up. You don't owe her an explanation," Jeff says to him. "Not her, especially."

"What's that mean?" They're both so much bigger than

me, I have to tilt my head back to get a good look at their deliberately blank faces. "Not me, especially?"

"You're one of them," George says. "Aren't you?"

I don't know how to answer that. The elevator doors open, and they shove me inside so that I stumble. I'm shaking. Jeff sees it, and his hand goes to the gun on his hip. He doesn't say anything. He doesn't have to.

I get the warning.

TWENTY-FIVE

"I WANT TO TALK TO OPAL."

Dr. Donna has been watching me eat my breakfast, and she's creeping me out. As usual, she's dressed more like she's on her way to some kind of fancy corporate fundraiser than to work in a research facility. Or a hospital, as she insists on calling it, even though I know the truth. She's half sitting with her butt propped on the edge of the dresser, and the toe of her black high heel tap-tap-taps on the tile floor.

"I'm sorry, but we can't allow that just yet."

I stab my spoon into the oatmeal, which is thick enough to keep the utensil standing upright. "When Opal and I were living in the assisted housing, we got an allotment of oatmeal every week. Enough for ten kids. We never finished it, and every week we got another carton, and I always took it home because I figured we had to. I really, really hate oatmeal."

"Funny how being hungry can change even the stron-gest preferences."

Her smirk makes me wish I'd been strong enough not to give in after three days.

"I'll eat it, but I'll never be hungry enough to *like* oatmeal."

"Funny," Dr. Donna says, "how a few good meals can make it so easy to forget what it's like to be hungry."

I nibble at the tofu bacon and drink the orange juice, but I leave the oatmeal alone. "You think a lot of things are funny."

"I guess maybe I just have a good outlook on life." She tilts her head to study me. "Unlike you."

"I have a great outlook on life!" I wave my fork to prove my point.

Dr. Donna's eyes narrow. "You think because you've . . . what. Survived? Had hardship? That your outlook is good? You're not the only one, you know."

We stare at each other, long and hard, but she doesn't give me one of her normal shifty-eyed looks.

"You think," she says in a low voice, "that you're the only person who's lost someone precious? You have no idea, Velvet, what it's like to lose everything and yet know you hold the key to getting it all back. That somehow, if only you'd been smarter, faster, stronger, if you'd been able to convince them to—"

She breaks off, clears her throat. Her gaze is glittery.

Bright. With an impatient shake of her head, she checks her watch and stands up straight. "It's time. Finish up so you can get started."

I don't hurry. Not for her. I take an extra long time brushing my teeth and washing my face until she raps on the door. I open it to face her. She's taller than me in those shoes, but if I knocked them out from under her, she wouldn't be.

"I want to talk to my sister."

"Your sister is fine. She's been placed in displacement housing and doing very well there. You'd only upset her if you called her."

"How do you figure that? She saw me get dragged away by armed soldiers. Gassed and hit on the head. Don't you think it would make her feel better to know I'm all right? Dillon, too. And Mrs. Holly. And my mom." I fall silent, thinking that my mom might not even know enough to miss me. I give Dr. Donna a long, hard look. "You've got me doing your stupid tests. I want to talk to my sister. And Dillon."

"We'll see," she says, in a way that tells me she has no intention of letting me talk to either one of them.

★ ★ ★

I've come to look forward to the running and jumping. Every night, they take me back to my room and leave me there to stare at the walls, but at least during the testing sessions I have something to do. I've taken to pulling a Linda Hamilton from *Terminator 2*. You know, the one in which she spends her time in the mental hospital doing pull-ups and getting fit, so when the time comes for the Terminator to travel back in time again and bust her out, she's ready.

I don't have a cyborg in sunglasses coming for me, but that doesn't mean I can't be ready.

I snag a pen from Dr. Billings when he's not looking, and sometimes I write as much as I can on the stiff, harsh sheets of paper towels from the bathroom. I fold them into tiny squares and hide them behind my dresser drawers. It does occur to me that they might be watching me. Hidden cameras or peepholes drilled behind the mirror on the wall. I don't care. If they want to confiscate my scribbled accounts of everything that's been happening, they're going to do it, anyway.

I like the manipulatives less than the obstacle courses, even when they get more and more complicated. Dr. Billings times me, and every time I complete one of the complicated puzzles faster than the last, he jumps up and down and crows a little. Sometimes, I deliberately mess them up to screw with his results, but he doesn't seem to notice that it's on purpose.

"It's okay, Velvet," he says. Sometimes, he pats my head or shoulder. "You'll get it better the next time."

I still have no idea what, exactly, they're testing me to see, just that every day the routine's the same. Breakfast.

Then the testing area, where they weigh and measure me and fit me with that headband that keeps track of my brain waves. Then they assign me different physical tasks until lunchtime. Then the cafeteria, where I load up on food and kind of gorge myself. Maybe that's why the after-lunch time with the manipulatives is so boring for me—I've eaten myself into a food coma, and all I want to do is sleep.

Today, they had spaghetti and meatballs on the menu. Garlic bread. Salad with oil and vinegar dressing. I gobble second portions of all of it, especially the meatballs. I know they have to be soy or something, but they're so good, so much like the ones my mom used to make, that I eat until I'm bursting.

"Can't I just take a nap?" I slump in the straight-backed chair they put in the room for me. No cushions. Hard metal. It should deter me from wanting to sleep, but it doesn't.

"No nap. But if you finish up the testing in good time, you might get to go back to your room earlier." Dr. Billings gestures, and the door opens. Jenny brings in what looks like an old tape recorder, the kind with round plastic wheels and thin plastic tape, except this one doesn't have any tape in it. Just two small silver pegs.

She puts it on the table and gives me a look I can't figure out. I can't understand Jenny at all, to be honest. She hardly ever says a word, but at the same time, her looks could kill a cobra. I never know if she hates me or Dr. Billings or just life in general.

"All right, Velvet. We're going to run you through a series of scenarios, okay? And I want you to gauge your emotional responses. Anytime you feel a happy reaction, I want you to twist the left-hand dial. When you feel a negative reaction, twist the right-hand dial. Okay?"

"What do the dials do?"

"They record your reactions. That's all." Dr. Billings has a certain soothing way of talking sometimes, usually when he's not telling me the whole truth about something. He has it now, so I give him a wary glance. Jenny won't look at me at all.

I sit at the table, a hand on each of the knobs. He begins talking, slow and soft. Kind of like the eye doctor . . . only instead of "Which is better: right or left?" Dr. Billings is asking me about how different things make me feel.

"Puppies." That's a left.

"Ice cream." Another left.

"School."

I look at him. "What if it's not a good or bad?"

"Pick the stronger feeling."

I choose right, though honestly I never hated school the way lots of kids did, at least not until the final days, and that was more because I was so burned out doing everything else that school didn't seem to matter much anymore.

The list goes on and on. My parents, Opal, Dillon. Left, left, left.

"ThinPro."

That's a sharp twist to the right, for sure.

"Winter. Spring. Fall. Summer. Heat. Cold. Darkness."

I twist the dials left or right, depending on what's going on. Dr. Billings makes his notes. I'm bored and tired, but right before I ask him how much longer, he says:

"Tony."

I hesitate. When I saw him last week in the cafeteria, I was happy. And once upon a time, Tony made me very happy. But he'd also made me really sad, too.

I twist the left-hand dial.

"Tell me about Tony, Velvet. He was your high school boyfriend?"

"Yes."

"And you had a special relationship, yes? How'd you get along with his mother?"

Right-hand twist, for sure.

"Tony speaks highly of you. Did you know that?"

I twist the left dial. "I'm glad."

"He says that even though you broke up with him because he cheated on you, he always really thought you were, and I quote, 'fantastic.'"

I hesitate. It's nice to know Tony thinks so, but remembering finding him in the school library with another girl still stings and might for a really long time. I twist the right dial.

"Very good." Dr. Billings makes a note in the file.

"He did say you were a terrible kisser, though," Jenny pipes up.

My fingers twitch on the right dial again.

Dr. Billings shakes his head. "Teenage boys can be so rude. Velvet, I'd like you to imagine that every time you twist that right-hand dial, you're sending an electric shock straight to Tony. Okay?"

Frowning, I take my hands away from the dials. "What?"

"Hands back on the dials, please. I want you to imagine you're shocking him every time you twist it."

"Can't I imagine I'm shocking someone else?" I picture Dr. Donna.

Dr. Billings keeps his soothing tone. "It will be more helpful if you picture Tony. Okay? Jennifer, as difficult as it might be for Velvet to hear this, we do have more information for her about Tony, isn't that so?"

"Yeah. My younger sister is best friends with Carly Tillman."

I don't know her, so I don't twist either dial.

Jenny sighs, looking put out. "She's the girl who was making out with Tony in the library."

"Don't forget to twist the dials," Dr. Billings says.

I give it a slight twist to the right.

"My sister says that Carly told her that she and Tony used to laugh about you."

Another harder twist to the right.

"She says that it was all over the school about what a loser you were, having to live in assisted housing, because you were a Conorphan and all that. And Tony pitied you, but didn't know how to break up with you. Because he thought you were such a loser, you'd never find another boyfriend—"

Right. Right. Right.

I think of how I went into the library, needing to talk to him, and found Tony lip to lip with that other girl. And they'd laughed about me? Laughed?

Right. Hard. Then harder.

"Can you describe what you're feeling, Velvet?"

"I'm really mad. And hurt. But mostly mad!" I twist the right dial.

"And imagining that Tony's getting an electric shock every time you twist the dial—how does that make you feel?"

"Good." It does. I twist it harder, biting on my lower lip a little.

"You'd like to hurt Tony? The way he's hurt you?"

"Yeah . . . I guess so." I twist the dial, thinking of a buzz and an electric tingle of sparks.

"Would you like to be able to hurt anyone who hurt you this way?"

I twist the dial. And again. Over and over, thinking of all the things that have made me sad or mad over the past year. "Yeah! I guess I would."

Dr. Billings pulls the cord on the blinds covering a window. I'm expecting one-way glass again, but this time I'm on the other side of it, looking to another white room, identical to the one I'm in. Same furniture, even.

Tony's on the other side of the glass.

He's just sitting down in a chair identical to mine. In front of him is a box that looks similar to the one in front of me, but instead of two silver knobs, it's got a bunch of wires coming out of it, and all of them connect to him.

I don't have to hear him to know he's screaming. His mouth is wide open, his head thrown back. I'm out of my chair and away from that box on the table before Dr. Billings can say another word. Tony slumps as soon as I let go of the dial, and I press myself against the wall as far from the window as I can get.

I clutch my stomach, thinking I'm going to hurl up all the food from lunch. My breath comes fast in my throat, scratching it. My tongue's suddenly so dry, I can't even wet my lips.

"Sit back down, Velvet. Put your hands on the dials."

"I'm not going to shock him!"

Dr. Billings gives me a strange, sort of sad smile. "You've been shocking him all this time. And you said yourself that you'd like to be able to hurt someone who hurt you."

"That was before I knew I was really doing it." I shake

my head, still feeling sick, though Tony seems to be recovering all right.

The woman who was with him in the cafeteria is offering him water and a cloth to wipe his face. She puts her hand on his shoulder as though to comfort him. To my disgust and sorrow, Tony starts to cry.

"Why is he doing this?" I look at Dr. Billings, who doesn't seem to take offense to my accusatory glare. "Did he know what could happen?"

"Yes. Of course. He had to sign a waiver, like all of our volunteers. As for why, I'm told the pay is quite good, the benefits attractive. And I believe, in Tony's case, he's trying to get some help for his family. His mother, particularly. I'm sure you can understand that."

I shake my head again. I didn't sign any waiver, and though it's not the first time I think Dr. Billings isn't telling me the truth, it's the first time I feel like he's flat-out lying. "I don't want to do this anymore."

"I'm afraid you don't have any choice, Velvet. Sit down."

"I won't. You can't make me."

"Tony signed up for this; he knew what was going to happen. If you don't do it, he doesn't get paid. And he doesn't get to help his mother."

I don't move even a fraction of an inch toward the table. "What's wrong with his mother?"

"She's one of the unfortunate number of people who've succumbed to one of the later waves of Contamination,"

Dr. Billings says, and now I know for sure he can't be telling the truth.

"Tony's mom never drank ThinPro. Never. I guarantee it."

He is silent for a moment. "All it takes is one sip, Velvet."

In the other room, Tony is still pale and sweating, but he's wiped his face. No matter how angry I ever was at him, there's no way I can twist that dial now. Even if it were Tony's mother in the chair, I couldn't bring myself to do it.

"Velvet, I'm telling you that you need to sit in that chair and turn the dials, and administer a mild shock to the volunteer in the other room. He is prepared for it. In fact, he wants you to continue. See?"

In the other room, the woman bends to murmur something into Tony's ear. He lifts his head and looks at the glass. His mouth is slack, eyes dull. But he nods.

"She could've said anything to him. That doesn't mean he's okay with this. And I'm definitely not, not even if he is. No." I stand firm for the first time since they'd tried to starve me for three days. Now I wish I hadn't been so easily bought for the price of a bowl of soup and some bread.

Jenny looks up from the table, where she's been messing around with a bunch of different instruments that they like to use to test my reflexes. Something in my expression sends her a step or two back. Without a word, she leaves the room.

"C'mon now. You don't want me to have to take away your privileges, do you?"

"You mean food and water? You mean my basic human rights? Is any of this even legal?" I gesture around the room. "Keeping me like this, against my will?"

"Oh, it's legal. Entirely." Dr. Billings nods.

"I'm not sick."

"No. But you are . . . special."

"Is that what you write on that clipboard?"

Before he can stop me, I snatch it from his hand. His handwriting is scrawling and hard to read, and I have to keep him from grabbing it back by pulling it away from him as I dodge him, getting far enough to scan what he's been writing about me.

There are long lists about strength, agility, progress in motor function and reaction to stimuli. *Reflexes, superior* stands out to me. *Adrenaline levels, elevated.*

Dr. Billings yanks the clipboard from my hand. He's breathing hard and sweating, red-faced. "Give me that!"

"Don't I have a right to know what you're doing with me?" I could grab the clipboard from him if I wanted to. He knows it, too. I can see it on his face.

"I'll have Dr. Donna talk to you about it. But rest assured, Velvet, it's merely standard testing procedures, nothing out of the ordinary—"

"I thought you said I was special."

His smile is totally false. "You are. Of course you are. Come on now, let's see how you do with this next series of tests."

"I said, no."

Dr. Billings frowns. I make a face. He backs up a step. I clench my fists.

The soldiers come and take me away.

TWENTY-SIX

I NEVER EAT DINNER IN THE CAFETERIA, WHICH is fine with me because I don't want to see Tony. Even if he doesn't know I'm the one who was electrocuting him. I'm served dinner in my room. A plate of Salisbury soy steak in thick, congealing gravy with a side of rice and corn. Chocolate pudding for dessert. It never tastes right, made with soy milk. It's kind of chalky and metallic, but I eat it because I can't force myself to choke down the disgusting fake steak. The gravy reminds me too much of snot.

I have no appetite. The day's testing left me sick to my stomach. I can't get the sight of Tony's slumped shoulders and open mouth out of my head.

The dial hadn't shocked me, but my fingers tingle anyway with the memory. Because it had felt good, hadn't it? At least a little. Imagining with every twist that I was sending waves of pain to someone who'd hurt me. There's only a little comfort in knowing that I did stop, once I found out.

But before that, before it became real, I'd liked it.

Arnaldo comes in to take away my tray. Something about the sight of him makes me laugh. He gives me a curious glance.

"Hey, Arnaldo."

"Hey, Velvet. You okay?" He comes a little closer and puts a hand on my upper arm. "You look a little—"

"Pudding." It's the only word I manage to say before the floor comes up and hits me in the face.

Sometime later, I swim up from darkness, unable to move my arms or legs. A blurred face comes into focus. Not Arnaldo, but Cody, grinning in a way that makes me want to punch him in the face. Right in it. Mash his lips with my fist, watch the blood squirt. . . .

"She's waking up. Good." That voice belongs to Dr. Donna, and I swing my head around to face her. "Hold her."

"You gave her enough sedative to almost kill her." That's Dr. Billings. He sounds worried.

"And she's still fighting. I said, hold her."

I blink away the fuzziness in my vision, focusing on Dr. Donna's voice. I stop pushing against the arms holding me down, not because I don't want to be free but because I can tell I'm not coordinated enough to get free. The slap of leather on my wrists forces a groan out of me, and I go still.

"Donna. She's awake. You can't—"

Dr. Donna's voice is diamond hard, sharp enough to

cut glass. "Arthur, I know what I'm doing. The dose was fine."

"Administered in pudding. You can't even be sure she took the right amount—"

She cuts him off again. I can see her sneer through the prison bars of my eyelashes. "First you were worried she had too much. Now you're worried she's had too little? You're the one who's been doing all the research on her. You're the one who's convinced her metabolism can destabilize any amount of sedatives in a quarter of the normal time, if they affect her at all. You're the one who thinks she's some kind of holy grail of test subjects."

I go very, very still.

"She's not sleeping," Dr. Billings says.

Dr. Donna bends closer and looks into my eyes, prying one open with her perfectly manicured fingernails. I keep my gaze unfocused, but don't close my eyes when she straightens. She gives Dr. Billings a look over her shoulder. If I were him, I'd want to slap the smug smile off her face. I want to, and I'm not him.

"Just because her eyes are open doesn't mean she's awake. You know that as well as I do. But if you insist, I'll be happy to make sure that Velvet is completely under. Or not."

Before I can breathe or move or do anything else, Dr. Donna places her knuckles on my chest and presses hard, rubbing straight up to the base of my throat. The pain is instant and immense, so overwhelming, I can't cry out from it—I can only writhe. My entire body bucks; my wrists, pinned down by the straps, burn and ache from how hard I yanked myself away from her. But I can't move.

She does it again, looking into my face with a grim, satisfied smile.

"Well," she says. "I guess she is awake, after all."

I shout out a bunch of insults. They rasp out of me like my tongue's rubbing a cheese grater, but Dr. Donna gets the point. Her smile gets a little wider.

"What a mouth. Arthur, you didn't tell me she had such a demure vocabulary."

My teeth clench down on the next set of words. My chest aches. My wrists, too. My head isn't fuzzy anymore, though there's a glowing sheen around everyone, and it seems like when I move my head, my eyes take a few seconds too long to catch up.

"Velvet, can you count backward for me from one hundred?"

I open my mouth to start, but Dr. Donna snaps her fingers in annoyance. "Forget that. She's not going to go out now, not without another dose of sedative. Do you want to give her one?"

Dr. Billings looks hesitant. "Not on top of what you gave her, no."

"What's going on?" I manage to say around what feels like a mouthful of cotton balls. I spit, but nothing comes out.

Dr. Donna's face wrinkles in disgust. "Stop that."

"Dry," I say.

Dr. Billings shakes his head. "I can't give you anything to drink, Velvet, I'm sorry. Not until after the procedure."

"Pro . . . seed . . . your?" I should know what he means, but I'm trying hard not to let my eyes slip shut against the bright lights. I'm not tired, but with every blink, my head hurts worse and worse. I force myself to keep them open, not wanting to be taken by surprise.

"Arthur. Hold her head."

Dr. Billings comes to the side of my bed and takes my head in both of his hands. They're very warm. He studies my face, and I wait for him to say something. Anything. But he stares only.

Dr. Donna holds up a black box. From inside, she takes out a long, thin needle attached to a small tube. She turns to me with a bright, fierce grin and takes something else out of the box.

"We've decided to make some changes to the testing," she says.

It's a StayCalm collar.

I don't remember when they tested me for Contamination by shoving a needle into my eye sockets, because I was unconscious. I don't know if they used any kind of anesthetic, but this time, all Dr. Donna offers is a nasal spray. It's cold and stinging, and I cough and cough. The taste of it runs down the back of my throat, choking me.

"Shhh. Settle down. This won't hurt. At least not very much." Dr. Donna tries to make her voice soothing but manages to sound more like she hopes she's wrong. She sounds like she hopes this hurts me a lot.

The needle slides in without effort, and she's right—I don't feel anything except a faint sting. But then Dr. Donna bites her bottom lip and pushes, hard, and my entire head pops with the sensation of the needle puncturing something deep inside my eye socket. I can't stop myself from jerking—it's not a pain, exactly, but it's horrifying, anyway. Dr. Billings holds my head still. I let my eyes roll up to look at him.

He offers me a smile that does nothing to make me feel better. The needle wiggles, going deeper. I open my mouth, but nothing comes out.

I see colors.

They pulse and throb for a few seconds, then fade. The needle wiggles again, and this time, I taste the pudding I ate for dinner. My throat constricts, burning. I gag.

"Hold her head still, Arthur, or else your golden goose won't be laying any more eggs," Dr. Donna murmurs, her face very close to mine.

I open my mouth to bite her, but all I can do is drool. Arnaldo would've wiped my chin for me, but Cody stands, staring only, his own mouth gaping. I didn't even know he was there. Dr. Donna pulls away. I can see the length of tubing coming from my eye. It attaches to a small syringe that she holds up so I can see.

"Just a little bit of pressure when the chip goes in," she says. "It won't hurt a bit."

She's right about that. It doesn't hurt a bit. It hurts worse than any pain I've ever had. The pressure is enormous. My head will pop, I can feel it. My head's an egg in a fist. Gonna explode.

Golden goose.

Egg.

Crush.

I writhe without being able to move, and I hear myself screaming, but there are no words. Only an endless, whistling cry that fades as I run out of breath.

My left eye has gone blind. Red haze. From my right, I see Cody back away, his face gone pale. Good. Let him faint, fall, let him remember this forever, what they did to me, what they're doing. . . .

Dr. Donna straightens. "There. All done."

The pain disappears as fast as it came, leaving behind a numbness that promises to turn into an ache. I gasp for breath. Dr. Billings holds my head so tight, I can't shake it. My stomach muscles hurt; I arched my body so hard within the restraints that I pulled something.

"Now. The other side."

"Nonononononono . . ." I can't even separate the words.

I won't be able to stand it. I won't be able. I will explode,

I will die, I would rather die, anything other than have her stick that other needle into my head.

"Perhaps another shot of anesthetic, Dr. Billings? What do you think?"

"It's topical, it should be fine." He sounds doubtful, and peers down into my eyes. "Velvet, you're not supposed to be able to feel anything with that spray Dr. Donna gave you. It's supposed to numb your sinuses completely. And with the sedative, you're supposed to be completely unconscious, actually. . . ."

"Please," I manage to say, putting everything I have into that one word. I can't manage another. That's all I have left.

He looks at Dr. Donna. "I'm not sure it's a good idea, Donna. She's already had far more medication than I had anticipated her needing. I'm not sure about the reactions. They could be worse than the procedure."

"Fine with me." She shrugs.

"Please," I think, but can't force my mouth to say. Please, oh, God, please give me something to keep it from hurting.

"Deep breath," Dr. Donna says.

She presses the needle to my other eye socket. This one stings worse. The popping sensation is worse, too, maybe because I already knew it was coming. But when she lifts the tubing to show me her fingers on the plunger of the syringe, I can't bear it.

I scream. And scream. And scream.

I'm still screaming when the colors beat against the inside

of my head, when my body shakes, when every muscle in my body goes tense and tight. The bed shakes. Dr. Billings's warm hands on my head hold me down.

Dr. Donna's shouting something at Cody, but I can't understand her words. Everything is pain. The smell of something burning. I think it's my brains.

And then . . . nothing.

TWENTY-SEVEN

"VELVET, CAN YOU HEAR ME? BLINK ONCE FOR yes, twice for no."

My eyes are open, I realize. And I can see. Blurred shapes, outlined by glowing edges. The stench of burning still coats my nose and mouth. I cough and spit.

"Velvet, it's Dr. Billings. You're fine now. I've given you some pain medication that should send you to sleep. Okay?"

Or kill me. That's what he said before, I'm sure of it. They gave me too much medicine before, too much could kill me, I could go to sleep and never wake up. So I won't go to sleep.

I blink, more than once or twice, over and over again, until Dr. Billings's face swims into view. Dr. Donna's next to him, and at least she's not smiling smugly. She looks genuinely concerned.

"Incredible," she says. "My God, Arthur. She can't possibly still be conscious."

Dr. Billings puts his hand on my forehead. "Velvet, I need you to let go, okay? Go to sleep. You'll feel so much better if you sleep."

But I don't want to slip into darkness. I might not come out of it. I tense my muscles, checking for pain . . . they all hurt. I feel like I've been hit by a truck, directly between the eyes. Blinking hurts, but since everything else does, too, I keep doing it.

"Come on. Let's get the collar on her and connected before she starts to struggle again."

Something tightens around my throat, and I can't cough it away. Dr. Donna's face is once again so close to me, I could bite off her nose, if only I could make my jaw cooperate. I would do it, if I could. Instead, my teeth snap shut against themselves.

She looks at me, startled. "Velvet?"

I don't answer.

She straightens, her fingers working at my throat. I hear a clicking whirr, and then that smell of burning again. Fainter, this time. Another pulse of color, though it's faded. Then Dr. Donna looks pleased.

"There," she says. "You're all set."

I don't feel any different, other than the slowly fading ache in my eye sockets and the constriction at my throat. I can't see the lights, but I hope they're blinking all a steady green. I swallow and find the collar doesn't restrict that. I turn my head from side to side and discover I can move without trouble, too. The collar doesn't seem to be keeping me from anything, but it's impossible not to know that it's there.

I close my eyes then. Tears burn, stinging in the spots where she'd slid needles only minutes ago. I hate for her to see me cry, but I can't stop myself.

"No tears," Dr. Donna says. "Just sleep. When you wake up, I promise you, Velvet, all of this will seem better. And you'll be a better girl for it."

I shake and shake and shake.

Dr. Donna's voice is soft against my ear. "My daughter's name is Alaina. She was beautiful, but no matter how many times I told her so, she didn't believe me. Oh, how we struggled with her. Diet pills, hospitals. She wouldn't eat. Do you know how many times I almost lost her?"

I want to tell her I don't care, but nothing comes out of me but a hiss of air.

"I thought ThinPro was a godsend. She lost weight without starving herself. She seemed to be back on track, getting healthy." There's a deep, shuddering breath from Dr. Donna, and I open my eyes to stare into hers. They are bright with tears, and her mouth is twisted. No more smug smile. No more predatory grin. "Now my beautiful daughter sits in a puddle of her own waste and doesn't know her own name, much less who I am. Instead of trying to kill herself, she killed four people. She should've been put down, but instead I managed to get her into a StayCalm collar. Just like this one. And I will do anything, Velvet. Anything, anything at all, to find a way to fix her. Do you understand me?"

I don't want to have pity for her, but something twists inside me. Whatever it is, it must show on my face, because Dr. Donna's cold sneer comes back in an instant. She jerks away from me like I spit on her.

"Put her to sleep."

"Velvet. You'll be fine. This is to help you." Dr. Billings puts his hand on my shoulder.

I'd roll away from him if I could move, but with my wrists and ankles still bound, the best I can do is to turn my face. I don't want to look at him. He's not my friend, no matter what he's ever said.

"Okay. Let's leave her for now."

He hesitates. His fingers squeeze my shoulder. "I should stay with her for a bit, Donna. Just to make sure she's all right. Cody, you can go, too."

Left alone with me, Dr. Billings pulls the chair up next to the bed and holds my hand while I cry. I hate him, maybe especially because he's trying to be so nice now. I can't wipe my nose, so he does it for me. The snot dripping down my throat tastes like the medicine Dr. Donna squirted up to numb my head.

"I need a drink," I croak.

He brings me water in a plastic cup, with a straw. I

sip greedily, then let myself fall back onto the pillows. Dr. Billings pats my arm.

"I'm sorry," he says after a while. "I tried to talk her out of the collar. But Donna's my superior. She's the one in charge. And she used to be . . . better. I've worked with her for years, and you won't believe me, but it's true. Donna was one of the most compassionate researchers I've ever known."

I don't answer him. For one, it hurts my throat to talk. For another, I don't have anything to say.

"You're special, Velvet. You don't know how much. And sometimes, people who are special have to do things they don't want to do. For the greater good. Sacrifices must be made. I know it's hard to believe. And right now I'm sure you hate us all. Maybe even me." He gives me a half-hopeful smile, like he wants me to deny it. When I don't, when I say nothing but turn my face away again, Dr. Billings sighs. "But you have to understand, Velvet. All of this is going to help people. I promise you that. I wouldn't be doing any of this if I didn't think we could figure out a way to really make a difference."

I believe he means it. I just can't bring myself to care. There is a collar around my neck that is sending wireless pulses of energy into my brains to keep me from caring. If I try too hard, it will batter my brain with more electricity until it kills me.

"I know you don't understand. But you will." He takes

my hand again, offering me comfort I don't want from him. "I barely understand it myself, but that's the beauty of science, Velvet. Discovery. Putting the pieces of the puzzle together, making it all fit. You know, I wanted to be a researcher my whole life, ever since I was a kid. I used to do science experiments in my room with beakers and chemicals. My parents hated it."

I want him to go away.

He stands to do something to the collar. I feel the pressure of it on my throat for a second, then release. "There. That should be better. You know, Velvet, so much of research is hard work, brutal dedication, the grind of experimentation. Over and over, changing the smallest variables to get a different result, trying to figure out what you want to achieve and how to get it. But sometimes . . . oh, lots of times, no matter how much work you do, how careful you are, how precise . . . it's all just a matter of luck."

He sits again, leaning forward to look into my eyes. Something wet is trickling out of them, and he snags a tissue from the box on the nightstand. It comes away stained crimson, and I'm not surprised to find I'm weeping blood.

"Luck was finding you, Velvet Ellis. Because out of all the people we've been testing, you are unique. Now, we thought there might be a chance, given your mother's rather remarkable recovery—"

"My mother?" The words are slurred, but he understands me.

Dr. Billings nods. "Yes. In all the test subjects, less than one percent of them ever showed any signs of recovery once they'd succumbed to the full effects of the Contamination. Those who'd suffered lesser gradations of Contamination naturally responded much better to the StayCalm collar, and of course the ones who'd been totally destroyed by the progression of their disease didn't have such a positive reaction. But invariably, all those fitted with the collars were able to control their reactions. Well"—he chuckles a little self-consciously—"not control them, really. Of course you know how the collar works. They're merely unable to continue reacting negatively to stimuli because the collar prevents it. But less than one percent ever showed any signs of improvement after being fitted with a collar. But your mother . . . her records showed that she was initially one of the worst hit with the disease. Her brain, simply riddled with holes. Just decimated."

I try to breathe, rasping harshly in my throat. "You had my mother's records?"

"Yes. Of course. She was released to the kennel. We do keep records on all the Contamination victims who were reunited with their families. Obviously, we didn't know her name or history when she was first . . . um . . . intercepted. But after you claimed her, we were able to retroactively cross-reference all the previous testing we'd done on her. And when we brought you both here . . ."

"She's still here."

"Yes."

I close my eyes. "She's alive."

"Oh . . . Velvet. Yes. She's alive." He sounds a little sad. "I'd have told you if she'd passed."

"Is she all right? You said remarkable recovery." Each word is like spitting out pebbles.

"Others tried to take the collars off, you know. And it never worked. They all died. All of them."

Even in my boggled state, I know there's no way they can possibly know for sure that's true. There could've been any number of people who never reported taking off the collars, who'd been just fine.

"But your mother . . . not only did she not die from the removal, but she actually seemed to recover once it had been taken off. Right?"

"Yes. She got better."

"Unfortunately, of course, the improvement was sporadic and not quantifiable, and she had a lot of regression. Though not to the point she'd been at her worst. The brain is an amazing organ. There've been many cases of stroke victims or patients with brain damage, sometimes even catastrophic injuries, recovering many motor functions that should've been lost forever. And there've been people who get what seems to have been a relatively minor bump on the head who experience complete personality changes, become incapable of the simplest tasks. Forget who they are. And we don't really know anything about why some people are able to adapt and others can't. But your mom, she definitely did."

I force myself to look at him. More wetness slides down my face, and he leans again to dab it. This time, the tissue's dabbed with pinkish yellow fluid, totally disgusting.

"And now?"

"Now," Dr. Billings says, and lets out a sigh. "Well, now I'm afraid she's not doing very well at all. She's quiet. That's the best way I can describe her. Your father, on the other hand—"

"Arthur." Dr. Donna's harsh voice cuts him off from the doorway. "I think it's time you left Velvet alone. Cody can sit with her. You should go home and get some rest."

Reluctantly, Dr. Billings stands, his hand still holding mine. He looks into my eyes, searching them. I close them to keep him from finding whatever it is he's trying to find, and after a few minutes, he goes away.

TWENTY-EIGHT

I'M NOT HUNGRY. DON'T WANT TO EAT. ARNALDO brings me a tray of oatmeal, a banana, some hot cocoa, and a glass of orange juice. I don't take a bite or a sip, even though he tries to tempt me into it with jokes.

I sit in my chair without moving. I'm not strapped down anymore. I could move, if I want to. I could turn my head and stand, make my feet go one in front of the other. I could even speak, if I want to. But I sit, the weight of the collar keeping me silent.

Without a window to show the rise and set of the sun and without a clock, the only way for me to mark the passing of time is by the swell of my hunger and my need to use the bathroom. But I'm not hungry, and I don't eat or drink, so I need to get up to use the toilet only once. Other than that, I sit. And sit. And sit.

Arnaldo goes off shift and Cody comes on.

"You look terrible," he tells me, almost kindly. "Man, you look like crap."

Dr. Donna comes in finally, looking stern. "If you don't eat, I'm going to have to hook you up to an IV or fit you with a feeding tube. Would you like that, Velvet? A feeding tube and a catheter and, hey, why not just put a colostomy bag on you while we're at it?"

"You'll do whatever you want, anyway." The first words out of my mouth taste like old blood.

She smiles. "Yes. True. But trust me, you'll like it much better if you just eat of your own accord rather than making me force you."

"I'm not hungry."

"You're being very petulant, Velvet. I'm sure your parents would be very disappointed in you."

This sparks me into anger, as I'm sure she knew it would. "My parents would never have wanted me to just give in to you!"

"Careful," she says gently. "You know what will happen if you let yourself get too agitated."

I brace myself for the rip of electricity through me. I wonder how bad it will hurt. I grip the sides of my chair, but nothing much happens other than a twinge in my head, and that could be left over from putting the needles in.

"So interesting. You're so much like your parents. Both of them." She studies me with a strange smile on her red-painted lips. "You're wondering how I know, right?"

I keep myself still. I'm not hungry, that's true, but I am achy and stiff from not getting out of this chair all day. And now for the first time since she put the collar on me, I'm not . . . blank. The cold oatmeal is stomach turning, but I pull it toward me and spoon some into my mouth, anyway.

"Good girl."

I ignore her and put another spoonful of nasty oatmeal in my mouth. Swallow. Another. I strip the peel off the banana and take a bite, and that's much better.

"Don't forget the juice," Dr. Donna says. "It's full of vitamins."

She leans against the dresser with her arms crossed over her chest. It's her favorite position, and she stares at me while I eat. "Arthur wanted to tell you as soon as we found out and put two and two together, but by that point, I wasn't sure what benefit it would have for you. After all, if we'd known from the beginning exactly what to look for, how to test you, and why, well, I'm sure we'd have started see-ing results weeks ago. How much time we could've saved, right? If only we'd known."

"Known what?" I wipe my mouth with the back of my hand; I'd been sloppy with the juice. Clumsy hands. I don't want to think about why.

"The reasons why you are unique. The way you are. It's because of your parents, Velvet. And of course we knew about your mother right from the start. As soon as you both were brought in, we figured out that Malinda was an anomaly. But if only we'd known about your father sooner . . ."

"What about my dad?" I cry out, and brace myself for an onslaught from the collar. Other than that same sort of twinge, there's nothing, but Dr. Donna's lips twitch.

"Careful," she murmurs. "You don't want to start blinking red, do you? Finish your juice."

I don't want more juice. "My dad's alive. Isn't he? He came to our house, and the Concops were after him. That was my dad, right?"

For a moment, I'm sure she's going to lie to me, but then Dr. Donna shrugs. "Yes. Some of my less-invested colleagues took umbrage with my methods. They claimed the results we were achieving were not worth the use of human subjects. So stupid. Such lack of forward thinking. There *are* no subjects that aren't human. The Contamination was an enormous random happenstance that we haven't been able to duplicate, not even in primates. The Contamination is limited to people who ingested ThinPro protein water in any quantity during a period of approximately eighteen months, from the first tainted batch until it was pulled from the market, and it's manifested itself in completely unpredictable ways we haven't even been able to effectively trajectorize. In other words, we have no idea what specific variables resulted in the Contamination, nor have we been able to accurately predict how it affects individuals, or what the long-term effects are in the exposed population."

"What's that got to do with my dad?" I'm having a hard time following her. I feel dozy and lazy, like my head wants to droop.

"After their termination from the research program, a few of my colleagues decided they were going to . . . remove . . . the patients from the more strenuous experiments. Several weeks ago, they loaded them into a tractor-trailer that was allegedly delivering supplies to the complex. Then they tried to get out of town by running one of the barriers, but they couldn't even manage that right. They wrecked the truck."

I choke on a breath, thinking of the truck barreling down on the concrete barriers, the soldier tossing out the razor strip. My dad had been in that truck, and I hadn't even known. "He got out and tried to come home, and you hunted him down like some kind of wild animal."

Her expression tells me that she thinks that's what he is. "We couldn't let him go, Velvet. Your father's too important to our research."

"What's so special about him?" I know the things that make my dad special. His goofy sense of humor. How good he was at fixing things when they broke. How he never made me or Opal feel less because we were girls, even if he did sometimes complain that being a guy in a house full of women was hard to deal with. But Dr. Donna wouldn't care about any of that stuff. To her, my dad's a test subject, nothing else.

"Your father was brought into one of the medical facilities during the first wave. According to his records, he showed signs of extreme disorientation, violent tendencies, and a severe lack of motor control. He'd been picked up during the rioting in downtown Lebanon, and had been witnessed breaking several storefront windows as well as assaulting police officers who arrived on scene. He was restrained, not given a field lobotomy or dispatched immediately, as so many of them were, because the arresting officer recognized him. Your father was unable to identify himself, though he had his wallet with him and the officer was able to confirm your dad's identity."

I stare at her for a long minute. "He was identified by name officially, but not released to us? Why not?"

"Your father, unlike ninety percent of the rest of the Contaminated, proved . . . useful." Dr. Donna gives me a grimacing grin. "He showed all signs of advanced Contamination, which progressed more rapidly even than in others. But there was a difference with him, something only few of the other test subjects experienced, so few, I think I could count them all on two hands. Your father, as rageful and aggressive as he was, as prone to violence, did regain his . . . sense of self, shall we say. After the initial confusion, your father was able to recall basic information about himself, as well as respond to simple tasks. He was able to use tools in order to complete tasks, and follow instructions to achieve rewards. When he wanted to, that is."

"You make him sound like a monkey." I push away the tray, not sure which is worse—the thought of my dad as a raging, murderous, and destructive Connie who didn't know how to stop himself, or one who did as he was told to get a banana.

"In many ways, yes, the training exercises we put your father through were based on previous experiments that had been completed, with varying levels of success, using primates. I myself ran one of those studies for many years before the Contamination, and let me say, Velvet, the results we were able to achieve with your dad were extraordinary. Beyond what we ever could've accomplished with apes, and so far above even the other human test subjects."

"What happened to them?" There's a buzzing in my brain I am sure is my imagination, but I try to make myself calm.

Dr. Donna doesn't seem worried. If my collar's blinking, she doesn't notice or care. She shrugs. "Oh. All of them experienced a brief period of cognizance, but it didn't last. They all died."

I swallow the bitter residue of the juice that had seemed so sweet when I drank it before. "How?"

For the first time today, she looks shifty. "That's really not . . ."

"How?" I demand. "How did they die? Was it something like a fever? Did they have seizures? What?"

"One committed suicide by strangling herself with her

own hair," Dr. Donna said bluntly. "One jumped into a stairwell while being transported from his room to the testing area. He fell eight flights. One gouged out his eyes with the end of his toothbrush and when that didn't finish him, he drowned himself in the shower. The two others both went into a catatonic state and couldn't be roused. Both died in their sleep."

A low, soft, and painful sound leaks from my lips. "But not my dad. He's okay? He's alive?"

"Well, he's alive," Dr. Donna says. "And we intend to keep him that way until we can figure out how the Contamination worked in him. It gave him superior strength and agility, the ability to withstand abnormal amounts of pain and still function, as well as a marked decrease in social and moral reasoning."

"And you act like that's a good thing?" I want to spit at her, but I keep myself from getting out of the chair. The collar beeps. Warmth floods me, and I smell that burning stink again, but this time it's undercut with the noxious smell of rotting flowers.

Dr. Donna's eyes narrow, her gaze going to the collar at my throat. "It has its practical uses, yes. I mean, think of it. If you could have someone with the ability to run for miles without tiring, withstand great physical distress and pain, and also not balk at being ordered to carry out tasks that most people would falter at . . . I'm sure you can understand why your father created such a great interest."

"You wanted to make him some sort of supersoldier? Something like that?"

Dr. Donna's grin is full of teeth. If she knew how ugly she looks when she grins that way, she'd spend the rest of her life frowning.

"Your dad, despite his amazing and interesting reactions to the Contamination, is far too volatile to be of any real use. And your mother, who is one of the only victims I've seen who was able to recover enough to speak, to comprehend, and at the same time somehow regain her former personality . . . well. As wonderful as all that is, she's weak and not at all capable of the same kinds of physical strength as your father experiences. But you, Velvet," she says, and I swear she swipes her tongue over her lips like she's getting ready to eat me, "you are something very special indeed. The best of both of them, aren't you?"

I'm shaking, my muscles tensing and releasing. The collar beeps again. My eyelids flutter against my will, making her look as she comes closer like one of those freaky ghosts from an Asian horror movie, the ones with all the hair and that jittering, scuttling walk.

"Dr. Billings's tests have confirmed what we thought might be true, and the results are honestly beyond anything we might've dreamed."

"Golden. Goose." My mouth pools with saliva I have to swallow hard. She's close enough again to my face for me to count her eyelashes and the wrinkles at the corners of

her eyes. She needs to pluck her eyebrows and use moistur-
izer.

"Yes. Have you finished your juice, Velvet?"

"Not thirsty."

She presses the glass closer to me. "You need to drink all of it. It's important. Lots of good stuff in there. Vitamins. Minerals. It's no ThinPro, but it's as close as we could get. Do you know what they will pay when I can figure out exactly how to re-create what happened to you?" Dr. Donna breathes against my face. "You're my million-dollar baby."

And that's when I headbutt her nose.

TWENTY-NINE

SCREAMING, BLOOD OOZING FROM THE GIANT
mess I made of her nose, Dr. Donna tries to punch me in
the face. But I'm faster than she is, and I duck out of the
way. I stumble forward.

She snags my hair, yanking my head back. I reach behind
me to grab her wrists, twisting my body to break her
grip. Her eyes are very wide, her mouth pulled back in a
snarl.

Her face doubles in front of me. Triples. The entire room
shifts out of focus, and I can't blink away the blur. Faintly,
like it's very far away, the collar is beeping. My hands go
to it, even though I know there's no way I can pull it off.
It feels hot against my palms. I stagger and go to one knee,
with a hand on the edge of the chair.

"Oh, no, no, you don't, you little brat. No Mercy Mode
for you! Cody! Arnaldo! Get in here! I need a thousand
milligrams of Rylaxin, IM, stat!" To me, Dr. Donna says,

"I've wasted too much time on you, Velvet. You're not going to check out so easily."

I can't concentrate. My muscles have gone tense and tight. I can't get up. I watch my fingers curl into my palm, the nails suddenly digging hard enough to cut my skin.

Breathe. Breathe. Breathe.

I get on my feet. Dr. Donna looks surprised. The door opens, and it's Arnaldo with a tray of syringes, followed by Cody with what I realize is a straitjacket, just like the kind you see in the movies.

She gapes, gesturing wildly at Arnaldo, who looks at me with less surprise than I'd expect. He nods, just barely.

"Arnaldo! Now!"

He has to move, but his hesitation gives me just enough time. I'm at the door with Dr. Donna's fingers snagging the back of my shirt, but Arnaldo and Cody block me. They pin my arms, but they forget about my feet. I kick Cody in the nose, breaking it. Blood sprays. Arnaldo dives for me then, but I'm fast. And strong.

All the running, jumping, leaping. All the climbing. All these weeks, they've done as much to train me for this as if they'd planned it all along.

I don't stop when I push past Dr. Donna; in fact, I keep going and make sure to shove her as hard as I can. She spins on those ridiculous shoes, teeters, and falls. Then I'm out the door and between the soldiers who have guns pointing at me, but I don't stop to think about if they're going to shoot or not, because behind me, Dr. Donna's screaming my name.

And also: "Stop her, but don't hurt her!"

The only reason I can outrun them is because I head for the stairs instead of the elevator, and I leap the railing. I hit the landing and slam through a door before anyone has time to get into the stairwell.

The hall's almost identical to mine, but the doors here are almost all open. I run past them, barely glancing inside. The rooms seem empty, beds and dressers the same as mine. Bricked-up windows. I reach the end of the hall, another set of stairs. They'll expect me to go down.

So I go up.

I take the stairs two at a time, hand on the railing to pull me along. The collar is hot on my throat, and every so often the pulsing bands of color flicker across my vision, but I ignore them. I push through the door at the top of the stairs and end up in a ward similar to the one I saw that first day they took me to testing.

This one's worse, though. No beds here. There are a couple of battered couches, some recliners. A TV playing old game shows on the wall. The room is full of collared Connies, all of them wearing soft tracksuits like the one Jenny gave me. Some of them shuffle around, some stand or sit motionless and staring. Most of them are slack-jawed, if not drooling. One, a girl of about my age, with pretty blond hair that's pulled back from her face with a harsh rubber band, stands facing the wall next to the door I just came through. She bangs her head against it, not hard enough to break the skin, but constant, monotonous, endless. *Bang, bang, bang.* Nobody stops her.

Some of them turn to look at me as I come skidding through the door, but most pay no more attention to me than if I were invisible. I should run, but facing these people, all ages, men and women and teens—though no kids younger than maybe thirteen—I can't move. Is this what I will become? I can't stay here. They're coming for me.

I walk quickly through the ward, not convinced that running won't trigger them somehow, even though I know the collars will keep them from doing anything to me. I slip through the door and into another hallway, this one L shaped. Dark, with flickering overhead lights, many of the bulbs burned out overhead. From the end of the hall, I hear murmuring voices, so I turn in the other direction. I pass open doors, rooms laid out like mine but with windows of glass. I guess they figure collared Connies wouldn't bother to jump out.

I pass another room, this one without a bed and dresser but instead with a set of big metal tubs covered with canvas laced up the middle with a space for someone's head to stick out. There are puddles of water on the floor and more dripping from an overhead pipe, and I'm so totally creeped out, I have to look behind me after I pass it, convinced there will be some gaunt and spindly thing coming out of that room after me. Another room, with a closed door and an observation window crisscrossed with metal mesh, has a stretcher and a series of machines with dials and wires and leather cuffs. . . . I'm running now, past these rooms of torture and pain. I'm heading for the stairs at the short end of the L, but before I can decide to take them or not, a door several feet away from me opens and a man in a wheelchair is pushed out by a white-suited orderly.

They don't see me when I duck behind an empty nursing station desk. But I see them as the orderly pushes the man past me. He's slumped over, wrists shackled to the arms of the wheelchair. Feet, the same.

But I know that halo of red hair, and even that haggard face. Those blue eyes. Even with the lines of age and rage and time etched into his face, I know him. It's the man who came into our backyard. It's my dad.

And I can see by the look in his eyes that he knows me.

THIRTY

HIS HEAD TURNS, BUT THE ORDERLY PUSHES him away so fast, there's no chance for him to say anything. The pounding of soldiers' feet comes next, and I press myself under the desk. The hallway is filled with the sudden shuffling of slippered feet, and when I peek out, I see the Connies being herded by the orderlies and nurses into their rooms. But the crowd keeps the soldiers from running down the hall, and I say a prayer to whoever's watching out for me—thank you for the delay.

I slip my fingers between the collar and my neck, feeling the heat of it. I never knew the collar burned. Now I feel even worse about all the times my mom's had gone off. I wait for it to send me to my knees again, but though I can still smell that faint burning and I hear a low, constant hum that comes from inside my skull, I'm no longer staggering. No more double vision. I breathe. In, out. Breathe and concentrate on being calm.

I hear Dr. Donna's voice barking out orders, but I don't dare peek around the desk.

"She can't have run very far. You, check the stairs. You, the elevator; she might've been stupid enough to try that. And you and you, start checking each and every one of these rooms! Get these people out of my way! Move it!"

They're going to catch me, and when they do, I'm sure that their starving me will be the least of my worries. At the thought of all the other things they might do to me, the hum in my head gets louder. I close my eyes against a sudden surge of red haze. Once, in gym class, I'd run too fast in heat without drinking enough and passed out in the locker room. This is the same red haze that overtook me right before I went down, and I can't afford to be unconscious now.

My hands run along the bottom of the desk, looking for a drawer. There must be one, where they keep the pencils and pens and paper clips. I find it, pulling quickly, no time for quiet. They're coming.

The drawer comes out too fast, spilling everything. I fumble, clumsy, trying to keep my eyes focused on the junk strewn all over the floor. I find a paper clip and straighten it, even though my fingers don't want to work. I drop it. Can't find it.

Breathe, Velvet, I hear my mother say. *Breathe, honey. You can do this.*

I find the slim piece of metal and slide my fingers along the collar, searching for that tiny, nearly invisible hole, but it refuses my touch. Desperate, the sound of pounding boots coming closer, I slip the paper clip in the laces of my sneaker and bend the wire just enough to keep it there.

Then I run.

I don't overthink it—I head for the room across the hall and directly for the window, where I slip behind the curtains. I unlatch the window, which opens out to a parking lot. This building is massive and I'm ten stories up. Surrounding the parking lot are the familiar green fields that dot most every place around Lebanon.

If I can get out this window and down to the ground, I can run, fast and far.

But the only way to do it is jump. I might be Contaminated, and so far it's made me furious and reckless, but it hasn't yet made me fearless. I don't have time to strip the bed of sheets and make a rope. I barely have time to squeeze out the window onto the narrow ledge that leads from window to window. I tug the curtains closed behind me to give myself some time, and then I'm clinging to the ledge with my fingers tight against the bricks.

It's like climbing the rock wall, except there are no soft mats to catch me and no conveniently placed grips. But I tell myself it's just like the rock wall so that I can keep moving. Slide my hands, slide my feet along the ledge to the next window, where there's nothing to hold on to but the glass, and I'm afraid to go across it in case the curtains are open and they can see me.

So I stay there, trying to force myself to move until at last there's nothing to be done but to do it. My fingers slip on the smooth glass, but I find a place to hold on to above the window. I go as fast as I can. Hand over hand. Feet sliding.

I fall.

At the last second, I grab, fingernails bending and breaking. It hurts, though I've had worse. I swing, first from one hand, then grab with the other and hang. My feet dangle inches above the ledge below me. Above me, there's a rattle of curtain rings, and a window, not the one I came out of, opens. I hear shouting and wait for someone to look out and down, but apparently they're not expecting me to have jumped out the window, because nobody does. At least not on this floor.

I do hear sirens, though. Not fire, nor police, more like an alarm going off inside the building. And, even though my fingernails are split and bleeding and I'm dangling from a ledge several stories above the ground, knowing that the fall could break every bone and probably kill me—and that's if I'm lucky—I start to laugh.

I laugh at the thoughts of Dr. Donna's face and Cody's broken nose and how I'm just a kid who got away. Wearing a collar, no less. I guess security doesn't have to be so tight when almost everyone inside the complex has been made incapable of fighting back.

I can't hang there forever. I work my way to the next

window, and the drainpipe there. I cling to that like a barnacle, waiting for it to break free of the brick and toss me to the ground, but it holds long enough for me to slide down it to the next floor. Then another. The rivets holding the metal brackets bite at me, tearing my skin through my tracksuit, but there's no choice. It's slide or fall. Or jump, I think when I ratchet down another floor and the agony in my thighs from the cutting metal makes me want to pass out. I'm still three stories up when I twist to the left and I see an open Dumpster. Can I do this? Hand over hand, my fingers cramping and aching, I climb out along the window ledges—these are bricked-up windows now, no longer glass—until I'm hanging over the Dumpster. If I've miscalculated, I will definitely break myself on the edge. Images of me hitting wrong and breaking my neck send me into a cold sweat, but I don't have a choice.

I drop.

I fall.

I land up to my waist in a mess of cardboard and coffee grinds. Shattered glass slices my calf, and both my ankles explode into agony, but when I test my weight on them, they don't seem to be broken. Breathing hard against the choking stink of the garbage, I crouch and try to gather my wits.

How long do I have before they come for me? Can they track me by the collar? I don't have time to figure it out.

I pull myself out of the garbage and land, legs buckling,

next to the Dumpster. The sirens are still going off inside. The collar settles on my throat, and I wait for another surge of shock to disable me, but though I can hear the humming and the red haze filters around the edges of my vision again, my muscles don't spasm.

I gather myself, looking around for any signs of something I can run toward. The parking lot is huge and mostly empty, but I'll be totally exposed. Even when I get into the field beyond, anyone looking out the windows could see me. I have no place to hide. Nowhere to run. They're going to find me.

I run, anyway, when a car pulls up next to me, and it keeps pace with me. The guy behind the wheel rolls down his window. "Get in."

I stumble over my shoelace and hit the asphalt on my hands and knees. At least I'm hidden now by the car, which is between me and the building. Panting, my sweaty, stringy hair in my face, I look up at him.

"Get in," he says again. "I got off duty twenty minutes ago, before the shit hit the fan, but when I heard what was going down, I thought I might find you. Get in."

I know this kid. It's the same young soldier who helped me get away that day when I tried saving those Connie kids.

I get in the car.

THIRTY-ONE

ELLEN'S SECRET ROOM SMELLS COMFORTINGLY of antiseptic. My wounds sting from her cleaning them, but it's not a bad pain. She's bound my ankles tight with sports wrap, and has me icing them with these neat chemical ice packs that mold around them. She offered me some pain-killers, but I didn't want to take them. I can't risk being woozy.

The soldier's name is Brice, and he's from Oklahoma originally. He has a girlfriend who still lives there, whom he'd like to marry, if he can finish his tour here in the black zone and get out of the army. The problem is that he enlisted just before the Contamination hit big-time, and they're not letting anyone out anymore without a really good reason. That's what he called it, too. A tour in the black zone.

"You make it sound like it's a war."

Brice, who doesn't look nearly old enough to be think-ing of getting married—and don't think I'm not aware of the irony of that thought—shrugs and gives Ellen a look. "Well. It is. Sort of."

"The stories they're telling us aren't true, are they?"

Brice shrugs again. "Some of it is. Oklahoma had hardly any Contamination. Wyoming, Montana, neither. Parts of Colorado were hit real hard. Denver is a black zone, but only to just around it. Not like out here."

"Almost the entire East Coast has gone black. Most of the West Coast. I'm guessing it's similar in other countries. The large population centers were hit hardest." Ellen pauses. "But I get my information from the Voice and Raven, same as everyone else. God knows you can't trust what the authorities say."

"They're not just keeping you all in," Brice says suddenly. "They're bringing people from the other places. Shipping them here. If you test positive, you get relocated. All that displacement housing, who do you think that's all really for?"

This seems to startle Ellen. "What about the people here who test negative?"

"If you have the money, you can get relocated to the green zone." Brice shakes his head. "Probably even if you test positive."

Ellen shrinks a little. "You're sure about this?"

"I was on a detail when they sent one of the trucks in. They're sending the really bad ones to the research center. Or . . . other places." Brice looks uncomfortable.

"They're killing them," I say.

His mouth works. "I don't know about that. I haven't seen it myself. But I've heard that, if you get sent to one of the containment facilities, you're better off dead."

"It's worse than the mental health system in the fifties and sixties. These people are declared incompetent, yet there is no treatment for them beyond the experimental, and there are too many of them even for the researchers. The sheer cost of keeping them fed and clothed and in good health . . ." Ellen shudders, putting a hand to her forehead. "Velvet, I'm not sure you understand, but you got the champagne experience. The others in the complex are not treated the way you were. And those who are just locked up, without being deemed of any benefit? Brice is right. I'm sure it would be more humane to have them all put down. The collars keep them in line, but the level of neglect in those places is horrifying."

"I've seen it." Quickly, I describe the wards, the room with the tubs, the stretcher. "But it's not worse than the kennels."

She makes a small noise. "Oh. Yes, it is. Much worse. There are all kinds of cages, Velvet, and not all of them have bars. And for the people in the Sanitarium, nobody is coming for them, ever."

We're all silent, thinking of it. I shake my head, which is enough to send a few waves of hazy red swimming around the edges of my vision again. I blink slowly to fend them off and slip a few sore fingers beneath my collar again. It's not hot anymore, but it is chafing my skin.

"Can we get this off me?"

"It's not that easy." Ellen offers me a drink, which I sip while she probes and pokes me. She touches the inside corners of my eyes gently, though even that soft pressure makes me wince. "My God. They butchered you, didn't they? Donna has no finesse. Never did."

"You worked with my dad, didn't you?" I've already told her everything Dr. Donna told me.

"Yes. I knew you looked familiar the first time you came here with Dillon and your mom."

Somehow hearing there's something of my dad in me that a stranger can see makes me feel better. "I need to find him. And my sister. I have to figure out a way to get my mom and dad out of there. . . ."

"Velvet." Ellen's voice is gentle. "You can't think about getting your dad. He's not . . . he won't be able to . . . he's not like your mom, kiddo. I can tell you with every confidence, he'll never be safe."

I shift on the table and tap the collar, not wanting to hear her say that. "Take this off me."

"I can't just take it off without the key."

"Paper clip," I say, stone-faced.

"I can't risk that." Ellen shakes her head. "The collars are not designed to be removed without the key. I know you got your mom's off without triggering Mercy Mode, but your mom is a special case. And we don't know how much better or faster she'd have recovered if you'd left the collar on. I know it seems like taking it off helped her—"

"How could it not have helped her? She was able to talk, and think!"

Ellen gives my shoulder a gentle squeeze. "With her unique reaction to the Contamination, there's no telling how your mom might've done without the damage incorrectly removing the collar caused."

I tap the collar again. "Dr. Donna said I'm the perfect mingling of my parents. Take the collar off me. I can't have it on."

"Calm down," Ellen says, but too late—the collar beeps. "Velvet, please."

I feel it sweeping over me, the rush and burn of paralysis. The twitch of muscles. The red haze. But I push back against it, refusing to give in to it, and in a minute, I'm breathing hard but still sitting upright. Ellen's mouth is hanging open. I fix her with a steady look.

"Take it off." When she doesn't move, I hop off the table, forgetting about my sprained ankles. I pull the straightened paper clip from my shoelace and limp to a mirror on the wall. I angle my head from side to side, trying to find the tiny hole. I still can't see it. In the reflection, I stare at her. "I'll do it myself eventually, but it's going to take longer."

We stare at each other. I can see the struggle on her face, but there's no way I'm going to spend another minute with this thing around my neck. I probe the collar again, my fingertips seeking the tiny hole.

"Fine," she snaps. "I'll do it. But I swear to you, if you die, I will kill you."

Suddenly, we're laughing. Brice snorts with it, his eyes red. Laughing hurts all the parts of me that have been abused today, but I can't stop it. And it feels good.

I hand her the paper clip, which she examines for a moment before shaking her head and opening the drawer to pull out a needle and a syringe. I flinch, imagining all the things needles have done to me lately, but Ellen makes a soothing sound and holds it up. She strips the plastic from it.

"It's harder than a paper clip and won't bend. And"—she demonstrates—"there's a small hole in the tip, which I'm not sure you know, is a part of the key. This will work better. I think. I hope."

I stand very still. "They didn't make them very secure, did they?"

"When you tell everyone that they'll kill the person wearing it if they try to take it off without a key," Ellen says as she leans very close, focused on the collar, "it kind of deletes the need for a whole lot of safeguards. Keep in mind, Velvet, they also kind of *want* people to . . . well."

"Die," I murmur, closing my eyes. "They want us to die."

It's the first time I've said it aloud to someone else, that I'm Contaminated. It doesn't feel so bad. At least, I don't feel any different than I did a few minutes ago, and it's not like Ellen doesn't know. There's actually a sort of weight lifted off me when I admit it in front of her and Brice. Because this is who I am, who I've become. Who I've been for a long time, I guess. And though there've been a lot of things that happened that have changed me, in my heart I know that no matter what's going on inside my brain, I am not a monster.

I'm still Velvet.

THIRTY-TWO

BRICE HAS GONE BACK TO THE BARRACKS, worried that, if he doesn't check in, he'll get snagged for helping me. But not so worried that he regrets it, he said before he left. Because it was the right thing to do. There are lots of right things to do, according to him, and someone has to start doing them.

Ellen has made some dinner. I never thought I'd want to eat again. She insisted, anyway.

"Dillon could have been assigned to any one of several displacement housing complexes. I haven't seen him, or I'd have told you already. They told you Opal had been placed in his custody?" Ellen watches me curiously as I dig into the plate of pasta she'd set in front of me.

My appetite's back. Roaring, in fact. My stomach feels like I haven't ever put food in it. I turn the fork in circles, loading it with pasta covered in sweet tomato sauce, then shove it in my mouth. After the weeks of bland hospital food, anything with flavor is like eating rainbows.

"Slow down," she murmurs.

"Yes. They told me she was with him. But that doesn't mean it's the truth, does it? They lied about everything else."

"They'd have no reason to have sent her anywhere else, and if you two were legally married, then he'd be the next logical choice for guardian. Everything's such a mess now, anyway. Tons of paperwork but nobody to follow up, and honestly, the people in charge don't really care. All the regulations, but most of it's going unenforced, except for the big stuff. The crime . . ." She shakes her head. "The crime is out of control."

I take a long drink of water, then another bite of spaghetti. This time, slower. I chew and swallow. "The Contaminated?"

"No. Regular people. That's what makes it so upsetting. It makes me glad I have a gun." Ellen shakes her head again.

I frown. "You have a gun?"

She lifts her chin. "Look. All it took was waking up one night with some yahoo standing over me asking me where I kept the good drugs, okay? I'm not proud of it, but, yeah, I have a gun. And it wasn't easy to get, either."

"I'm not judging. Do you know how to use it?"

"Yes." Her eyes go steely. "Definitely."

I sit back in the chair, my stomach so full, I think I

might pop. "I need to get to Dillon. I need to find out what happened to Mrs. Holly, too."

"Velvet, you know it's very likely that Mrs. Holly is . . . gone."

"At least I'd know," I tell her. "Instead of always wondering."

It's been close to six hours since Brice picked me up in the parking lot and brought me here. I need sleep, but I don't want to even take a nap. My stomach's full. My wounds are taken care of. The collar's off.

I push away from the table. "Tell me where the displacement housing is."

"Velvet, it's everywhere. I mean, he could be in any one of the complexes. Or, hell, even in one of the regular houses. So many are empty because of people being sent away."

That's when I know exactly where to find him. It doesn't matter where they assigned him; I'm sure that Dillon will have gone home. "He went to his parents' house." Heart racing, I take my dish to the sink because it would be so rude not to, and when I turn to face her, Ellen's giving me a weird look.

"What?"

"Go," she says, with a wave of her hands. "I shouldn't let you. I should worry about you more. You're in no condition to be running around this time of night, and there's every chance you'll get picked up by some patrol and all the good work I did on you today will have been a waste of my time. But . . . go. I can't stop you. But do me a favor, at least. Let me give you some better clothes, okay?"

That makes sense. My tracksuit and sneakers offer little protection. Ellen outfits me in sturdy jeans with a denim shirt, gloves, and a pair of heavy-duty lace-up boots that are a little tight in the toes, but will have to do.

"Not for fashion," she says as she hands me a leather jacket with a thick collar like the kind old-time pilots wore. The leather is soft and smells good, though the jacket's obviously not new. "But in case you have to do any sort of jumping through bushes or climbing or . . . well. Whatever it is you're going to end up doing."

I shrug into the jacket. The sleeves are a little too long, but everything else fits great. "Thanks. For everything."

"Someone has to start doing the right things, like Brice said. I tried, or I thought I did." For a moment, Ellen looks sad. "Then I got scared."

"You've done a lot. You took care of my mom that day. And Dillon said you took care of a lot of other people, too."

"I could do more. I *should* do more. Go now."

From outside comes a sweep of bright light through the windows and the crackle of a speaker-boosted voice. Ellen goes to the window and tugs the curtain aside. When she looks back at me, her face seems very pale.

"They tracked the collar. I wondered if they might— it's the sort of thing Donna would've done, just to be safe.

The normal collars don't have tracking devices in them, but she'd custom-built something so she didn't lose her cash cow." Ellen pulls open a closet and takes out a shotgun. I'd been expecting a handgun; seeing her with that thing makes me take a stumbling step back, especially when she racks it. "Get out of here. Back door. Hurry, you're only about five steps ahead of them at this point. Go!"

I go, fast as I can, out the back door and across the yard. I take a running leap at the fence, glad for the gloves, which help me grip and protect my hands from the splintery wood. I dig the toes of my borrowed boots into the fence and push upward, managing to get myself to the top, where I swing myself over and drop into the yard on the other side. My ankles twinge, but the pain is fading. The house on this side is dark; the grass and weeds grown so high, it's clear nobody's lived there for a long time. There are lights on the street in front of it, too. Sweeping white lights and the murmur of those crackly voices.

I zigzag to the right, into the backyard of the next house. There are lights on in this one, but I don't even peek in the windows. I keep going. Into the yard of the house after that, keeping low, leaping bushes and tricycles and a sand-box. I trip over a collapsed lawn chair, but manage to land on one foot, and keep running.

This hurts. The pounding of my heart is so loud, it's impossible to hear what's going on around me, but it's not like any of the soldiers are trying to be secretive. From behind me, I hear gunshots. I can't tell from what kind of gun, but I don't let myself turn around even for one second.

I run and run, at first through backyards, then daring to cross the street to get to the next row of houses. I'm not sure where I'm going, or how far it is until I get to Dillon's house. I was there only once. But I run faster, staying away from the soldiers and keeping out of sight of any lit windows, until at last I stumble out onto a street I do recognize. I orient myself while I try to catch my breath. I bend, hands on my knees while the world, topsy-turvy, curves around me.

Everything's quiet here. If they're on a manhunt for me, they're not doing any better a job of it than they did keeping me in the Sanitarium. I stretch sore muscles, feeling the wrappings around my ankles loosening. The boots are laced tight enough for now, but I'm going to be in agony later, and it's unlikely Dillon's going to have any ice for me. Certainly nothing stronger for pain than aspirin, if he even has that.

I take the time to make sure I'm heading in the right direction. Down one street, then the other, keeping to the sidewalk this time so I don't get lost. I count the house numbers. This street is almost completely dark, which isn't a shocker, considering what time it is, but the signs of neglect everywhere tell me that almost all of these houses have been abandoned. One, two, three, his house is a few down from the corner. It's too dark to see the color, but I recognize the concrete gnome in the front yard.

I stop in front of it, desperate and eager to get inside but uncertain about how to do it. Do I knock? I try the handle to see if it's unlocked, and the door jerks open hard in front of me. Hands are on me, and I don't think, I react. I dip and turn, twisting, grabbing at the shadowy figure. My nails dig deep into bare skin. Hot breath washes over me, and strong arms pin me.

I will kill him.

That's what I think in the seconds before the voice in my ear says my name, low and urgent, and I know who's holding me so tightly. But I can't stop myself from chopping his throat with the side of my hand. At the last second, I pull my punch so that even though I still hit him, it's only enough to make him cough and gag. Not enough to end his life.

"Dillon, I'm sorry. I'm sorry." I say it over and over, but somehow doubt it could ever be enough.

And then he has me in his arms, his hand on the back of my head, and he's kissing me, and somehow, I know he will forgive me.

THIRTY-THREE

"THEY CAME AND TOOK HER A COUPLE HOURS ago." Dillon's voice is still raspy, but his eyes have stopped watering. "I couldn't stop them."

"It's not your fault."

I want to go to bed and sleep forever. I want to take a hot shower. I want, at least, to have a cold drink. Instead, we are stuffing backpacks with supplies in the dark so we don't alert any passing soldiers.

"I should've run with her. Done something." Dillon rolls up a T-shirt and shoves it to the bottom of the pack. His shoulders hunch.

In the dim light coming from behind the curtains, he's a shadow, but I can see him—better than he can see me, I think, and I wonder if this is something else that's happened to me because of the Contamination. I put my arms around him from behind, pressing my cheek against his back. It takes him a few seconds, but then he turns and hugs me. I can't make him feel better. He can't change what happened.

"We'll get her back," I say finally. "I got out. I can get back in."

"And out again? Velvet. No."

"She's my sister, Dillon." I step away from him.

"They'll catch you!"

"They won't expect me to go back inside." I say this with more confidence than I feel.

From outside, I hear shouts and the rough rumble of the truck engines. We don't have time to argue about this. They might not be tracking me anymore, but how long before Donna realizes where I must've gone and sends them directly here? If they came here for Opal, they'll be here for me any minute.

I shove a few cans into my backpack, then weigh it in my hands. Too heavy. I take out most of the food, leaving only the granola bars and small packages of cookies. I shove in a handful of socks, bandages, tubes of antibiotic ointment, a pair of scissors. A pocketknife from the junk drawer Dillon dumped onto the kitchen table. We need to run, travel light. We can scavenge along the way, if we have to. Right now all I can think about is getting to Opal.

I can't think about my parents.

Take care of your sister, I hear my mom say, and though it kills me, I know I have to think of Opal first. My parents, later. They would expect it of me.

Dillon steps in front of me as he shrugs into his backpack.

"Velvet, stop. Listen to me. There's a supply train leaving Lebanon at dawn. I know about it because Mario, that guy I told you about, got switched to a different route. Now he's doing pickup at the unloading docks for the supply station. The one where the trains drop off stuff. He's taking his family and they're getting out on that train, heading for a green zone. Raven says there are people waiting there to take us in."

"Us?"

"People escaping from the black zones."

"Is it safe? Of course it's not safe." Before he can answer, I shake my head with a laugh. Stupid. It's not like we can buy a ticket and reserve a seat. Still—"We have to be on that train, Dillon."

"We'll never make it."

I grab him by both arms and turn him into the sliver of light coming from outside so he can see me, my face, how serious I am. "We'll make it."

★ ★ ★

Dillon can't keep up with me, and I have to shorten my strides. His pack is heavier, because he insisted he could carry more. I don't want to embarrass him, but when his breath starts rasping in his lungs and he falls behind as we duck through the backyards, I finally turn to him.

"Switch with me."

"No—"

"I'm strong," I tell him. "I've been doing nothing but

running, jumping, and lifting stuff for weeks. Plus, I'm . . . well, I'm strong, Dillon."

I want him to understand, but how can he when I barely understand myself? And I don't want him to be afraid of me. Dillon bends, hands on his knees.

At that moment, a ray of white light sweeps the yard. I'm on my knees a second after that, pulling him down beside me. We both hit the ground, our faces pressed into the dirt. I'm glad for the leather coat and gloves Ellen lent me, but all Dillon has on is a denim shirt and jeans.

The light sweeps back and forth. The truck moves on. We, I think, are *so* going to get caught.

I wait a minute or so before I sit up. I'm trying to gauge by the light in the sky how close we are to dawn, and what that means, exactly. Five a.m.? Six a.m.?

"Did he say the train left at a specific time, or just at dawn?"

"Just at dawn, but I'm sure there's a schedule."

I peek through the bushes. The trucks have gone around the bend, leaving behind the stink of exhaust. I sit back on my heels.

"Can you run again? We have another couple miles to go before we get to the Sanitarium. How far is it from the train station? Do you know?"

"The train station is behind the old YMCA, across the street. They converted all those old factory buildings into storage and offices."

"A few miles?" I try to calculate how far, but I can't. I can run and jump and lift heavy things, but the calculation of distance escapes me.

Dillon pulls me close. "This is crazy. You know that? You're going back in there. Get Opal out. And get to the train by dawn?"

"Yes." It's the only answer I know to give.

Incredibly, Dillon grins. He kisses me. We don't have time for this, but I let him, because suddenly I want to cling to him and never let go.

"Hey," he says. "Shhh. Hey, Velvet, don't cry."

"There was so much blood."

Dillon holds me tighter. "We're going to get through this. Together."

I hold on to him like I'm drowning and he's pulling me out of the water. A year ago, I didn't know him, and since then I've married and lived with him, I've made him my family. He's made me laugh, he's helped me survive.

"I love you," I tell him, and can't believe I never told him this before.

"I love you, too." He laughs and pulls me close for a kiss. "I thought I'd never see you again."

We stare at each other with dirty faces and the sound of trucks and soldiers roaming the streets looking for us. I link my fingers with his, squeezing. Everything hurts, even the breath I draw in.

"What if I can't do it? I'm so tired," I say. He was right

before. This is an impossible task. Get there, get Opal, get out, get to the train. All without getting caught. All in the space of a few hours. Dillon frowns. "You can do this. You're right; the last thing they'll expect you to do is go back. And you *are* strong, Velvet. You're the strongest girl I've ever met. But you don't have to do this alone, remember that."

It feels so good not to be alone. But as I move, my arms and legs are practically screaming with weariness and the built-up agony of everything I've put my body through. It's like someone flipped a switch inside me, and I've gone from being made of titanium to aluminum foil.

Another rumble reaches my ears, different from the army trucks'. At first, I think it's a tank, and my stomach sinks, but then Dillon's looking through the hedge. I try to pull him back, to keep him from giving us away, but he turns to me with a grin.

"I know how we're going to do it. We'll get in and out and away, and nobody will even notice us at all."

I'm so tired, I can't tell if he's making any sense. "How?"

"Garbage truck," he says. "Nobody ever pays attention to the garbage trucks."

THIRTY-FOUR

"I DON'T WANT ANY TROUBLE." IT'S JUST A young kid behind the desk, a bandanna around his forehead and the beginnings of wispy growth that's trying hard to be a beard on his chin. He wears a Waste Disposal Department coverall, but was dozing with his feet on the desk when we came in. He looks guilty now.

Dillon hasn't even threatened him. All we did was come into the office and knock on the desk. The kid woke up, tossed his hands in the air, and looked like we were waving guns.

"I need the keys to one of the trucks," Dillon says. "Gimme Mario's."

He wouldn't need it, that's what we're both thinking, but the kid behind the desk has no clue. He blinks rapidly, taking in the sight of both of us. Then he shrugs and gestures at the rack of keys hanging on hooks behind him.

"Take it," he says. "I hate this job. They don't pay me

enough to deal with crap like this. I wanted to work with the ration trucks, but, no, instead I gotta smell garbage all day long."

"It's worse on the truck," Dillon says with a scowl. "And in the dump."

The kid shrugs. "Yeah, I'll bet. Hey, can you punch me in the face or something? Make it look like you mugged me?"

Dillon and I share a look. The kid sees it and lets out a long, hissing sigh. He shakes his head.

"I can't just say I gave it up."

"Dude, I'm not gonna punch you in the—"

I punch the kid in the nose. His head rocks back, and he lets out a strangled yelp. Blood starts to leak from his nose, and he claps a hand over it.

To be fair, I did think twice about it. But the kid has a point. We can't let him get in trouble to help us.

"Ouch," he complains, then looks at me. "Give me a black eye, too."

Dillon puts out a hand to stop me. "We don't have time to play punching bag! Just give me the keys!"

"Fine!" The kid snags a key from the rack behind him and tosses it toward Dillon, who catches it midair. "Freak."

"I'm not the one begging for a punch in the face," Dillon mutters as we head out through the back door to the parking lot. When I try to get in the cab, though, he shakes his head. "No. You need to ride in the back."

"With the garbage? What about the crusher thing?"

"You'll be fine. Just lay still. I won't crush you. I promise."

I trust him, of course I do. But settling into the back of the garbage truck, which isn't full but smells so bad, I think I might faint, still freaks me out. I breathe in shallow gasps, holding my nose. The noise blocks out everything, except my thoughts.

We drive.

I'm already going over the plan Dillon and I came up with on the way to the WDD office. He will drive the truck around the back of the hospital, outside one of the service entrances. And after that . . . I will find her.

Dr. Donna's the one who took her; I'm sure the soldiers have brought Opal to the same floor where they kept me, the special one without windows so nobody can jump out of them. Dr. Donna will have already put Opal in a room, maybe drugged her. It's too early in the morning for experiments with Dr. Billings, but that doesn't mean they won't be getting her ready.

One thing is different between my sister and me—Opal isn't Contaminated. Not a bit. I drank a bottle or two of the ThinPro, swayed by the ads that promised a "beach body" in a few weeks. But Opal had never worried about stuff like that; she was just a kid when everything started, and honestly, that kid lived on juice boxes and chocolate milk. You couldn't have forced a bottle of water down her throat. But she *would* drink orange juice, and that's what Dr. Donna had been giving me to pump me full of whatever proteins had caused the Contamination in the first place.

I have to get to Opal. It's the only thought I can hold on to as the truck jostles and bounces. At one point, I'm sure my teeth will rattle right out of my head. When we finally stop, I'm not sure I can move until Dillon helps me out. I sag in his arms.

He looks at me, worry painted on his face. "Velvet, are you all right?"

I want to tell him I'm okay, but all I can do is shake my head.

"C'mere." He tugs me around the side of the truck, between it and the brick wall of the hospital. He pushes me gently to lean against the truck. He lifts my chin and looks into my eyes. "Your pupils are like pinpoints. Are you okay? What's wrong?"

I swallow around a sudden dryness like cotton balls on my tongue and in my throat. I rasp out, "I don't know. I feel . . . funny."

"You can't do this, not in your condition."

I force myself to straighten. I shake my head to clear it of the haze, but it's not working. "I have to. I have to find Opal."

"I can find her."

"You have no idea where to go or where she might be. I'm the one who was in there, I'm the one who got out—"

"You can tell me," he says. "Trust me. Nobody pays attention to the garbage guys, anyway."

Again, I shake my head, which doesn't do anything but make me dizzier. The ground is going to come up and hit me in the face at any second. I can already feel it sliding away under my feet.

I bite my tongue.

Hard, on purpose. Blood squirts. I bite again, harder this time. The pain is huge, enormous, ginormous, as Opal would say, but everything shifts back into clarity. I spit to the side and expect to see a fountain of red gush out of me, but it's not so bad. Just a little pink.

I look at Dillon. "Let's go."

THIRTY-FIVE

WHEN I STAND INSIDE THE BIG, ROLLING GARBAGE can, it comes up to my chest. I can't sit down all the way in it. The best I can do is crouch, but I bend and twist until I can fit and Dillon can put the lid on it. It's way better than being in the back of the truck was, at least. It doesn't smell nearly as bad, and even though the bottom's encrusted with a layer of matted paper and stuff, the rest of it's pretty clean.

I feel bad at first, when he starts to pull the can. Even though all the weeks of everything Dr. Billings and Dr. Donna had me do left me in the best shape I've ever been in, I'll never be a small girl. But then I realize something I hadn't noticed. Dillon's used to pulling heavy cans. The long months of working in the WDD have made him stronger, too.

"Maintenance elevator," he says calmly.

I don't know if he's saying that to someone or just to let me know what's going on. I stay quiet, anyway. The wheels rumble under me. My neck's getting a crick in it, so I brace my hands against the side of the garbage can and breathe through the pain, which is really nothing compared to the ache in my tongue. I rub it against my teeth every time I start to feel hazy again, which is every few minutes at first, but starts to get better when I feel the elevator moving.

Dr. Donna and Dr. Billings kept me on the eighth floor, and I'm sure that's where Opal will be, too. They wouldn't have put her in the other sections with the Connies. Dr. Donna will be testing her the way they did with me. I know it. I have to believe it, just like I have to believe I still have time to get to her before they do anything to hurt her permanently.

The maintenance elevator is slow and stops at every floor. I listen to the heavy door open and shut while I sip air through my parted lips and try to keep pushing away the desire to sleep. Finally, Dillon murmurs, "Here we go," and the can moves again. My weight shifts unexpectedly when he tips it, and I bite against my tongue again to keep from crying out.

I told him to find the nurse's station and see if he could find a list with Opal's name on it, but the can comes to an abrupt stop that sends me thudding against the inside of it again. I hold my breath, trying to make myself small, even though everything hurts so much from being squeezed up in here that I'm about ready to pop out of the top like a jack-in-the-box.

"What's this? What are you doing?"

It's Dr. Donna. I'd know that voice anywhere. I force myself not to move.

"Switching out the receptacles. Got an order you needed a larger bin for this floor." Dillon sounds bored. "Got the order for new cans for each of these rooms, too, but they'll come later. Got a back order. You know how it is, everything's on back order—"

"I don't know anything about garbage," Dr. Donna snaps. "Just put it where it belongs. And get out of my way!"

"Sorry," Dillon says in that same bored tone. "It's a real big bin."

"I can see that. I'm trying to get through . . . fine, just go." She sounds exasperated, and I love it.

"You can move your cart first. I'll wait."

"I can't get my cart around that can!"

All I can picture now is Dr. Donna and Dillon pushing the can and the cart against each other, dancing from side to side, and laughter threatens to explode out of me, so I clap my hands over my mouth to keep it inside. Then we're moving again. Faster, this time. *Clack, clack, clack,* on the tiles. I don't know what room she'll be in. Dillon pauses at every door, long enough to look inside.

"Sorry," he says once. "You need a new can in that room? I'm placing an order."

"No, this one's fine."

At the sound of Arnaldo's voice, I again want to pop out

of the can. He was always good to me. I want to ask him to help me, even though I'm not sure he would. I force myself still.

"Hey," Dillon says then. "Aren't any of these rooms in use? I'm only supposed to get new cans for the rooms that are being used. All these look empty."

He's a genius.

"The only one in use right now is that one, second to the left at the end of the hall," Arnaldo says.

"Thanks, man. I'll get out of your way now."

"Hey. Hang on a—"

There's a grunt, then a thud. Oh, poor Arnaldo. I'd always liked him. Cody had been a real jerk, but Arnaldo had always tried to make life at least a little easier for me.

A few more tiles, another couple of minutes. The can moves, then tilts upright. I wait, listening hard.

"Shhh," I hear Dillon say. "Don't say anything. We're here for you, Opal."

That's when I push upward, knocking off the lid to leap out of the can.

THIRTY-SIX

"VELVET!" OPAL'S ACROSS THE ROOM AND IN my arms so fast, she knocks me back, and I stagger.

It's impossible that she's grown so much again in the time we've been apart, but she has, by at least another few inches. I push her hair off her face and take it in my hands to stare into her eyes. I'm not sure what I'm looking for. Bruises on the inside corners of the eyes or signs of Contamination, maybe—not that you can see that on a person. It's not like a scar or stain. It's always hidden.

"I told that bad doctor you'd come for me," Opal says.

"Of course," Dillon says from behind me. He's at the door, watching to make sure nobody's coming. "But we have to go. Fast. I'm not sure I hit him hard enough to keep him down for long. And where is everyone else?"

That's a good question. Even for a small staff, someone other than Arnaldo should be on this floor.

"In that?" Opal makes a face. "Gross."

I laugh and hug her. Hard, until she squirms free. "Yeah. In that. C'mon."

"We won't both fit." She looks inside the can, then at both of us. "Are you freaking kidding me?"

"Get in," Dillon says—not yelling, his voice low and calm but urgent. "Someone's coming."

I get in first and press my knees against the inside of the can. I can't crouch, not yet, but as soon as Dillon lifts Opal inside and fits her next to me, I try to hunker down. She was right; there isn't enough room. I get an elbow in the face, then in the gut. Opal doesn't seem to be cooperating, and even though a few seconds ago I was overjoyed to see her, now I'm ready to snap at her to stop digging her bones into me.

Without warning, Dillon slams the lid down on my head. It's hard enough to shove me deeper into the can with Opal wedged in next to me. In the next second, we're moving, tilted on our sides so that I have to brace myself hard against the walls with my hands, or else I'll crush her. She cries out, and I manage to press my arm against her face. It's not enough to silence her if she really wants to yell, but she gets the hint.

We're moving too fast. Dillon must almost be running, and that can't be good. I can't tell which direction we're going in, and it's hard enough to keep myself from completely squishing Opal every time the can tilts. From the sound of her breathing, she's either crying or trying hard not to. I don't blame her. I want to cry myself.

This is stupid. So stupid. I'm convinced Dr. Donna won't hurt me or Opal, at least not too bad. But Dillon . . . what will happen to Dillon if we get caught? I never should've let him help me.

With thoughts filling my head of their taking Dillon away, putting him in jail, or worse, I can't stay still. I hear the elevators chime and tell myself to count, to breathe. We will be out of the hospital in only minutes now. And then, once we're in the truck, we are out.

We'll be free.

It can't be that easy, can it? Of course not. Someone will notice Opal is missing, or poor Arnaldo will wake up, and then we're in trouble. I got away once, by myself and because fighting back surprised them. What will we do if this time, Dr. Donna has more soldiers?

"Almost there." Dillon's voice is low and faint and cut into pieces by his heavy breathing.

The can shifts and jerks. Again, I try not to completely crush my sister, but I can tell I'm hurting her by the way she wriggles and the squeak that leaks out of her. I press against the can. I'm breathing hard, too. Everything is getting hazy again, but I refuse to pass out.

The elevator dings again. Then something else: a rising, bleating siren. Fire alarm.

The can tilts upright. The lid comes off. Dillon looks in

on us, and the expression on his face has me stretching up to get out of the garbage bin as fast as I can. He looks grim-faced and determined, but also terrified.

"The elevators won't work if the fire alarm's going off," he says. "We'll have to take the stairs. C'mon. Get out of there, before—"

Somewhere not far from us, there's an explosion. The floor rumbles and dust sifts from the ceiling, making us cough. There's no smell of smoke or anything, not yet, but a second explosion comes fast behind the first, and suddenly the three of us are moving. No more hesitation. The can falls behind us, bouncing as we run out of the elevator.

That's when black smoke starts pouring out through the overhead vents. Thick, choking, with a strong chemical stink. Opal, at once, starts waving a hand in front of her face. My eyes sting. Dillon bursts into a fit of coughing that has him bending over, hands on his knees.

"Stairs!" I point, then stop to look over my shoulder. "Opal, why wasn't anyone here with you, other than Arnaldo?"

"They all got called away to help out with something that bad doctor said was a . . . a . . ." She falters, looking uncertain. Her face scrunches. "I don't know what she called it, but she was really mad, said all the other people in here needed to be put down. I was afraid that's what she was going to do to me!"

"No. I would never have let her." We don't have time for this, I know that much, but again I look down the hall. We never even got off the eighth floor. To Dillon, I say, "We can't leave Arnaldo here."

Dillon, eyes red and streaming, straightens. "Velvet . . ."

"He was nice to me! And if there's a fire—" Another explosion, this one closer. Maybe on the floor directly above. More dirt hits us, and this time, a ceiling panel falls down. Wires dangle, spitting sparks. I give Dillon a desperate, determined look, and he nods, already running with me down the hall, Opal in tow.

Arnaldo's sitting up, groggy, when we go into the room. We get him to his feet. He's bleeding a little from the corner of his mouth, and a giant bruise is swelling on his forehead. Black eye. I look at Dillon, just quickly, and he's looking apologetic. Now I hear not only the fire alarm but a far-off popping, and I know it's bullets.

"C'mon, man. Let's go," Dillon says.

"They told me I had to make sure the kid was okay," Arnaldo mutters. Blinking, he focuses on me. Then, instantly, he's awake and fighting us until I grab his arm.

"Arnaldo, something's happening. We have to go!"

Together, we hustle him out into the now-smoky hall. Opal's shifting from foot to foot and looks so relieved to see us that I think she might cry. Arnaldo reaches for her, but Dillon hauls him back. I know Arnaldo; he's not trying to hurt her.

"We have to go!" I shout, and bang open the door to the stairs.

They're not as smoky as the hallway, but the lingering stench of chemicals is there. Also, something just as bad. The deeper, disturbing smell of unwashed bodies, sour breath, incontinence. The fire alarm is louder here, echoing off the concrete walls, and there's another sound. Shouting and shuffling feet and bare hands slapping on the metal railing. I don't wait another second. I shove Dillon and Arnaldo and Opal ahead of me down the stairs, because above us, someone is coming.

A lot of someones are coming. The shouting comes from the orderlies, who are trying to urge along the collared Connies down the stairs ahead of the fire or whatever it is that's happening upstairs. They can't move very fast. Most of them wear those tracksuits that are too big for them, along with soft slippers that keep falling off their feet. The orderlies are trying to keep them in single file, but they're bunching up in twos and threes, taking one step at a time. All of us make it down the first set of steps to the landing on the seventh floor, and that's when another explosion rocks through the stairwell.

The orderlies behind us are shouting again. The Connies shove, and a few fall, knocking down the ones in front of them. It's like being in front of a relentless wave that's trying to sweep us away. Arnaldo is still not quite steady on his feet, but he has a protective hand on Opal's shoulder, while

Dillon is directly behind them. I'm bringing up the rear, and I look over my shoulder at the tidal wave of Connies behind us.

In the earliest days of the Contamination, watching the news on TV, I'd always believed I'd caught sight of my dad in the crowd. A hint of his red hair. A flash of the tie I'd bought him for Father's Day one year, the one printed with pictures of Rubik's Cubes. Until the day I saw him in my backyard, I'd been sure he was dead and tossed into one of the mass graves they'd dug in the fields along the highway.

That's why, when I catch sight of my mom in the crowd, toward the back, I don't doubt for an instant that it's her. She's moving as slowly and uncertainly as the rest of them, and though I search desperately for any sign that they've put a collar on her again, it's impossible for me to tell. I look automatically for my dad, but don't see him. Now the crowd reaches me, and I'm being pushed along. Another set of stairs. Another landing. I try to look behind me, but there's no way to pay attention to the crowd and where I'm going, and before I know it, we're all caught up in the wave. I lose sight of Opal, but I can see the back of Arnaldo's head and hope he's still holding on to her. Dillon is in front of me one minute, then a burly Connie with a slack jaw and vacant eyes has pushed between us, stepping on my toes, and I'm pinned between him and the railing for a moment long enough for the crowd to push Dillon away from me.

Everything is noise and stink and the crush of bodies. We pour down the stairs and out the door at the bottom, into the parking lot that is filled with fire trucks and ambulances and cop cars, all with lights flashing. From down the road comes the rumble of something bigger, tanks or maybe just big trucks. Behind us, as we all surge into the lot, the building is on fire. Glass has blown out, scattering on the asphalt. Smoke pours from the empty spaces. The orderlies shout, and the Connies shove and stumble, but I manage to grab Dillon's elbow and we both grab hold of Arnaldo and Opal, too. We are caught up in the swelling crowd and confusion. I fight it, looking for my mom, but I can't find her again. I spin and shoulder a few Connies out of the way, desperate for a glimpse of her, but there are too many of them. It's like trying to stand against a tidal wave.

A pair of firefighters runs past me, pushing Connies out of the way. The police officers, two women and a man, stand back by their cars with expressionless faces, their hands on their guns.

An army truck, the kind with the canvas back, pulls into the parking lot. Soldiers pour out of it, each of them carrying a gun. They're going to start shooting, and there's no way we won't be hit.

All around me, the collars start flashing yellow. Then red. And finally, at last, they're all a steady, unblinking crimson just as I get to the garbage truck, where Dillon has already started the engine. Opal and Arnaldo are in the front seat. Arnaldo grabs for my wrist and hauls me inside, yanking the door shut behind me.

"Wait! My mom!"—I fight him, but Arnaldo's too big for me. I slam against the door, but Dillon's already driving.

All the Connies start to twitch and shake and fall to the ground. The sound of the garbage truck's engine is lost in the louder roar of everything else. Dillon pulls out, past the fire trucks. Past the police cars. Past the Connies on the ground, some of them already gone still.

None of the soldiers pays any attention, though one of the police officers turns to look at us as we pass. Her face is still stolid and neutral, but she sees us; I can tell by the way her stance shifts, just for a moment. Then she turns away without so much as lifting her hand from the gun on her hip, and Dillon keeps driving. Out of the parking lot. Down the road. More trucks pass us, some with sirens, army trucks overflowing with soldiers, another ambulance, lights off. Behind us, another massive explosion rocks the hospital, and all I can see in the rearview mirror is more smoke and the red-orange glare of fire.

Dillon drives past empty fields and houses, past the memorial site where I'd thought my dad might be buried. Dillon's waved right through the roadblocks without so much as a second glance, though I force Opal to duck down below the level of the dashboard until we're through. He drives past empty neighborhoods with boarded-up houses and long grass in the yards. A gas station, also abandoned long enough for weeds to cover the parking lot, the glass broken in the convenience store.

Nobody stops us.

It's true. Nobody pays attention to a garbage truck, not even one with four people in the front seat. We drive through downtown Lebanon. I haven't been here in months. Everything's empty and silent. We cross the train tracks and head for the warehouse.

The train's leaving.

"We'll have to run," I say to Opal.

"I can do it, Velvet."

I'm not sure she can. She's grown taller, but her legs are still short. But we'll try. I'll carry her, if I have to.

And so we run. The four of us, Arnaldo still a little unsteady, but keeping his feet. Dillon links an arm over his shoulders to help him along. I grab Opal's hand, pulling her. Dillon shoves Arnaldo ahead of him, and Arnaldo grabs at the hand at the open door to the train car. He pulls himself onto his belly and rolls. For a few seconds, when he disappears, I'm sure he will forget about us or even push us away—Dillon did knock him out, after all. The train's picking up speed now. We won't be able to catch up. . . .

But then another hand reaches out. "Opal! C'mon!"

And Dillon and I take her hands like she's a toddler, not eleven, and we're going to swing her between us. Together, we yank her forward so that Arnaldo can grab her by the wrists. He hauls her onto the train, and Dillon is right there behind them both. He dangles, feet skidding on the gravel, ripping at the toes of his sneakers while he tries to get on board. Opal and Arnaldo grab at his shirt, pulling him inside. And then there's only me, and the train is going faster and faster, and I will never be able to catch it.

I run.

Fast as I can, full out, legs stretching, arms pumping. I have never run this fast, but this time I am running for my life. My boots hit the gravel, sliding under my feet, but I keep my balance. I focus on the open train car and my sister's face. My Dillon's face. Even on Arnaldo, who should've been an enemy but had become something of a friend. Pushing myself with everything I have, I swipe at their reaching hands, but miss. Again. I have maybe another minute of stamina, another thirty seconds before the train picks up enough speed to leave me behind for good. I reach again and miss again.

I jump.

I slap Dillon's wrist with one hand, Arnaldo's with the other. They both grab me tight, yanking me forward. My belly and hips slam the edge of the train car and my feet strike the tracks, but my toes are protected by Ellen's boots. In another second or so, Dillon and Arnaldo are pulling me on board just as the train lets out a long, warning whistle, and I tuck my legs inside.

"We did it!" Opal cries. "Velvet! We made it!"

Then all I can do is hold on to her as tight as I can.

THIRTY-SEVEN

OUT HERE IN THE GREEN, THERE'S NO VOICE or Raven, but there are other voices. Other tellers of the truth. And there are other people like us, who've fled and escaped from the black zones.

There was an uprising at the Sanitarium. The official word is that a group of radicals fighting for Connie rights set off a series of chemical bombs in the hospital in order to release them. The damage was extensive, and everyone who'd been under care there died during the explosions or in the fires afterward. That's the official version, anyway, but I don't believe it.

No mention of Dr. Donna or Dr. Billings, but I know they might have been killed. I feel sad about Dr. Billings, and not so much about Dr. Donna.

I have no idea if my parents are alive, though all I can think of is how they each could always finish the other's sentences. How my dad unfailingly managed to buy my mom the exact right birthday gift every year, things she claimed she didn't know she wanted until she opened the box. How no matter who got home first, each was ready to greet the other at the door. I believe my dad would've found my mom, even in the crowd. Even if both of them had lost their minds, they'd have found each other, and protected each other.

I want to believe they are alive.

The truth is that someone on the inside did instigate a revolt and set off the bombs. And then the government activated Mercy Mode on all those Connies and slaughtered them instead of trying to save them when the building went up in flames and became debris.

Nobody knows who led the revolt, but I think I know.

"You can't be sure," Dillon whispers into my hair when we are finally alone. We are in our tent together; it's late; and all I can do is think of sleep and know I won't be able to find it. "It could've been anyone."

"It was my dad. I know it."

"Velvet . . ." He sighs, but says no more. He holds me instead, and I let him, because I love him and we have to stick together. We might be in the green, but we aren't out of trouble. Not yet, not entirely.

We're considered refugees, so we've been put into one of the tent cities springing up in mall parking lots. We've been given job assignments, new clothes, food rations. Opal is going to school again. We've been vaccinated, fumigated, medicated, and indoctrinated. We've been tested for Contamination, but whatever makes me special doesn't show up on their tests. Inconclusive.

I guess I'm lucky.

But it's only a matter of time before they figure out what I am. What I think Opal must be, too, if Dr. Donna succeeded in Contaminating her. Every day, I look for signs of it, but Opal is who she's always been. Funny, sarcastic, smart, kind of a brat. If she is Contaminated, she's got it the same way I do, and I'm cynical enough to believe that there are people on this side of the barriers who'd want to use us in just the same way Dr. Donna did.

For now, though, I sink into the stiff, unyielding cot and listen to the sound of Dillon's breathing go soft and slow. Opal was asleep when we came to bed—she's still eating like a pig and outgrowing all her clothes, so I think she's going through yet another growth spurt or something. I can't sleep. There's too much going on in my mind.

The people here are nice. They tell us that, soon enough, after a while, we'll be allowed to leave the tent city and find real jobs and housing in the green zone. But I'm not sure I believe them. It's the people in the green who are sending all their Connies into the black, after all.

I try to relax and let sleep find me, and at last, my eyelids start to drift closed. Tomorrow, as Scarlett O'Hara says, is another day, and while I don't have to wear a dress made of curtains, I sure won't be hungry, either. I might have to wear hand-me-downs and eat bland, cafeteria-slop kind of food, but I'm warm and dry, with a roof of sorts over my head and people who I love near me. We are safe.

At least, we're supposed to be.